This book is dedicated to my wife and editor, Jen, who gave me constant encouragement, as well as reasonably low-cost editorial services. If I didn't dedicate the work to her, I would be permanently stuck with the most loathsome household chores, like collecting poop in the backyard from Max, Milo, and Bear. To be clear, Max, Milo, and Bear are dogs, not children—our kids left home years ago.

Max, Milo, and Bear deserve some credit too. After all, they slept tirelessly under my desk while I wrote the book, offering groans as literary advice. It was excellent bonding between a man and his dogs, but unfortunately, one of them has a serious gas problem.

SPECIAL THANKS

I would like to thank Dr. Chen Chung Ming, a Taiwanese immigrant to the United States. Dr. Chen's technical brilliance, commercial smarts, devotion, Yankee hat, and trouble with plurals inspired the main character in this story. In addition, I would like to thank former colleagues Billy Martin of Tennessee, Cleveland Ngan of Shanghai, and Dr. Deyuan Miao, formerly of Beijing, for their friendship and for allowing the use of their names or likenesses in the story. As an aside, Cleveland and Dr. Miao taught me the Chinese-style "bottoms-up" toast, which I highly recommend be limited to beer.

Fortunately, I had several good friends who helped with several iterations of this book and gave me invaluable editorial advice: Peter Schaff, Lynn Clarke, Richard Ford, Denis Roy, Phil Beard, Jim Frew, Al Noyes, and Sallie Stanley. I cannot thank them enough for laboring through really bad versions.

1

THE "A" TEAM

When Jack Thompson, president of Lund Plastics, decided to create a research and development department for the division, his decision met with universal enthusiasm.

"Why the hell do we need R & D?" bellowed Dirk McAllister, Lund's vice president of manufacturing, over a plate of chicken-fried steak, gravy, and curly fries.

"Keep it down, will ya?" responded Jack *sotto voce* as he looked sheepishly around to the adjoining tables at the diner while shoveling a load of fries into his mouth.

"Why?"

"Because we're in a frickin' restaurant."

"It's just a low-rent Nashville diner, Jack."

"Where I happen to have lunch every day."

"Every day?"

"Every gosh darn day."

"No kidding. What's your cholesterol?"

"Only 190—I just had a physical."

"That's amazing."

"Yep, and my triglycerides are good too. Could you please pass the ketchup?" Despite Jack's daily ritual with gravy and fries, he was a fit man in his early sixties with a gray crew cut.

"You're a medical miracle, Jack. Anyway, why R & D?"

1

"Dave Lund ordered me to do it. He's the boss."

"Just because his family owns the business?"

"It's a good reason; plus, he's the new CEO of Lund."

"But he's young, new to the business, and doesn't know jack."

"What?" Jack asked with a puzzled look.

"It's an expression. He doesn't know jack about us. We make plastics for industrial coatings. It's as basic as it gets. What does Dave Lund think R & D can do?"

"I dunno—maybe develop some new products."

"Jack, this is all a bunch of Dave's Harvard Business School bullshit. He probably learned about this in some ivory-tower course about innovation. He's a former management consultant and hasn't done anything himself. This isn't frickin' Apple—we're a plastics company! And he's no Steve Jobs."

"I know, I know. He's doing a bunch of Harvard stuff that won't work, like talking about our core competencies."

"Our what?"

"Core competencies—it's business-school speak for 'what we're good at.'"

"We're good at one thing, Jack: making plastics, and lots of it, at the lowest cost. We don't need a Harvard MBA to figure it out, but creating an R & D department will only get in the way and increase our costs."

"I know."

"Well, what lucky sucker on your staff gets to manage R & D?"

"That's what I wanted to talk to you about …"

Dirk McAllister was a gruff man in his mid-fifties who had spent his entire career in plastic manufacturing. He welcomed change like the National Rifle Association embraced universal background checks. After getting his orders from Jack about R & D, Dirk devised a simple plan to handle the situation: hire the cheapest, most innocuous scientist possible and make sure he stayed out of the way.

To accomplish this task, Dirk needed to assemble an unusually weak team to screen and interview candidates. His first choice was obvious: Darrell Hartman, Lund Plastics' vice president of human resources and chief people officer. Darrell had a strong reputation for intellectual mediocrity. On the management team, he had no equal. Some of his Lund colleagues even speculated that Darrell bought his clothes for full price at Jos A. Bank Clothier. He was equally known for political correctness and sentimentality—his title of chief people officer being a prime example.

The second choice was more difficult, but Dirk wanted to augment the soft side of his team with a woman. For this, he picked Lund's vice president of finance, B'linda Mae Jones. B'linda, whose nickname was Trophy (short for "Apostrophe"), was the clear intellectual superior of Darrell, but she was a die-hard women's libber, a perfect bias for hiring a gentler, more innocuous scientist. Trophy was legend around the office, and not just for her financial acumen. In her late thirties, Trophy was a looker with a beautiful face amid a wild frock of long, curly blonde hair. She stood five-foot two without her signature stiletto heels and had a figure noted for slender hips and waist to complement an upper half whose most prominent parts were nicknamed Bonnie and Clyde.

To round out the team, Dirk asked the Nashville office receptionist, Beverly Stroup, to join. Beverly was a petite, likable woman in her mid-thirties who idolized Darrell for his advanced sensitivity and executive capacities—an obvious sign of her dimness.

Dirk decided to locate his new scientist in Lund's manufacturing plant in Dalton, Georgia, a three-hour drive from the Nashville headquarters. The location would minimize Dirk's interaction with him or her. To keep the new scientist even further at bay, Dirk would build a cheap lab in the attic of the Dalton plant, a desolate place with no windows that was full of plant fumes, a location sure to dissuade any capable candidates from taking the job.

Challenges like this brought out the best in Dirk.

To initiate the search for the new scientist, the team engaged a recruiter who had retired as a human resources manager at a Georgia manufacturing facility. He was a sole practitioner in his sixties, and Darrell had met him at a sensitivity-training workshop in Atlanta years earlier. The choice exceeded Dirk's hopes for incompetence.

Fortunately for Dirk, recruiting scientists in the world of plastics was nearly impossible—industrial plastics companies simply didn't have R & D. Plastics had become as differentiated as sand, but the recruiter persisted and introduced several candidates. The team rejected all for being under-qualified, despite Dirk's insistence otherwise. Dirk decided not to overrule his team, lest his strategy become too apparent.

Several weeks later, the team met in Nashville to review another batch of resumes. The Nashville office was in a one-story business park outside the city, with dirty carpets, horrible coffee, and motivational posters that Darrell had acquired to improve the morale of the organization. His favorite was a colorful skydiving formation with the caption, "Teamwork: Aim High."

Darrell, Trophy, and Bev sifted through piles of resumes, growing increasingly despondent that none had the right qualifications for the position. Trophy suddenly took an interest in one and queried the team, "Hey, have y'all seen this one? It's from a Dr. Chen, who's apparently Chinese. He's doing a postdoc at Michigan Tech."

Darrell looked up from his pile and said, "No, I haven't. What's his background?"

"He has a PhD in plastics science from Beijing University and is now at Michigan Tech researching how to make plastic composites lighter and stronger."

"Dr. Chen, huh?" Darrell said, thinking out loud. "That would be good for our diversity. What's his first name?"

"It just says Chen."

"Maybe he's like Madonna," Bev offered.

Two weeks later, the team assembled at the Dalton plant to interview Dr. Chen. The plant was a monstrosity, with giant machines, and more than 150 employees. Its conference room had a large, rectangular table with cheap veneer, mismatched chairs, and motivational posters about teamwork and leadership. Dirk had arranged for coffee, Coke, and Diet Coke for his team and Dr. Chen, as well as chocolate doughnuts and bags of Doritos, Trophy's favorite. Darrell had brought detailed interview guides for each team member, complete with a color-highlighted list of topics not to broach, like asking the candidate if he was pregnant.

At 10:00 a.m., the plant receptionist, a woman in her twenties named Billie, knocked on the conference room door and entered.

"Excuse me, y'all, but Dr. Chen is here."

Walking behind her was a slightly rotund Chinese man about five feet, six inches tall, in his mid-thirties, wearing black plastic-framed glasses.

"Hello, my name is Chen," he declared with a warm smile and heavy Chinese accent.

Chen wore a white lab coat with his name inscribed above the many pens in his front pocket. He also wore an old blue tie.

Darrell was the first to greet Chen, and he introduced him to Dirk, Trophy, and Bev.

"Please sit down, Dr. Chen," Darrell said, offering a seat on the opposite side of the table.

"Thank you, Darrell. I am very happy to be here in Daltons."

"Dr. Chen, would you like some coffee or perhaps a Coke and doughnuts?" offered Bev. She and Trophy were already sipping Diet Cokes and munching on Doritos.

"Do you have hot waters?" asked Chen as he pulled out a red tin adorned with Chinese characters. "I have tea from China, a present from some friend in Beijing."

"We'll get you hot water right away," Trophy responded. "Is it sweet tea?"

"No, it's Chinese oolong tea, good for healths."

"Maybe I should try some," Dirk said, chuckling.

"Be my guests," Chen said as he passed the tin to Dirk. Dirk handled it like a live grenade and gave it back to Chen.

After Bev brought back a mug of steaming hot water, Chen grabbed a pinch of tea from his tin and put it in the water. The leaves floated for a couple minutes before getting soaked and sinking to the bottom.

"Chen," Trophy asked, "don't y'all use tea bags in China?"

"No, B'lindas, we just add some leaf and drink it."

"Extraordinary!" Bev exclaimed.

Trophy decided to start the interview. "So, Dr. Chen, you're from China?"

Darrell immediately turned red and gave Trophy a dirty look, pointing to the colored warnings in the interview guide. Dirk chuckled; Bev looked confused and concerned.

"Yes, B'lindas, I am from Beijing, the capitols."

"How's the weather over there?" Bev asked.

"Very hot and humids in the summer and freezings in the winter."

"How do you like America?" Bev continued.

"Michigan Tech is also freezings, and I like *The Today Shows*."

"Well, Dr. Chen," Trophy explained, "Georgia has very nice weather, and we also have *The Today Show*. Katie Couric was my favorite, but she left the show."

"Yes, I liked her, but my favorite is Al Rokers."

"He's great with the crowd outside!" Bev interjected.

"Yes, Bev, somedays, I would like to visit the studio."

Bev was absorbed in thought and came up with the next question. "Dr. Chen, are there still any Communists in China?"

"Yes, many Communist."

"Oh, my! Do you know any?"

"Yes."

"Are they dangerous?"

"No, Bev. I even have some cousin Communist."

The group's attention was riveted.

"Seriously?" Bev asked incredulously.

"No jokers."

"Well, I'll be!" Bev exclaimed. "Are you a Communist?"

Darrell shuffled through the interview guide and papers, searching for guidance on the Communist question.

"No, I am just some plastics doctor."

Darrell interrupted to steer the interview in a different direction. "Dr. Chen, can you explain to us your postdoctoral work at Michigan Tech?"

"Yes, Darrell, I do some experiment to understand how to make plastics composite stronger by changing the structure of the polymers."

"Oh, my," Bev said in amazement.

"How do you do that?" Dirk asked.

"We make some plastic with different polymers and then measure the strength with machine."

Bev stared at Chen like he had invented gravity.

"Could your work help us at Lund?" Dirk continued.

"Yes, Mr. Dirks, maybe you could make some plastic lighter with same strength—to save many dollar."

"Now you're talkin'," Dirk said.

"At Michigan Tech, we reduce plastic weights by 15 percents."

"My word!" Bev said.

After a brief pause, Bev continued. "So, Dr. Chen, do you have any hobbies?"

"Yes, I make fortune cookie." Dirk sat up straight, thinking the interview was getting really interesting.

"With the fortunes inside?"

"Yes, Bev, I write the fortune and put them inside some cookie."

"How do you know?" Bev asked.

"Know what?"

"How do you know each person's fortune?"

Dirk chuckled; Darrell looked confused; Trophy smiled.

"It takes many practice, Bev," Chen explained.

"Good Lord!" Bev commented.

Darrell chimed in. "Dr. Chen, do you have a staff at Michigan Tech?"

"Yes, Darrell, I have two assistant."

"Did you hire them?"

"Yes, I did some interview, like this."

"Can you describe them?"

"The first is master student from Upper Peninsulas of Michigan. He is a man about twenty-five year old—"

"His gender and age are irrelevant, Dr. Chen. How do you manage him?"

"We have tea in the mornings and talk about doing some experiment. Then he does it and put result in computer."

"Do you agree on his objectives?"

"What objective?" Chen looked confused.

Darrell continued. "Do you have forms to describe his objectives that you both sign?"

Dirk interrupted. "Darrell, it's okay. Chen can learn how to use forms here." Clearly, Dirk had found his man.

After an hour, Dirk asked Chen if he would mind waiting in the reception area so they could talk. As soon as Chen left, Dirk said, "Well, what do you all think?"

"He's perfect," Bev responded. "Chen is so smart!"

"He's really nice, too," Trophy added. "I don't think he'll make waves here, especially since he's not a Communist."

This was music to Dirk's ears.

"Darrell?" Dirk asked.

"Well, his work is impressive, and I agree he's nice. I'm concerned that he doesn't use forms to define objectives."

What a moron, Dirk thought. *I better think of something.*

"Good point, Darrell, but remember, he works for a university in the Upper Peninsula of Michigan—not a sophisticated corporation like Lund. I'm sure you could train him in no time."

"Yea, Darrell," Bev said, "Look what you did with me."

Trophy interjected, "She has a point, Darrell; when it comes to forms, you're world-class."

Darrell accepted Trophy's derision as a strong compliment. "Gee, I'm flattered. You've convinced me. Chen will be great."

"It's settled then," Dirk exclaimed. "Bev, go get Dr. Chen and let's give him the good news!"

2

FUMES

The afternoon before Chen's first day at Lund, Darrell drove to Dalton to prepare for Chen's indoctrination. Chen was the most senior hire in years, and Darrell felt strongly he had to handle this himself. He packed a large box of forms into his 1995 blue Volvo station wagon, along with his gag-a-maggot-smelling safety boots and overnight bag, and headed for Georgia. Darrell's wagon was notorious among the Lund team, most notably for foot odor, a pungent mixture from his omnipresent tennis shoes and the safety boots. He had a pine-tree air freshener, which was like a BB gun against panzers.

On the dashboard, Darrell had a bobble figure of a bearded man in a robe, Andy Gibb of the Bee Gees. It was a visible warning to new riders to beware of Darrell's music collection. Unsuspecting riders found themselves trapped for hours listening to *The Best of the Carpenters*, John Denver, Helen Reddy, The Bee Gees, and other pieces known for sentimentality.

The next morning, Darrell arrived early to set up in the plant conference room. Remembering that Chen favored tea over coffee, Darrell brought a jug of sweet tea and a dozen assorted doughnuts. As he was arranging ten piles of forms on the conference table, the human resource manager for Dalton, Sophie Garibaldi, joined him. Sophie was in her early thirties. A recent MBA graduate from the University of Georgia, Sophie had head-turning good looks with her wavy, dark-brown hair; fetching, big brown eyes; perfect smile; and trim, athletic figure. Sophie wore little makeup and dressed casually with tight jeans and a black button-down shirt. Sophie ran intellectual laps around her boss, Darrell, which was why Dirk intentionally kept her off the R & D interview team.

"Good morning, Sophie," Darrell said.

"Hey, Darrell. What's up?"

"I'm glad you're here. Today is a great development opportunity for you."

"How so?"

"A critical skill for advancement in human resources at Lund is the mastery of forms. As you can see, I've laid out ten piles for Dr. Chen. For the next hire, I'd like you to be able to lay out the forms yourself."

"Do you think I can pick it up that fast, Darrell?"

Sophie's sarcasm escaped Darrell. "All good development is a stretch, Sophie, but I would never throw you out of the boat and ask you to swim. I'll be there, just in case."

"What a relief."

"I think you have great potential, Sophie. In seven to ten years, you could be the HR manager for a bigger plant, and in another ten, you could be ready for my job."

"That soon?"

"Absolutely. You are on a fast track."

A moment later, Dr. Chen walked into the room wearing his glasses and white lab coat with his name above its pen-infested front pocket.

"Good morning, Darrell," Chen said with a smile.

"Welcome, Dr. Chen. I'd like to introduce you to the human resource manager here in Dalton, Sophie Garibaldi."

"It's some pleasure, Miss Sophie."

"The pleasure is mine, Dr. Chen."

"Please, call me Chen."

Sophie was immediately smitten by his modest demeanor, sartorial simplicity, and major diction issues.

"It's great to have you here, Chen!" Sophie beamed.

"Thank you. I am very happys to be working for Lunds Plastics."

"How was the trip from the Upper Peninsula?" Sophie asked.

"Since this is my first business jobs, I listened to the Jack Welch business CDs the whole way."

"He's one of my favorites," Sophie replied. "How did you like the CDs?"

"Very good. I am ready to make Lund like General Electricity," Chen answered.

Darrell interrupted. "Would you like some tea, Chen?"

"Yes, thank you."

Darrell poured sweet tea into a plastic cup while Chen watched with a perplexed look. He took one sip, grimaced, and held the cup before his eyes.

"Is something wrong, Chen?" Sophie asked.

"I do not know this tea. It is not hot and is full of sugars."

"It's sweet tea, typical in Georgia. Would you prefer hot tea?"

"Yes, please, Miss Sophie."

Darrell just stared vacantly at his forms, unaware of the tea issue, and then started. "Okay, Chen, let's start with your information forms. Please complete three copies of these forms and provide a copy of your passport and work permit to Sophie."

"Why three copies?" Sophie queried.

"You're new to this, Sophie; let me explain. One is for the Nashville files, one is for the Dalton files, and an extra is in case one gets lost."

"Why not have him fill out one and then make photocopies?"

"His signature must be original on all. It's a requirement of Lund Human Resources."

"I see," Sophie lied.

"You'll catch on, Sophie; don't worry."

Darrell proceeded to have Chen fill out several original copies of myriad forms related to insurance, beneficiaries, emergency contacts, etc. After two hours of filling out forms, Darrell turned on his computer to give Chen a presentation on Lund values. The presentation started with Lund's logo and a picture of a dozen employees of obviously different ethnic backgrounds and job levels with arms interlocked and big smiles. Lund's corporate values were: People, Profits, and Possibilities, and Darrell read standard Lund speaking points for all three, including examples.

"Darrell," Chen asked, raising his hand, "is the addition of research and developments at Lund Plastics about some possibilities?"

"Exactly, Dr. Chen. Your hire shows Lund's major commitment to possibilities."

Sophie said, "Dr. Chen, we all hope you're the beginning of big changes around here."

"Thank you, Miss Sophies."

At the conclusion of the values presentation, which included lunch, Darrell looked at his watch and said, "Well, Dr. Chen, it's only three; we did orientation a couple hours faster than normal. If you'd like, Sophie can show you your new lab."

"Yes, please."

Sophie and Chen donned safety hats and earplugs for the trip to the lab. The entrance was near the giant steel mixing machines. It was hot, noisy, and full of fumes. They entered on the ground floor and climbed two flights of old, rickety stairs with loose handrails to an entrance door at the top. The lab was a dump. It was a small, misshapen room whose walls and ceiling were made by the upper contours of the plant. The walls were made of exposed wood composites, and plant fumes filled the air. There was a table, a few mismatched metal chairs, and a couple workbenches with a few machines. Two old computers were on the workbenches.

Dirk's instructions to prepare a cheap, dirty lab had been fulfilled with gusto by the cost-conscious plant manager, Billy Lansing.

Sophie was embarrassed by the shabby lab. "I'm afraid this is it, Chen. Sorry it's so Spartan."

"I like it, Miss Sophie. We will make it some Chinese lab."

"Well, at least it smells better than Darrell's shoes."

"Good points." They both laughed.

3

唐人街

(CHINATOWN)

During Chen's initial days, he arrived early in the morning, often carrying boxes of equipment and supplies, stayed in his lab, and left late at night. No one knew what he was doing. Dirk was delighted; Chen was harmless and stayed completely out of his way. They hadn't met in person. Chen never bothered to call Dirk or visit the Nashville office, and no one in Dalton complained to Dirk about Chen because he didn't bother a soul.

Things with Chen are perfect, Dirk thought.

Sophie was Chen's mainstay in Dalton; she was the only visitor to the smoky attic. She took him out for lunch often and introduced him to Southern BBQ, hush puppies, and fried catfish. Chen was an eager student, asking Sophie about all things American, particularly NASCAR and country music. Chen reciprocated by teaching Sophie to use chopsticks over Chinese takeout in the lab. Their friendship grew rapidly and was purely platonic.

Sophie saw that Chen had been marginalized by Dirk and resolved to spoil the plot. For starters, she commandeered an intern from the University of Georgia, previously earmarked for the plant, to help Chen. Since it was a temporary position, it kept Chen from having to attend two days of Darrell's training on managing subordinates. Sophie had been forced to take the course, and she compared it unfavorably to waterboarding. "Even Dick Cheney would consider it torture," Sophie confided to a friend.

Chen and Sophie interviewed several candidates and selected Travis Green, a homegrown Georgian who drank Mountain Dew in his interview and sported a two-day beard growth. This augured well for Chen's assimilation into southern American culture. Chen liked Travis and was excited about his promise to introduce Chen to Red Man Chewing Tobacco.

For two weeks, Chen and Travis worked on the lab. They refurbished the machines on the workbench, bought new chairs for the conference table, added a small refrigerator for Mountain Dew, purchased a teapot for oolong tea, and refinished the floor. At Chen's instruction, Travis painted the entrance door red to resemble a Chinese temple. Chen brought statues of two foo dogs, the frightening lion/dog hybrid traditionally used to guard Chinese buildings, and placed them on each side of the door. Sophie made a sign saying 唐人街, which meant "Chinatown" in Mandarin. She thought it added authenticity, though she worried whether the name violated Lund policies about race or national origin.

While Travis and Sophie were admiring the finished lab, Chen posed a question.

"Travis, Sophie, do you know what Chinatown need now?"

"An industrial air filtering system?" Sophie asked.

"No, some party for new house."

"An open house?"

"Yes."

"That's a good idea, Chen."

Travis created electronic invitations for "The Lund Plastics R & D Open House." The invitation featured a picture of the red lab door, complete with foo-dog guards and the Mandarin Chinatown sign, and announced a special Chinese lunch to celebrate the opening of R & D at Lund Plastics. Sophie e-mailed them to Jack Thompson, Dirk, Trophy, Bev, Darrell, several of the Dalton plant supervisors, and even Dave Lund. According to rumor, Dave Lund was the driving force behind R & D at Lund, and she thought he should be included.

Everyone accepted the invitation, even Dave Lund.

For the open house, Travis, Sophie, and Chen decorated the lab with posters of The Great Wall and The Forbidden City, paper dragons, and several framed displays of Chinese landscape art and calligraphy. They ordered a variety of Chinese dishes from a Dalton restaurant, and Chen brought homemade spring rolls and fortune cookies. Sophie brought large pots of Chinese tea and two gallons of sweet tea as emergency back up.

At eleven forty-five on the day of the open house, Jack Thompson, Darrell, and Dirk entered the lab. Jack was coughing.

"Dirk, what the hell kind of place is this? I can barely breathe."

"It's the only place where we could put the lab, Jack. I don't think Chen minds."

"No," Chen interrupted, "it's just like Beijing in summer—hot, humids, and full of smokes."

Dirk gestured to Jack. "Dr. Chen, this is Jack Thompson, the president of Plastics."

"Helluva pleasure, Dr. Chen. Welcome aboard."

"Nice to meet you, Mr. President."

"Please, call me Jack."

"Deals."

Just then, Trophy, Bev, and several Dalton supervisors arrived, all wearing safety glasses and earplugs.

"Come on in, everyone," Sophie offered. "We're happy to have y'all. Who would like tea?"

All raised their hands enthusiastically. Travis, Chen, and Sophie poured steaming oolong tea into Chinese cups and passed them out to the guests. Everyone looked into their cups like they had just been served fresh urine.

"What's this?" Jack asked.

"It's some oolong tea," Chen explained. "From Beijing."

"And Dr. Chen doesn't even use tea bags!" Bev explained proudly.

One of the plant supervisors whispered to another. "It looks like frog piss."

"Do y'all have any sugar?" asked Billy Lansing, the Dalton plant manager.

Sophie saved the day. "You don't put sugar in oolong tea, y'all, but if you prefer, we have sweet tea over there."

Everyone but Bev and Trophy put down their cups and lined up for sweet tea.

While the group gulped tea, Dave Lund arrived. He had driven from Lund's corporate headquarters in Memphis. There was sudden silence—many of the plant's folks had not met Dave before.

"Hey, everyone," Dave said affably. "Sorry I'm late—got lost in the plant."

"Welcome, Dave. I'm Sophie Garibaldi from Dalton HR. Would you like some Chinese tea?"

"Nice to meet you, Sophie. Yes, I would love some Chinese tea."

"Probably an Ivy League thing," Dirk muttered to Jack.

Dave was in his mid-forties, a handsome man six feet tall with a medium build and brown hair. Dave had joined his family firm a year earlier when his uncle, Johann Lund, retired after being CEO for thirty years. He had a strong strategic background, having been a management consultant at the prestigious McCutcheon Group for more than ten years after graduating from the Harvard Business School. Dave's warm personality masked his keen intelligence.

Dave scanned the room full of Caucasians. "Okay, which one of you is Dr. Chen?"

Chen stepped forward with an extended hand. "My name is Chen."

"Pleased to meet you, Dr. Chen. Welcome to Lund. We're excited to have you here and know you can make a big difference."

Dirk stared at the floor.

"Thank you, Dave. I am excited to be part of Lunds. My plan is to make some new product for Plastics."

"That's why we wanted you, Dr. Chen. New products are key for us, especially here."

Sophie announced, "Lunch is served!"

Everyone lined up and loaded their plates with Chinese food kept hot by Travis's ingenious use of Bunsen burners. The dishes smelled fantastic, even among the plant fumes, and everyone dug in. The plant supervisors added sweet sauce liberally to everything, even the sweet 'n sour chicken. Sweet tea flowed freely. Chen's experiment with chopsticks failed miserably—several chunks of sweet 'n sour chicken ended up on the floor—but Sophie came to the rescue with forks.

While everyone finished their lunch, Dave Lund rose to address the group.

"First, I'd like to formally welcome Dr. Chen and his assistant, Travis, to Lund. It's great to have you here. Second, I would like to thank them and Sophie for hosting this lunch. What a great idea and terrific food! It was worth the trip over from Memphis. Many of you may wonder why we are adding R & D here at Plastics."

That would include me, pondered Dirk.

"Well, as you know, we are much smaller than many of our competitors. In fact, we are the number-six player in our industry. It's very difficult for us to compete on cost against the big boys, so we have to be different. We think the best course would be to develop new products."

Dirk rolled his eyes at Jack.

Dave continued. "Thank you again. It's been great seeing you, and I look forward to great things."

At the conclusion of Dave's speech, Travis and Sophie passed out Chen's homemade fortune cookies. One after another, they opened the cookies and chuckled at the fortunes inside.

"What's so funny?" Jack asked.

"Read your fortune," Billy Lansing responded.

Jack opened his cookie and read his fortune out loud. "'May you have some good healths.'"

The group laughed. Trophy read hers next. "'Your love burn brighter than some candle flame.'"

"You're lucky, Tr—I mean, B'linda," Dirk commented.

Dirk read his. "'When you looks down, all you see is some dirts.'"

Bev followed. "These are *sooo* true. Listen to mine, y'all: 'If you are afraid to throw dice, you will never throw some six.'"

Trophy said, "These are great! They sound like Chen."

"I wrote fortunes on my home computer," Chen explained, "and put them in some cookie."

"Was it difficult?" Trophy asked.

"It took many time to get the right size, but no matters what, I had some squiggly line," Chen explained.

"What squiggly line?"

"Every times I write fortune, the computer put green or red squiggly line under some word."

On the way out, Darrell pulled Sophie aside under the Chinatown sign.

"Sophie, about this sign. You know it's against Lund policy to make distinctions based on national origin or race."

"It's not like that, Darrell."

"What's it say?"

"Lund Research and Development Center. We thought Chinese might make Chen feel more welcome in a predominately white plant."

"Oh, very sensitive thinking. Nice work."

4

BISCUITS AND CAPPUCCINO

After Dave Lund's encouraging words at the "Chinatown" open house, Chen and Travis resolved to make a difference at Lund. They conducted several lab experiments, focusing on new structures for plastics, as well as antimicrobial additives. Dirk stayed out of their way. Chen kept things under wraps so he could surprise Dirk with a product breakthrough.

Because Chen had grown quite popular in Dalton, albeit somewhat as a curiosity, he was given wide latitude in the plant. Chen had even convinced Billy Lansing that his work on new, lighter structures would increase plant throughput, a major temptation for the manufacturing department.

Chen's approach was to change the chemical composition of the plastic and cure it under much higher temperatures. This increased the speed of the process noticeably, but it also greatened the risk of fire. Chen's sales pitch to Billy Lansing had omitted this critical fact.

The trial run of Chen's new product went well for the first fifteen minutes. The machine operator loved the faster run rate—until the higher-temperature plastic ignited, shutting down the process and triggering the large overhead sprinkler system that flooded the area.

By the time Billy Lansing responded to the emergency call, it was apparent that Chen's promise of enhanced productivity was not to be. Furthermore, the plant would be shut down for a day to clean and drain the machinery, which would cost tens of thousands of dollars in lost profit and extra labor.

When Billy saw Chen, he yelled, "What the hell happened?"

"So sorry, Billy. The machines did not like some hot temperature. Sometime, it happen."

"Do you realize what this means? I've gotta call Dirk."

Dirk appreciated the quick heads-up from Billy. "What the hell do you mean, the machines stuck and started on fire?"

"We were doing a trial run on Chen's new product."

"What? You did a trial run without talking to me first?"

"It was supposed to increase production. I didn't think it would be a problem."

"You didn't think? I could've told you in two seconds about this risk. Why do you think no one does that?"

"Sorry, Dirk."

"From now on, Chen does nothing—I mean *nothing*—in the plant without my permission. Got it?"

"Yes, sir."

For the next several weeks, Chen and Travis stayed in Chinatown, conducting experiments to learn what went wrong with the plant trial.

***

Back in Nashville, Jack and Dirk continued their weekly lunches at the diner. Jack had become fast friends with a young waitress named Kim, a freckled brunette with a strong Southern accent who wore short shirts to expose her midsection. Kim had warmed to Jack, viewing him as a best customer and father figure.

After Jack and Dirk had settled into their gravy and fries, Kim approached their table.

"Jack, do you notice anything different about me?"

Jack looked her over and said, "No, Kim, why?"

"Look real close."

"You look the same to me."

Kim pulled up her already short shirt, exposing a new belly-button ring that was surrounded by hideous bruising.

"Jesus! What's that?"

"My new belly-button ring. I got it at the state fair last weekend."

"Does it hurt?"

"Not anymore. My boyfriend loves it, and so does Mama."

"Wow."

"Well, gotta run. *Bon appetito!*"

"Jack," Dirk said, "I just lost my appetite."

"Me, too. Anyway, Dirk, there's something I wanted to talk to you about. It concerns Chen."

"I told you: since the fire, we don't let him do plant trials."

"It's not that."

"What then?"

"Dave Lund and I met last week, and we decided that Plastics could use a strategist."

"Was this Dave's idea?"

"Yes, but he convinced me."

"Jack, our strategy is clear: make lots of plastic at the lowest cost. It's worked for years."

"Dave thinks it won't work in the future. He wants us to come up with something different."

"I've gotta bad feeling about this—"

"He convinced me to hire a new vice president of strategy, reporting to me."

"That'll be expensive, Jack."

"I know, but hopefully, it'll be worth it."

"If it's done deal, let's make sure to find someone who won't screw us up. Darrell has this recruiter he met at a sensitivity conference—"

"Too late for that. Dave already has the guy."

"Who?"

"Someone he worked with at McCutcheon. Name's Derek Vogel."

"Shit."

"He sounds good."

"Another McCutcheon consultant. Are you kidding me?" Dirk replied incredulously.

"Apparently, he's strong with strategy."

"I bet. He'll take my watch and tell me the time."

"Give him a chance, Dirk. He might be good."

"I'll try. What's this got to do with Chen?"

"Dave and I decided that it would be best to have Chen report to Vogel instead of you."

"Are you kidding me? The guy hasn't been here one day, and he already steals one of my direct reports."

"Vogel doesn't even know about it, and you've been against Chen from day one, more so since the fire."

"That's beside the point."

"Sorry, Dirk; it's settled."

***

Derek Vogel was a thirty-five-year-old management consultant from the Boston office of the world's premier consulting firm, The McCutcheon Group. A graduate of the Stanford Graduate School of Business, Vogel had worked on two strategy projects with Dave Lund at McCutcheon. Vogel had developed significant respect for Dave Lund—enough to leave the elite consulting firm to join an unknown $200 million plastics division of Lund Industries. Dave had matched Vogel's pay, touted the wonderful Nashville lifestyle, and hinted at promotional opportunities at Plastics.

Derek was eager for a new lifestyle. For years, he had traveled to meet with clients Monday through Friday, returning to Boston on weekends only to catch up on sleep and laundry. His social life had been in tatters until he met Carol Bennington, a tall, dark beauty and eldest daughter of the Peter Bennington family. The Benningtons defined Boston blue bloods, known for lavish parties and kissing cheeks without actual contact. But Carol rebelled against her roots and took up "slumming," which explained her attraction to Derek. They developed a tight bond over the Red Sox, night bowling, and peanut butter omelets for breakfast. Carol's parents were horrified by her marital choice and viewed Derek and his midwestern roots as a form of social leprosy.

When the prospect of moving to Nashville arose, Carol jumped.

"Derek, it's perfect. Nashville is a nice city, and my parents refuse to travel south of the Mason-Dixon Line. They think the South is uncouth."

"Can you get that in writing?"

Derek's first day at Lund was a career highlight for Darrell Hartman. He had never oriented a vice president before, and Derek's senior status necessitated extra forms and a more in-depth exploration of Lund values. The orientation soured Derek a bit on Lund, but Carol easily persuaded him to hang on.

"My parents want us for brunch every Sunday if we stay in Boston."

"Okay, I'll stick it out at Lund."

Jack and Derek had never met, an unusual situation for a new hire. Just for kicks, Jack invited Derek to his diner for a special "welcome to Lund, watch out for Dirk" lunch. He discussed the idea with Bev.

"Bev, I think I'll take the new guy to the diner as a cultural test."

"What do you mean?" asked Bev.

"Because he's a Yank—oh, never mind."

It was Derek's first experience with sweet tea, and he marveled at how so much sugar could remain dissolved in a cold liquid. Jack considered it a good sign. When Derek ordered fried chicken steak, fries, and gravy, Jack was impressed. But when Derek complimented Kim on her belly-button ring, Jack was sold.

"Derek, you're kinda unusual for a Yankee."

"Why's that?"

"No problem eating at a place like this. You like sweet tea. You order fried chicken steak and gravy, and Kim likes you."

"Well, my parents are from Minnesota."

Jack had no idea what he meant but nodded and said, "Ah, yes. Now I get it. Hey, Derek, I know it's your first day and everything, but would you be interested in a little road trip tomorrow? A few of us are going to the Dalton plant."

"Sounds like a great opportunity to meet people and start learning the business."

"It's a three-hour drive. We're all meeting at the office at seven; we'll stop and get a biscuit on the way."

"It sounds perfect. What's a biscuit?"

At seven the next morning, they were off in the company van. The driver was Bobby Ray Petry, the director of environmental health and safety. Bobby had light-red hair and wore a plaid shirt with khaki pants and loafers. He was a "good old boy" who hailed from a small town in the Tennessee hills and was a graduate of the University of Tennessee. Bobby had a Tennessee Volunteer football helmet on his desk, and according to rumor, Peyton Manning's jersey number tattooed on his left butt cheek.

Jack rode shotgun, and Derek sat in the middle seat with Darrell Hartman. In the third row were Dirk McAllister and Larry La Croix, the vice president of sales and marketing. Larry was an intense, fit man in his mid-forties. Jack introduced Derek to the group, and off they went.

On the outskirts of Nashville, Bobby pulled into the parking lot of a small restaurant called Billy's Biscuits 'N Gravy.

Jack got out and said, "The usual, fellas?"

Everyone nodded; Derek looked confused.

"How about you, Derek?"

"Um, I guess I'll have a biscuit—and a cappuccino."

Jack said, "I'll see what I can do."

Jack emerged with three bags of biscuits and a cardboard tray filled with drinks.

"They didn't have cappuccino. The closest thing was sweet tea."

"Okay, thanks, Jack," Derek replied.

Their road-trip conversation turned from NASCAR to the organization in Dalton. After a while, Jack turned to Derek and said, "There's someone in particular that I want you to meet today."

"Great. Who?"

"Our director of research and development, Dr. Chen. He's an Oriental fella."

"Okay—any reason you want me to meet him?"

"Well, now that we have a vice president of strategy—you—I thought R & D ought to report into your organization."

"My organization is just me. Where does R & D report now?"

"To Dirk back there."

Derek turned to look at Dirk, who averted his eyes.

"What's this Dr. Chen like?" Derek asked.

"You'll see," Jack responded. "He's a nice fella, but his ideas are sometimes a bit far-out."

"Like what?"

"He believes in Chinese superstitions and the crazy stuff they do down there."

"Down where?"

"China."

Derek turned around to face Dirk and asked, "What do you think, Dirk?"

"I think his pupu platter is missing a few spring rolls."

Around ten thirty, the van turned into the Dalton plant parking lot and pulled up to the building entrance. Once inside, the group said hello and got ready for a tour. At tour's end, it was time for lunch. After hush puppies, pulled pork with hot sauce, and tea, Jack said, "Derek, it's time to visit Dr. Chen."

Jack led Derek up the very rickety stairs at the back of the plant. He told him they were going to Chinatown (Sophie had told Jack the real translation after he swore not to tell Darrell).

"What's in Chinatown?" Derek asked.

"Not much—only Chen, his technical assistant, and some lab machines."

"How long have we had it?"

"Not long. Folks don't think they can come up with anything."

"Great," Derek said, thinking that Chen must be a colossal screw-up.

"Just a word of caution: Chen talks funny, has trouble with plurals."

They climbed to the top floor and approached the red door. Derek immediately noticed the Chinese foo dogs guarding the entrance. To Derek, foo dogs were disturbing evidence of opium abuse in ancient China and another sign that Jack was passing Derek a piece of shit.

Jack opened the door, revealing a small area with no windows filled with smoky plant fumes. Its décor was distinctly Chinese, an oddity for Georgia, in Derek's mind.

Standing before a lab bench was Chen, wearing his signature white lab coat and glasses with side shields. He was sipping oolong tea from a blue Lund Plastics mug. Next to him was burning incense.

Derek said, "Dr. Chen, I presume?"

He smiled, nodded, and said, "Are you Derek Vogel, the new vice presidents of some strategy?"

"Yes, I am. Nice to meet you."

"My name is Chen. I am the director of research and developments."

Holy shit, Derek thought, *Jack was right about the plurals.*

Chen introduced his technical assistant, Travis Green. Travis spoke with a pronounced Georgian accent, had a three-day growth, was drinking Mountain Dew, and had a chewing-tobacco bulge in his left cheek. Derek wondered about his new organization.

Trying to start the new relationship, Derek asked Chen about his background.

"I have some PhD in plastics sciences from Beijing Universities."

"That's impressive, Dr. Chen. What's your first name?"

"Everyone just calls me Chen."

"Like Cher."

"She is very good. I really like 'I've Got You Babes.'"

"'Half Breed' is my favorite, no offense."

"No offenses," Chen replied.

"Hey, Chen, can I ask a question?"

"Shoots."

"What's with those wild-looking Chinese dog-lions outside the door?"

"Those are some Chinese foo dog. They keep away the evil spirit."

"No kidding. Have they been on vacation?"

"What?"

"Never mind. Can I ask you something else?"

"Sure."

"What's with the incense?" Derek asked.

"It's to hide the fume from the plant."

"I see. Do Lund safety rules allow you to burn incense in a plant?"

"No, it is against some rule, but the safety inspector never come here."

"Why not?"

"Because it's too dangerous."

5

THE KOOSH

With Derek on board, Jack decided it was time for a Plastics strategy off-site meeting. A contributing factor was Dave Lund's order that Plastics develop a new strategy. The prospect didn't frighten Jack because he had a strategy-development method that had worked throughout his career: Dave Packer, PhD, a facilitator known as "Dr. Dave." Dr. Dave was not a business guru—he was a former therapist with a doctorate in abnormal psychology—but he excelled at generating discussion and finding points of agreement in groups.

Though Jack now had a qualified vice president of strategy, he felt Dr. Dave's experience would be critical to developing a strong strategy. He decided to break the news to Derek over lunch at the diner.

Once they had been served, Jack broached the topic. "Derek, I've decided it's time for Plastics to have a strategy off-site meeting."

"Great idea, Jack. I've been working on some analytical frameworks and things."

"I'm sure it's good work, but since you're still new, I'd like to do it the way I've always done strategy."

"Oh? How?"

"First, I like to involve the top fifteen to twenty folks in the business."

"Good idea."

"And take them off-site—someplace really nice, to stimulate creative thinking."

"Sounds good. Where?"

"Myrtle Beach, South Carolina."

"I've never been there."

"It's top notch—restaurants, golf, good hotels, the works."

"Good. Then how do you do strategy?"

"We take the best ideas from the team and distill them into a strategy."

"Would you like me to present any analysis, like an assessment of the plastics industry, our competitive position, and whatnot?"

"That won't be necessary. Dr. Dave and his team know how to do this."

"Dr. Dave?"

"He's our strategy consultant. Out of Macon, Georgia. One of the best."

"What does Dr. Dave do?"

"He'll go around the room asking what we're doing wrong with the business and how we can improve."

"What about strategy?"

"Derek, this is strategy—we put everyone's ideas together, pick the best ones, and bodda-boom-bodda-bang, we have a strategy."

"Bodda-boom-bodda-bang?"

"Yes, siree."

Everyone was excited about the off-site strategy adventure, except Dirk. While talking to Derek in the office kitchen, Dirk groused, "We don't need to pay for a high-priced consultant like Dr. Dave. We already have a proven strategy."

"What's that?" Derek asked.

"Simple. We produce the best plastics at the lowest costs— lower than our competitors—and our customers love our quality."

"Dirk, we're the sixth-largest in the industry—the big guys don't even know our name. How could we have the lowest costs?"

"This isn't some Ivy League business-school case, Vogel. Welcome to the real world. I've seen this work for years. Trust me."

"Stanford isn't in the Ivy League."

"Same difference."

***

Bev was in charge of off-site logistics and arrived at the Myrtle Beach Marriott two days early to set up. She arranged welcome bags for each participant, including name tags, a meeting agenda, protein bars, two drink tickets for the bar, an engraved Lund Plastics notebook, a Lund water bottle, and a package of peanuts.

The team arrived on Wednesday afternoon in time to shower and get ready for the welcome dinner. Chen came with Travis, Sophie, and Billy Lansing; they had taken the Dalton van for the long drive.

Derek greeted Chen in the hotel lobby. "Dr. Chen, great to see you. How was the trip?"

"Long but very goods," Chen replied.

"Have you had anything to eat?"

"Yes, thanks, Derek. We stopped for some nice lunch on the way."

"Oh yeah, where?"

"McDonald."

At six p.m., the team met in a large room on the hotel's second floor for appetizers and drinks. Larry La Croix was thrilled the bar had Miller Lite and complimented Jack on "going all-out for this important meeting." Trophy and Sophie went for the house chardonnay, while Jack and Dirk had scotch. Chen drank a Budweiser while Travis destroyed the appetizer tray and six Bud Lights.

After an hour, Jack stood in front to address the group.

"Before we start, I'd like to thank all of you for making room in your day jobs for this meeting. Your participation is critical to developing a great strategy for Lund." He held up his scotch and said, "Cheers!"

"Cheers!" the group echoed.

Chen shouted *"Ganbei!"* and chugged his remaining half beer.

"Good God; what was that, Chen?" Jack asked.

"It mean *cheers* in Chinese."

"But why did you chug your beer?"

"In China, we always do bottom-up after we say *ganbei*."

"That could be dangerous."

"Yes, especially with strong Chinese white liquors."

After the chuckles subsided, Jack continued. "Now let me introduce you to Dr. Dave Packer. Dr. Dave has a PhD and has worked with me on several Lund strategies over the years. He is a renowned strategist, and we are lucky to have him this week."

The group applauded enthusiastically.

Dr. Dave stood next to Jack, held up his right hand, and said, "Thank you for the warm applause. Welcome, Team Lund. Over the next two days, we will delve deeply into your business and tap each of you for ideas on how to make Plastics great. But tonight, let's really get to know each other as people."

The lights dimmed and the screen behind Dr. Dave lit up. Darrell had a remote and was orchestrating events.

"As you know, Bev asked each of you to e-mail her a picture that has special meaning to you. I would now like everyone to introduce his or her picture to the group."

There was a buzz in the group.

"Darrell has volunteered to start."

Darrell pushed a button on the remote, and a picture came up on the screen. It was a photo of Darrell with his wife, son, and daughter hiking on the Appalachian Trail the previous summer.

"Hi. Y'all know me. My name is Darrell Hartman, the chief people officer of Lund Plastics. I've been at Plastics for more than twenty years in a variety of HR positions, culminating in becoming CPO two years ago. This is my wife, Abby—my soul mate and the love of my life—and our son, DJ (for Darrell Junior) and our daughter, Jillie. This picture is from our Mother's Day trip into the Blue Ridge Mountains. When Lund becomes too stressful, I find great comfort in going back to nature with my family."

Trophy whispered to Sophie, "He works thirty hours per week doing forms. Where's the stress?"

"Not everyone does them right," Sophie said with a giggle.

Dr. Dave commented, "Thanks for sharing, Darrell. We all know about stress. Who's next?"

"Bob Davis," Darrell explained, pushing the button.

Bob Davis was the director of sales, Larry La Croix's number-two man. He was legendary at Plastics for his maniacal focus on customer entertainment, which involved copious amounts of food and alcohol and often included strip clubs. Bob was in his mid-forties, pudgy, and had thinning brown hair. He had gotten divorced a couple years earlier when his wife found an e-mail to him with topless photos from a stripper named Cyndi (with a smiley face to dot the *i*).

Bob's picture showed him wearing a Lund Plastics button-down shirt at the American Plastics Show the previous year in Las Vegas. He had his arms around two very attractive women, probably booth models. Next to him were several chubby middle-aged men.

"Hi, I'm Bob Davis, director of sales. This picture is meaningful to me because it shows what I love most: our company and our customers. Those boys up there are from Knoxville Tools, one of our largest customers. The girls are ... heh, heh, some of their sales professionals."

Sophie and Trophy looked disgusted; Darrell turned beet red, and as he was about to chastise Bob, Dr. Dave spoke up. "Thanks, Bob. That's quite a contrast to Darrell's Mother's Day photo."

The other photos were similar to Darrell's: pictures of family doing some favorite activity and descriptions like "love of my life, best friend, soul mate." Travis broke the streak with a picture of him in hunting camouflage, rifle in one hand and the bleeding head of a ten-point buck in the other.

Sophie couldn't resist. "Is he your soul mate, Travis?"

"No," joked Bob Davis, "Travis prefers females—ha!"

"Bob, have you read Lund's policies about sexual harassment?" Darrell scolded.

"No, but I think that buck might get a bang out of it—ha, ha, ha."

Jack interrupted. "That's enough, Bob. There are ladies present."

Chen went last, showing a picture of him standing next to a familiar older American man holding a book. "Hello, I am Chen, the director of research and developments. I am very happy to be in Americas and part of Plastics."

"Who's in the picture, Chen?" Trophy asked.

"Jack Welch, famous CEO from General Electricity, at his books signing at the Georgias Tech. The picture is special to me because I want to learn how to become some good capitalist."

"What a great segue way to our meeting," commented Dr. Dave. "Well, that's it. Please enjoy dinner and, if you want, each of you has two drink tickets for the bar after the meal."

After dinner, the group, minus Dr. Dave and Darrell, migrated to the hotel bar and burned through drink tickets like they were flash paper. Bob then started a tab, and momentum accelerated. By midnight, Jack, Chen, Sophie, and Trophy called it a night, but the rest powered on. With every drink, they became more optimistic about the strategy meeting. Derek thoroughly enjoyed bonding with his colleagues for the first time.

At 1:00 a.m., the bar closed, and the bartender gave Bob the bill with the walloping total: $567.35.

"Would you like to put that on your room?" the bartender asked.

"You betcha," Bob slurred.

"Just put your name and room number at the bottom with a total and sign it."

"Okey dokey," Bob giggled. He grabbed the chit, added a hefty tip, printed some information, and signed it. He handed it back and said, "Thanks, pal. You did a grrrreat job."

Looking at the generous tip, the bartender said, "It was my pleasure, and *thank you* for the nice tip, Mr. … eh, Mr.—"

"Chen," Bob finished.

"Yes, thanks, Mr. Chen."

On the way up the elevator, Billy Lansing asked Bob, "Did you do what I think you did?"

"Whadya think I did?" Bob slurred.

"Did you put the tab on Chen's room?"

"Yessirrree. Room 523—I watched him check in."

"How much was it, Bob?"

"A shitload."

The next morning, the team met in the main conference room. Eyes were red, cheeks were pale, and coffee disappeared at record speed. Travis brought a case of Mountain Dew, which was surprisingly popular that morning. The room had flip charts, round tables with chairs, water pitchers, Marriott notepads and pens, and stacks of colored Post-it Notes. Dr. Dave stood in front in a dark-blue shirt with a red tie and gray pants. He was assisted by another PhD in psychology, Terry Gregory.

Dr. Dave started, "I trust everyone got a good night's sleep— heh, heh—and we're ready to go." Bob Davis and Billy Lansing made eye contact and snickered.

The Docs had several flip charts to record the meeting flow. The first was titled "Lund Strengths." The second was "Lund

Weaknesses," and the third was "Improvement Ideas." The last was "Vision."

Dr. Dave explained the process. "Over the next day and half, we'll work as a team to fill out these charts. Before we start, I suggest some ground rules. First, there are no bad ideas. No criticisms. Build on each other's thoughts. Second, remember that Lund can be anything you want, if you work hard and truly believe. After all, Apple was just a couple guys in a garage.

"I will facilitate the discussion. Dr. Terry will transcribe your ideas on the flip charts. He's been working on his penmanship since last time. Right, Dr. Terry? Ha, ha." There was the sound of very weak laughter, except for Darrell's guffaw.

"After doing each area, we will vote on the top three ideas using colored Post-it Notes. Dr. Terry and I will count the votes. Once we have agreed on the top areas, we will work together to draft a vision for Lund Plastics."

Jack whispered to Derek, "See what I mean?"

Dr. Dave continued. "I know this is a lot of work, but it's a tried-and-true process. Most strategists consider it world-class." Dr. Dave paused for effect and then pulled out a Koosh ball, the soft rubber ball with dangling rubber strings that was easy to throw and catch.

What the ...? Derek wondered.

He continued. "We will use the Koosh to indicate whose turn it is to speak. Just raise your hand, and I will toss it to you. Any questions?"

Chen raised his hand.

"Yes, sir—Dr. Chen, is it?"

"Yes, Dr. Dave. What if I cannot catch some goose?"

"It's called a Koosh, and don't worry—it's easy to catch."

"Okay, I will give it some best shot."

"Great. Let's start with Lund strengths. Who would like to begin?"

Larry La Croix raised his hand and caught the Koosh.

"Our customers. We have very high customer loyalty." Dr. Terry wrote "Lund Customers" on the flip chart for "Strengths." Larry tossed the Koosh back.

"Very good. Who's next?"

Bobby Ray raised his hand and caught the Koosh. "We have the safest plants in the industry." Dr. Terry wrote down "Operational Safety."

Billy Lansing was next and said, "Lund has the lowest costs in the industry."

As Dr. Terry recorded this, Derek asked Billy politely, "Billy, no offense, but we are 1/7th the size of the largest producer. How can we be the low-cost producer?"

Dr. Dave immediately interrupted. "Derek, you are not allowed to speak without the Koosh. Also, remember: there are no dumb ideas."

"Just dumb people," Bobby muttered to Derek.

Dr. Dave continued. "Let's keep going. We will all get our chance to vote at the end."

Dirk got the Koosh and said Lund had the highest-quality plastic. The group nodded in vigorous agreement.

Then Chen raised his hand. Dr. Dave smiled and tossed the Koosh to Chen, who thrust his hand up to catch it. The Koosh bounced off his fingers, hit Derek on the forehead, and fell into his water glass with a splash.

As Derek wiped water off his shirt, Chen said, "Sorry, Derek, but I have some buttersfinger."

Dr. Dave resumed. "What were you going to say, Dr. Chen?"

"Lund has some R & D centers—our competitor do not."

"Very good, Dr. Chen. Just for my edification, how big is your R & D staff?"

"We are two peoples."

"Including you?"

"Yes, Dr. Dave. Travis and me."

"Interesting. Dr. Chen, you seem to view the glass half-full."

"What do you mean?"

"It's an American expression. Optimists view the glass half-full, and pessimists see it half-empty. How do you see it?"

"It depend."

"On what?"

"What's in the glass."

The group erupted in laughter; Derek marveled at Chen's wisdom.

Darrell was next and caught an errant pass from Dr. Dave. "Our people are our biggest strength," explained Darrell. "Without our people, our plants wouldn't run, and we wouldn't have any customers or any safety record—or R & D." This evoked applause from the room. Dr. Dave beamed.

And so it went. After more than two hours, there were twenty proposed strengths listed.

Dr. Dave called for a lunch break and asked the team to vote for three strengths when they returned. After eating lunch and checking e-mails, the group gathered around the easels with the list of strengths. Each thoughtfully placed Post-it Notes on his or her favorites. Voting took nearly an hour, and people agonized over their selections, frequently moving their Post-it Notes and observing the others' voting patterns, especially Jack's.

While the group took a bathroom break, the Docs tallied the votes and announced the winners: "Lund People" had by far the most votes, followed by "Quality Products" and "Low-Cost Producer."

Dr. Dave summarized. "We're making great progress, y'all. All we have left today is to define Lund weaknesses. This isn't the fun part, but we have to face reality if we're going to improve. We'll use the same approach. Who would like to start?"

Bobby got the Koosh and said, "Our 'silo organization.' Our functions are in silos and don't always work together." There was a strong murmur of assent. Dr. Terry wrote "Silos." Dr. Dave gave a knowing, condescending smile and said, "Don't worry—this comes up in almost every strategy session of mine."

Larry asked for the Koosh and said, "We only have three plants: Maine, Georgia, and Michigan. Our customers love us, but in some regions, we can't serve them. They reluctantly go to our competitors." Dr. Terry wrote "Regional Constraints."

The group stalled in finding more weaknesses. Darrell squirmed visibly in his seat, raised his hand, caught the Koosh, and said, "Communications."

"What do you mean by 'communications,' Darrell?" asked Dr. Dave, smiling smugly.

"How we talk to each other, you know? E-mail, how we don't talk clearly. Stuff like that." Heads nodded furiously.

"Very good." Dr. Terry wrote "Communications"—double-underlined.

"This is a very common issue," Dr. Dave explained, "so don't be ashamed. Lund is not alone. Okay, do we have any others?" Everyone looked at each other, pleased with the list.

Dr. Dave continued. "I guess we don't really need to vote since there are only three: organizational silos, regional constraints, and communications." Derek became increasingly worried about the meeting's output—specifically, how he was going to explain the Plastics strategy to Dave Lund.

Jack stood up and brought the day's meeting to a close. "Good work, everyone. Nice job. It's a little after four. We have free time until six. Several of us are planning to explore the boardwalk and beach. Bev, can you tell us the logistics for tonight?"

Bev stood at the back of the room and said, "Meet in the lobby at 6:00 p.m. sharp to take the bus to Ruth's Chris Steak House! Yea!"

There was a roar of approval.

Larry raised his hand. "Yes, Larry?" Bev answered.

"Bev, will we be getting more drink tickets for after dinner?"

Darrell stood up. "Let me take that one, Bev. As you may have heard, the Lund Electronics Division had an incident last year during their sales meeting in Las Vegas when several people drank too much and ended up skinny-dipping in the hotel pool with some exotic dancers."

"Sounds good!" Bob roared, to great laughter.

"Since then, corporate HR has prohibited open bars at all Lund meetings."

"What?" Larry cried.

"It's unfortunate, but this is why we gave drink tickets. Everyone here got two."

"Two? You gotta be kidding! We finished those in thirty minutes," Larry bellowed.

"I know, I know, but you can blame Electronics. Anyway, Bev has arranged for us to have a welcome drink at the restaurant and wine with dinner."

After a big steak dinner, the group returned to the Marriott and headed for the bar, like horses to the barn. No one had any drink tickets left, so Bob started a tab, giving Billy a knowing nod. The group got louder and louder, and after an hour, Sophie, Trophy, and Chen retired to their rooms. Darrell and Jack followed a few minutes later, but the rest carried on.

At midnight, Bob asked for the tab. Once again, the total was more than $400. Bob added a 20 percent tip and signed the bill to Chen's room again. He and Billy giggled the whole way back to their rooms.

At eight the next morning, the group reconvened for stage three of the process: "Lund Improvement Ideas." Bob, Billy, and several others were a bit subdued and took full advantage of coffee and Travis's Mountain Dew nap-killers.

Dr. Dave started. "Yesterday, as you remember, we agreed on three Lund strengths and found only three Lund weaknesses. Today, our job is to develop improvement ideas and then consolidate our work into a vision statement, which will be our strategy. Okay, are we good to start?"

Darrell raised and waved his hand vigorously and caught the Koosh. "We have to improve our communications."

The group nodded with approval.

"Since communication is such a big issue, why don't we get more specific?" Dr. Dave suggested. This unleashed a string of ideas from the rest of the team members. Dr. Terry wrote furiously.

"No using all-caps in e-mails to make a point. It's like e-shouting." (Murmurs of agreement swept through the crowd.)

"Let's switch functions for one week a year to understand what others go through."

"Why don't we do a ropes course to build teamwork?"

"No blind copies on e-mails. It's kinda sneaky." (There was loud applause for this one.)

"Why don't we have group coffee breaks? It might would help people talk to each other."

"I think we should have an e-mail etiquette class, and everyone has to take it." (Applause.)

"Let's hire a communications consultant. Um, no offense, Dr. Dave, but you're more a strategist."

"Why don't we have 'lunch 'n learn' sessions, where everyone brings their lunches and one function makes a presentation on what they do?"

"Let's take some operation peoples to some customer to see what happen if they use the wrong polymer in manufacturings." (This was Chen's suggestion.)

"Can we create a social committee for each location?"

"We don't need computers. If you have something to say, walk down the hall." (This was met with roaring cheers.)

"Let's have more meetings like this!" (Bev's suggestion)

The group decided to implement every communication idea immediately.

When discussion turned to the "silo organization" weakness, Darrell landed a human resource haymaker punch: "Hey, y'all, if we do all the communication stuff well, would we have a silo issue?"

"That's brilliant, Darrell," Dr. Dave responded. "Great thinking."

Just like that, the issues of "Communications" and "Silo Organization" had been slain by the same swift HR sword.

The "capacity" discussion was straightforward. The team wanted to build a fourth plant without further analysis. Jack cautioned the group. "Remember, a new plant would cost $100 million. Before we go to Corporate with this request, we better have a detailed analysis to support it." The group nodded and looked around.

Larry stood up and said, "We're all pretty busy these days running the business. Let's have Derek do the analysis. Though he doesn't know the industry, Dave Lund trusts him."

Bobby turned to Derek and whispered, "Derek, that's a ringing endorsement if I ever heard one."

There were smiles all around, and Jack agreed. With that, the "improvement ideas" were done. It was time to write the vision statement. Group composition is never easy, and the group experienced typical difficulties. Some wanted to pack the statement with everything possible. Others argued over every comma and word. Still others wanted nothing left to imagination or interpretation, insisting every word be carefully explained.

After hours of arguing and a working lunch, the team ended up with the following vision statement:

Living by our belief in People, Profits, and Possibilities,
Lund Plastics will be recognized by our customers, suppliers,
Communities, and competitors as the world
leader of the plastics industry by:

*Being the lowest-cost producer of all our products,
*Offering customers the consistently highest-quality products,
*Having world-class customer service,
*Having the most advanced technology for
developing new products, and
*Communicating, both internally and externally,
with all our constituencies, without silos.

Dr. Dave had masterfully worked the crowd to make sure no one was disappointed or felt left out of creating "The Vision." Any reasonably trained observer would, however, have concluded that the statement deviated substantially from reality and offered a perilous lack of direction.

As the meeting broke up in the early afternoon, Dr. Dave stood and closed the meeting. "First, let's give a round of applause to Bev for putting this together."

"Here, here!" Darrell said as he stood up.

"Thank all y'all. It's been a great pleasure," Bev responded, blushing. "You are all set for late check-out, and make sure to take your receipt."

Dr. Dave continued. "Congratulations, ladies and gentlemen. I've been doing this kind of strategy work for about twenty years, and I've got to say, this is the best vision statement and strategy I've ever seen. Wouldn't you agree, Dr. Terry?"

"Absolutely, Dr. Dave," Dr. Terry replied. "World-class."

With that, everyone left the room to get their bags and check out.

Chen was first in line to check out, and when he received his bill, his face turned white.

"Is there a problem, Dr. Chen?" the receptionist asked with concern.

"I do not understand. I only had two water and some M&M from the minibars, but there is bill for more than one thousand dollar."

Bob and Billy overheard the discussion and giggled.

Looking at the bill, the receptionist said, "Well, there were two charges from the main bar—one last night and one from the night before. Both charges were for room 523 and signed by Dr. Chen. That's you, right?"

"Yes, I am Chen, but I did not sign some tabs. I used Bev's drink ticket."

"What?" asked the baffled receptionist.

"I never had some bar tab."

"Let me call over to the bar to verify these charges. Just one minute." She dialed the phone, and the bartender from the first night answered.

"Jimmy, hi, it's Gloria at the front desk. Listen, we have a problem at reception. There's a Dr. Chen checking out who has two big bar charges on his bill but says he never had a tab."

While listening, she looked at her computer: "Really? You were on duty that night? I don't know. Maybe it's a language issue." Whispering and cupping the phone close to her mouth, she said, "He's an Oriental fellow and doesn't speak English good."

Gloria continued, acting surprised. "What? Are you sure? Hold on."

Turning back to Chen, Gloria said, "Dr. Chen, the bartender says the man who signed your name wasn't Oriental. Did you give your room number to someone who isn't Oriental?"

"What is Oriental?"

"Someone like you, from China and places like that with … you know." Gloria moved her hands across her face, mimicking slanted eyes.

"No, I did not give my rooms to somebody who is not Oriental."

"Our apologies, Dr. Chen, for this mix-up. I'll take those charges off your bill, and tell you what: the M&Ms are on the house."

"Thank you, Miss Gloria."

"Our pleasure, Dr. Chen. Could you do me a favor?"

"Yes, anything."

"When you get contacted for a customer survey about the front desk, will you be willing to answer five—absolutely excellent—for every question?"

6

THE DEATH STAR

A few days later, Derek walked over to Jack's office to debrief about the session. Bev was speaking to Jack.

"And the bartender said he wasn't Oriental."

"Chen wasn't Oriental?" Jack asked.

"No, whoever signed Chen's name wasn't Oriental."

"So who was it?"

"The bartender described him as slightly pink, a little pudgy all over, and very tipsy."

"That describes half the men in the Carolinas."

"That's why the hotel isn't very close to solving this, and they're out more than $1,000."

"They must be upset," Jack said.

Bev noticed Derek and said, "Oh, hey, Derek. We were just talking about a problem over Chen's bill from the Myrtle Beach meeting."

"Maybe I can help," Derek offered.

"Do you think the bartender could have mistaken Chen for someone who is not Oriental?"

Derek chuckled. "You know, Bev, some people think the term *Oriental* is offensive."

"Really?"

"Yea, but don't sweat it. I think the bartender got it right—it wasn't Chen."

"How do you know?"

"Because I saw Chen leave the bar an hour before everyone else."

"Who signed it, then?"

"Bob Davis was last to leave. I bet he's playing a prank on Chen."

"Good Lord! That would explain the perpetrator not being Oriental," Bev said.

"Yep—Bob is definitely not, um, Oriental. I would just ask him; he'll fess up."

"Gee, thanks, Derek."

After Bev left, Derek sat down across from Jack.

"Thanks for clearing that up, Derek."

"No problem. I'd hate to have Chen get in trouble over some drinks."

"Good points." They both laughed.

"How are things, Jack?" Derek asked.

"Great. I was really impressed by Dr. Dave and the new strategy."

"Yeah?" Derek commented without conviction.

"Yea, in your experience at McCutcheon, did you ever see such a strategy?"

"Not even close."

"That's what I thought: damn if the Docs didn't nail it!"

Jack continued. "Derek, don't you think we should present our strategy to Dave Lund in person?"

Dave Lund was an honors graduate of the Harvard Business School and a strategy whiz. Derek was sure he'd gag on the new strategy. Standing firm on his conviction, Derek said, "You're probably right, Jack. It would be best to talk to Dave in person about it."

Jack continued. "The new strategy's really exciting! Dave and the corporate folks will be impressed."

"Yes, they will be," Derek answered.

"Derek, I won't be around Lund too much longer, and you're the new strategist. It would be great for your development and standing for you to go to Memphis and present it—by yourself."

"Me? Alone? Do you think so?" Derek responded, nervousness clearly in his voice.

"Yes. So does Dave Lund. I called him about it yesterday."

"Really?"

"Yep. It's good news. He'd like you to come day after tomorrow."

It wasn't a trap; Jack was a believer and so were others. Just before lunch, Larry visited Jack's office.

"Jack, I just don't get why you're sending Derek to Memphis," Larry complained.

"For cryin' out loud, Larry, he's the vice president of strategy."

"Yeah, but he's new and didn't contribute much to our new strategy. He shouldn't get the credit."

"Don't worry; Dave Lund is smart enough to know that the strategy is the work of the entire team and not just Derek."

With dread, Derek set out for Memphis to meet with Dave. On the way, he called Chen.

"Chen, can I ask you a serious question?"

"Shoots."

"What do you think of our strategy?"

"I did not like the goose."

"Apart from that. What did you think?"

"To be franks, we cannot do this strategy. Lund is too small to do all these thing. We must do some specializations."

"What do you suggest?"

"Some new product."

Lund's world headquarters were on the top floor of a sleek skyscraper in downtown Memphis. The lobby was plush, and photos of generations of Lunds decorated the walls. Dave Lund's assistant, Barbara, escorted Derek back to the corner office, a spacious office with a beautiful view of the Mississippi River.

After small talk about Carol moving to Nashville, sweet tea, and the Atlanta Braves, Dave's favorite baseball team, Derek and Dave got down to business.

"Dave, as Jack probably told you, we had our Plastics strategy meeting," Derek started, dreading the inevitable strategy revelation.

"I'm really curious about how it ended up, now with you there to improve the thinking."

"There was good participation," Derek offered weakly.

"Good participation? That describes most food riots."

"Well, um, we had this facilitator named Dr. Dave."

"The guy from Macon?"

"Yes."

"With that crazy Koosh?"

"You know him?"

"Jack invited him to lead a corporate strategy session a few years ago. All we did was list ideas on charts and vote on them."

"His, um, methods haven't evolved much."

"You didn't use any of our McCutcheon strategy frameworks?" Dave asked incredulously.

"Unfortunately, no."

"I hate to ask, but what did you all come up with?"

Meekly, Derek summarized the strategy and recited the new vision statement.

Dave responded immediately. "That's the shittiest business statement ever written. Derek, you can't be the low-cost producer when you're sixth-largest, and you can't promise to do everything in a strategy; you have to make choices."

"You're right, Dave."

"Derek, I hired you to be the strategist, not the village idiot."

"I know."

"You need to find an angle or niche where we can compete successfully."

"New products may be the way to go, but no one has been able to do it in our industry."

"How's your R & D coming along?"

"It reports to me now but still only has Dr. Chen and his assistant, Travis."

"The guy with the fortunes cookie?"

At least Dave kept his sense of humor, Derek thought.

On the way out, Dave introduced Derek to Lund's chief financial officer, Miles Templeton. His office was twice the size of Dave's and ornately decorated. Miles was a big man in his late fifties wearing suspenders and large cuff links, and his well-oiled hair was combed back over his head, like Gordon Gecko's in the movie *Wall Street*. He carried an air of power and extreme confidence, despite being passed over for chief executive officer in lieu of the much younger and less experienced Dave Lund. He was quite unhappy about the choice and determined to prove everyone wrong.

Miles greeted Derek with a big smile. "Please sit down," he said.

"Thanks, Miles, it's nice to meet you."

"Likewise. I've heard a lot about you from Dave. How are things going for you at Lund?"

"Pretty well, thanks. It's a big change from The McCutcheon Group, but I enjoy the people and learning the business."

"That's good to hear," Miles said through obviously enhanced dentistry. "Though Dave has spoken quite highly of you, he hasn't told me much about your background."

Derek summarized his career. As Derek spoke, he noticed Miles's facial expressions change. Derek thought he could read Miles's mind: *Another young, lightweight Ivy League consultant with no experience in the real world, similar to Dave Lund, who beat me out of the CEO job only because he's family.*

When Derek finished, Miles simply said, "That's interesting."

"So, Miles," Derek asked, trying to change topics, "what do you do at Lund?"

"Technically, Derek, I'm the chief financial officer, which is probably self-explanatory, but I'm also the chief operating officer."

"What's that?"

"Dave doesn't follow the details too much—he's still learning our businesses, after all—so I manage the details of the company, including reviews of the financial results of all divisions."

"Plastics, too?" Derek asked.

"Of course. Unofficially, I'm Jack Thompson's boss, and he knows it."

Miles kept smiling, but there was venom in his eyes. If Dave was Lund's Luke Skywalker, Miles was its Darth Vader, brooding in the Death Star.

7

CITY FOX

Despite Dave's scolding about strategy, he endorsed Derek's lead of the new plant project, provided he had strong analysis to support such a large investment. "The Lund Board of Directors would not authorize $100 million in capital based on the gut judgment of a team who wrote that vision statement."

Derek gave the project a code name: Project Skywalker, and assembled a team comprised of Chen, Bobby, Larry La Croix, and Dirk McAllister. Over the strenuous objections of Larry, Team Skywalker decided not to hire Dr. Dave as a strategic consultant. The team did the work themselves and ultimately got approval from Dave and the Lund board of directors for the investment.

For the new plant location, Team Skywalker selected a small town in northeast Tennessee called Jackson Hill. The town had a population of 867, two restaurants, and a private club called Pickin' It for playing banjos and "visiting." The town was very rural, surrounded by beautiful mountains and forests.

Derek and Bobby made the first political overture to the town and went to meet with the mayor, Billy Ray Martin, and the chairman of the Chamber of Commerce, Tommy Ray Jackson, over tea at the Jackson Diner. Bobby explained the $100 million investment in the town, 150 permanent jobs in the plant, and another three hundred jobs for companies serving the operation. Billy Ray and Tommy Ray practically drooled with excitement.

"Bobby Ray," said Billy Ray to Bobby, "this sounds like an economic boom for our town. Tommy Ray and I are very excited. However, there are other considerations."

"Sure," answered Bobby, "what are they?"

"This has been a quiet, peaceful area," Billy Ray continued. "Folks will worry about noise, truck traffic, plant emissions and such."

"Billy Ray, I should tell you more about Lund. We are a family business and believe in doing the right things, even if it costs us more in the short-term."

"Glad to hear it, Bobby Ray. Would y'all be willing to have a town meeting and explain all this?"

To help plan the meeting, Bobby hired a public relations firm from New York. The firm was eager to have Lund as a long-term client and assigned one of their top professionals, Genevieve London, to the case. For weeks before the town hall, Bobby and Derek worked with Ms. London by phone to plan the presentation, including poster-sized pictures of the other plants, a large banner that listed Lund's values, testimonials from other communities, and a slide presentation showing the positive economic impact the project would have on Jackson Hill.

Meanwhile, Bobby purchased an option on one hundred acres outside Jackson Hill. The land was called Milton Place and was largely wooded. Its only structure was the Milton family's house.

Very early on the morning of the town hall meeting, the team took the company van to Jackson Hill. Bobby drove and Dirk rode shotgun. Chen and Derek sat in the middle seat to brainstorm about new products. Larry and Billy sat in the third row. For breakfast, Bobby brought doughnuts, Mountain Dew, and beef jerky. Chen brought a thermos of oolong tea, triggering efforts to convert him to drinking Mountain Dew.

Bobby started. "Chen, I highly recommend you switch to Mountain Dew."

Chen was perplexed by the suggestion. "Why, Bobby?"

"Mountain Dew tastes great, gives you a good buzz, and it's all-American! Don't you want to be American, Chen?"

"Good points, Bobby. I also would like to learn about NASCAR racings and the Atlanta Brave baseball team."

"Well, you're in the right crowd, Chen," Bobby continued. "Now, try a Dew."

After two Mountain Dews, Chen was a human blur, asking questions about all things American, from NASCAR to Dolly Parton to University of Tennessee football.

About halfway to Jackson Hill, the conversation turned to business. Derek asked Larry his opinion on Lund customers' biggest problems with Lund products.

"Well," Larry said, "the biggest issue is what's called microbial growth."

"What do you mean?" Derek asked.

Chen interrupted. "Many applications of plastic coating are exposed to fungis or some bug."

"What do you mean, 'bug?'"

"Some bad bacterias, like *e colis*."

"And fungi, too," added Larry. "This is bad for many surfaces. For example, black mold grows on home siding and is a health hazard, as well as an eyesore."

"It costs many dollar in sanitations to clean some mold," Chen added, sipping his third Dew.

"I see," Derek said. "Is it possible to make plastics so the bugs can't live on them?"

"It may be possibles," Chen said.

"How?" Derek asked.

"Maybe by using some differents structures that make liquid fall off. So some bug have no house. Or maybe add ion from silver to the plastic to kill the bug," Chen explained and then said, "Bobby, could I please have some more beef jerkies?"

"Are there market possibilities for this?" Derek asked.

"Several," added Larry. "One of the largest is fixtures, like toilets. Imagine if fixtures had no bacteria."

"Carol wouldn't freak out at gas stations," Derek responded.

Dirk entered the conversation. "The problem is, Derek, these plastics are difficult to manufacture without wreaking havoc in the plant, and the silver ions are very expensive. Before you joined Lund, Chen and Travis almost burned down the Dalton plant because of the high temperatures. This is why we don't mess around with these ideas."

Not too far from Jackson Hill, the team stopped at McGhee Tyson Airport in Knoxville to pick up Genevieve London, who was flying in from New York. None of them had seen her before and didn't know what she looked like. Bobby, Chen, and Derek waited outside security. Chen held a sign that read "G. London."

No sign was necessary. Out walked the archetypical Manhattan professional woman, about forty years old, tall, thin, and beautiful, with shoulder-length, straight brown hair, slightly streaked. She wore a tan suit with a matching purse and light-brown suede boots. Ms. London was a fox—a big-city fox.

Bobby spoke first. "Genevieve, I'm Bobby Ray Petry. Welcome to the great state of Tennessee, home of the Volunteers."

"Thanks, Bobby; it's great to meet you in person. I'm absolutely delighted to be here."

"Genevieve, this is Derek Vogel."

"It's a pleasure, Derek."

"Welcome," Derek responded.

Finally, Bobby turned to Chen. "Genevieve, this is Lund's director of research and development, Dr. Chen."

"What a pleasure to meet you, Doctor."

"Please, call me Chen. The pleasant is mine."

Back at the van, Genevieve met the rest of the team, all of whom were stunned by her New York beauty. She was the most elegant woman they had ever seen.

It was only noon when they drove into Jackson Hill, five hours before the town hall. Bobby suggested lunch at the Jackson Diner, and the team enthusiastically agreed. Walking in, Genevieve said it was her first barbecue experience.

Chen said, "Miss Londons, I would be happy to do some order for you."

"Why, how nice of you, Chen."

Chen ordered two pulled-pork sandwiches, fries, and two sweet teas. Genevieve beamed in gratitude, but it was obvious from her looks and physique that she had never eaten these foods.

As the group settled at a table, Genevieve opened two sugar packets and poured them into her tea. She stirred and stirred and stirred, but the sugar fell to the bottom of the glass.

Derek said, "Hate to break it to you, Genevieve, but it's physically impossible."

"What's impossible?"

"You can't get any sugar to dissolve in the tea."

"That's crazy. Why not?"

"It's already saturated."

"With what?"

"Sugar."

Genevieve took a sip. She was shocked and held up the glass in disbelief.

"Told you," Derek said.

Chen interrupted. "I prefers the oolong tea from China, but they only have some sweet tea."

"Too bad," Genevieve said with a smile.

After lunch, Bobby suggested a tour of the town. Bobby drove through Jackson Hill and slowed to show everyone Pickin' It, where several locals played banjos on outdoor benches, while others whittled wood with small knives. Several large piles of whittlings were scattered around the area.

Bobby steered the van out of Jackson Hill and, a mile later, turned onto a dirt road. The road meandered into a hilly, wooded area with an old wooden sign that said "Milton Place." There were bullet holes in the sign as well as in the mailbox by the entrance. Genevieve's face grew long with concern. Bobby turned into the driveway, which was a wide dirt trail through the woods. On the right side of the van, there was an old, rusty car in the woods with its hood and wheels gone.

In fact, both sides of the driveway were lined with abandoned, rusted, and partially dismembered cars. It was like an auto graveyard. Genevieve stared in awe. Bobby noticed her in the rearview mirror and turned to look at Derek. He mouthed the words *watch this* and smiled.

A quarter-mile down the driveway, patches of shiny metal covered the road. Dirk asked Bobby about it, and he stopped for a look. Chen opened the sliding door, and everyone looked out. There were hundreds, if not thousands, of crushed Budweiser cans. Everyone howled except Genevieve, who looked ill.

Chen was mystified. "Bobby, why are there so many Budweiser can here?"

"It must be the Miltons' recycling program."

"They must be very greens."

Bobby drove over a hill to the Milton house, a gray, rotting abode. There were many pieces of junk under the front porch, like truck tires, engines, and bathtubs. Some windows were missing, and in several places, the curtains didn't match, even in the same windows. The trail of beers led to a circular driveway, where an old, red pickup was parked. It had a gun rack and Confederate-flag stickers. Bobby had been here before, and he was enjoying himself tremendously. Genevieve's face had lost all color.

Just for kicks, Bobby said, "Hey, any of y'all seen *Deliverance*?"

At that moment, the group spied a severed deer head hanging from a tree next to the driveway. Blood still dripped from its neck. Genevieve covered her mouth with her hand in horror, her gaze following the dripping to a pool of blood. She grabbed Bobby's shoulder and said, "Let's get the hell out of here!"

The din of tires spinning on crushed Bud cans was matched by laughter in the van. Ten minutes later, back on the highway, Genevieve became giddy with relief and said, "Boys, you sure know how to show a city girl a good time."

About one hundred people attended the town hall. Their nametags revealed that a majority, both male and female, had *Ray* in their names. Lund's Bobby (Ray) felt right at home. For the first hour, Team Skywalker split up and mingled. About twenty men gathered around Genevieve, like seagulls to a dumpster. Derek wanted to chat with Genevieve but felt compelled to keep an eye on Chen to prevent a serious cultural misstep.

Chen was talking with a town elder, a ninety-year-old named Johnny Ray. They conversed energetically. Using two nearly distinct languages, they discussed American cars. Derek overheard Johnny Ray say, with a very heavy Southern accent, "It has 350 horsepower and a V8, Dr. Chang."

"That's many horse, Mr. Ray. Does it have some pickups?"

"So much that the sheriff and his deputies know me well, heh, heh, heh."

Soon afterward, the town-hall meeting started. Bobby did most of the talking; he spoke their language, and the folks loved him. He introduced the Lund team by name and position. All went well until he came to Chen, who had disappeared. While the Lund team and town folk looked around for Dr. Chen, one of the locals spoke up.

"Is Dr. Chen the Oriental fella?"

"Yes," Bobby answered.

"Ol' Johnny Ray's givin' him a ride in his Cadillac."

A few minutes later, Chen and Johnny Ray rejoined the group, both grinning ear to ear. As they shook hands, Chen said, "Thanks, Mr. Ray, for the great rides."

"My pleasure, Dr. Chang. Make sure you tell Chairman Mao about my Caddy."

Nothing could have greased the wheels of the new relationship better than news of Ol' Johnny Ray taking a shine to Chen. Connie Rae summed it up at the end of the meeting when she said, "If Lund's Oriental fella is okay with Johnny Ray, then, by golly, everything's gonna be just fine with the rest of y'all."

8

BAD FORM

Due to progress on Project Skywalker, Derek's stock had risen considerably with the Plastics team. Trophy and Bev loved his style and ideas for the business. Larry began to trust his judgment, but Dirk still questioned the need for new products, repeating ad nauseam his strategy of high volume, low costs, and quality. Derek ignored him politely, vowing to develop some products that might change his mind.

Jack even viewed Derek as a possible successor for him when he retired. One day, he asked Darrell for his views on Derek's management style.

"It's difficult to say," Darrell noted. "Derek has only one direct report, Chen, and the R & D organization only has one other."

"Damn, you're right, Darrell. We need to accelerate Derek's development as a leader. Do you have any ideas?"

"How about my management-development class? Derek hasn't taken that yet."

"He's too senior. Let's give him more intensive individual attention."

"Like what?"

"Maybe Dr. Dave and you might could mentor Derek on management."

Darrell paused in thought, then said, "It could work. I have some ideas that might help."

"Well, why don't you call Dr. Dave and work it out?"

Jack broke the news to Derek the following day at the diner. The next step was for Derek to have monthly mentoring meetings with Darrell and Dr. Dave. In Derek's mind, these meetings made Guantanamo Bay seem like a Club Med. At the first meeting, Derek learned "Managing By Objectives" (MBO), which involved having Derek's direct reports (Chen) complete a "Personal Performance Objectives Form" (PPOF). Chen would then send a copy to Derek and schedule a meeting to discuss them. At this meeting, Derek and Chen would agree on and prioritize objectives. Chen would then rewrite the form, sign it, and forward it to the people department (Darrell), who would initial it and forward it to Derek. Derek would then sign it, keep a copy for his files, and send one copy to Chen and another to Darrell. Every quarter, Derek was supposed to meet with Chen to assess his progress versus the objectives. He would write an assessment, initial it, and forward it to Chen with a copy to Darrell. Darrell's job was to make sure the progress was "SMART," which stood for "Specific, Measurable, Actionable, Realistic, and Timely." If the progress was not SMART, he would return it to Derek to start over.

"Any questions?" Darrell asked after his explanation.

"I don't know what to say," Derek commented.

"I'm glad you're impressed, Derek," Dr. Dave added. "This is a world-class process that all great leaders follow."

Derek's first foray into MBO/PPOF/SMART ("MOFMART," for short) involved calling Chen.

"Chen, this is Derek. How are things?"

"Not too bads. Travis and I develop some interesting products prototype that I like to show you next weeks when you're down here."

"That's not why I called, but great. What are they?"

"You know how we talk about developing plastics that kill some fungis?"

"You mean the ones that Lund hasn't been able to make?"

"Yes, the sames. We experiment with different polysmer, ion, and temperature, and maybe it work."

"That's pretty cool. I can't wait to see it."

"We show you next week. Okay? Bye."

"Chen, before you go, you and I have to complete the Lund MOFMART Process."

"MUFFART?"

"MOFMART. Can you write down your objectives for the year in order of priority?"

"I just tell you now: 1. Develop and commercialize product that some bad bug do not like; 2. Develop lists of some highest potentials new products for Lund futures; and 3. Help the Manufacturings complete the Jackson Hill plants on time."

"You're good at this, Chen."

"Great; done now?"

"Do you mind just writing the list on the PPOF, which is a form in the MOFMART process, and sending to me? We have to sign it and give a copy to Darrell."

"No problem. I'll fax you some signed copy this afternoon."

When Darrell got the form, he seemed happy. "Derek, we are all pleased to see how well you are handling your first MOFMART process."

The day before the trip to meet with Chen, Darrell visited Derek's office, his malodorous tennis shoes betraying his arrival by a couple seconds. Darrell suggested they travel together.

"Three hours in a car alone would be a good time to coach you on how to manage Chen. I can drive."

The next morning, they left in Darrell's Volvo, which was smellier than Derek feared, due to confinement and Darrell's well-worn safety boots behind the driver's seat.

An hour into the journey, it happened.

"So, Derek, what kind of music do you like?"

"Well, my tastes vary. I like stuff like Boston, The Talking Heads, Madonna, Jimmy Buffet, and Fine Young Cannibals."

"Reach behind your seat. There's a box of CDs. I don't have any of those groups, but there's some good stuff in there."

With great trepidation, Derek found the box that held about thirty CDs, including The Bee Gees, Cat Stevens, The Carpenters, Linda Ronstadt, Barry Manilow, and John Denver. Darrell grabbed one, popped it into the player, and handed Derek the cover.

"This is a good one," he said. It was *The Best of the Carpenters*.

While listening to "We've Only Just Begun," Darrell pounced. "Derek, do you know Lund's number-one problem?"

"I'm not sure."

"Communications."

"That's what you said at the strategy conference. I thought Dr. Dave took care of it."

"It's still a problem. People are sending e-mails instead of talking, using all caps and other stuff."

"I don't really understand."

"You see—even the two of us have a communication issue."

Derek didn't know what was worse, *The Best of the Carpenters* or Darrell's touchy-feely bloviating.

After a long pause, all Derek could say was, "Darrell, I gotta pee."

They arrived at the Dalton plant for an all-hands meeting with Derek's organization—Chen and Travis. Darrell asked to observe so he could assess Derek's management style. As they passed the foo dogs en route to Chinatown, Derek silently prayed they'd keep out evil human resource spirits. As usual, the attic was full of plant fumes and incense. They sat around Chinatown's lone table. Chen wore his usual lab coat and side shields for his glasses. He sipped a Mountain Dew—his cultural conversion was underway. Travis also wore a lab coat, looked like he hadn't shaved in several days, and drank Mountain Dew. His left cheek bulged with chew.

After talk about the weather and Mountain Dew as a tea replacement, Derek got down to business.

"Chen, I am really excited to see the product prototypes you and Travis have developed."

"Good, let's start some meetings," Chen said enthusiastically. From under the table, Chen pulled out five small samples.

"Derek, Americans Siding is by far the leadings residentials siding company in the North Americas," explained Chen. "They have some strict products specs for sidings the bug do not like, and we can't meet them."

"Why not?" Derek asked. Darrell watched passively.

"Because they are very picky about the bug, like black mold. Black mold make some house ugly and not good for the healths. We haven't been able to meet this criterias."

"Do you know why we can't?"

"We thinks some combinations of polysmer and temperature, maybe chemicals additive too."

"So, what are you and Travis trying to do?"

"We made some products sample in the laboratory. In each, we use differents polysmer and differents temperature in some machine and add some silver ion too. These are five sample. Very promising."

"Have you tested them for mold?"

"Yes, all much better than our regular products."

"Good enough for American Siding?"

Chen smiled a little. "Yes, two are clearly bad home for the bug. Three are close."

Derek grinned.

"Chen, are you telling me that you and Travis solved the problem? This product could be 20 percent of our volume, no?"

"No? Do you mean yes?" Chen asked.

"It's an expression, Chen. No means yes sometimes."

"English is tougher than the Mandarin sometime. Derek, we still have some problem."

"What?"

"We can't make it."

"But what's this?" Derek asked, pointing to the samples.

"These are the lab's products prototype. We can't make it in the plants."

"Why not?"

"Manufacturings doesn't want to. They like their polysmer and don't want to hurt their productions with temperature or some chemical ion. Remember what Dirk said on our roads trip about the fire?"

Darrell started fidgeting in his seat. Chen continued.

"Derek, we have some another problem, too."

"Worse than that?"

"Maybe."

"What?"

"Sale and Marketings won't let me talk to Americans to work with them."

"Why not?"

"Maybe because I'm Chinese or not in sale. I dunno."

"Let me get this straight, Chen: Manufacturing won't try making it, and Sales won't let you talk to the customer."

"No offenses, but I don't think they let you talks to some customer either, Derek."

"No offense taken. So we have some organizational issues, Chen. Let's not get all bummed out by this."

"But, Derek—"

"Listen, Chen. Travis. You guys have really come up with something. You may have cracked the code. This could be 20 percent of our business and much more profitable than our other products. This is really exciting! You guys should be psyched. Chen, this is great!"

Just then, Darrell broke his silence, leaned forward, and said, "Dr. Chen, have you completed your MOFMART process?"

Foo dogs are worthless, Derek thought.

"Huh?" Chen asked with a stunned look.

"Have you done your objectives and filled out the PPOF?"

"Yes. I wrote my PPOFs and faxed some to Derek," Chen explained.

"Well, you need to make your PPOF SMART and send the original."

"My PPOFs is not SMART?" Chen asked.

"No, which in this case means no. It must be specific, measurable, actionable, realistic, and timely. Your objectives were missing some dates and specifics about end products."

Chen was severely wounded by the allegation. He frowned, and his eyes watered.

"So sorry, Darrell. I do it now."

9

OPEN ARMS

Jack and Derek had lunch at the diner the next day. Kim brought them open-face turkey sandwiches with gravy, fries, and tea.

"So, Derek, I heard you had a good trip to Dalton yesterday with Darrell."

"Yeah, it was very interesting and encouraging, despite the shoe odor."

"Don't you know it. I try to catch a cold before road-tripping with him."

"That's tough to time just right."

"You're not kidding, and I've gotten strange looks licking door knobs."

"I wish I had a picture. Anyway, Jack, the trip was encouraging."

"How so? Do you mind passing the ketchup?" asked Jack, who bathed his fries in Heinz magic.

"Chen and his team have developed prototype plastic that appears to solve the microbial specs of American Siding."

"Darrell mentioned something about that."

"Jack, if we got a quarter of American's volume, it would be about 20 percent of our business. And at higher margins."

"I heard there are issues."

"Manufacturing won't try a new polymer and ion additive system, and Sales won't let anyone talk to American to learn what they truly need. It's hard to be successful with those constraints."

"Both Dirk and Larry talked to me about it. They think it's high-risk. Remember the fire? Plus, we are selling everything we make now at good margins."

"Jack, we're small. We must be different."

Jack suddenly stared at the French fries and got very quiet.

"Is there something wrong with your fries, Jack?"

"No, sorry. There's just something I would like to talk to you about confidentially."

"Sure."

"I'm turning sixty-five next month, and after talking to Dave Lund, I decided to retire."

"Who will take your place?"

"I spent an afternoon with Dave Lund last week talking this through. We decided that you are ready to take over as president."

"Me? Really?"

"We know you're young and new to the industry and all, but as you said, we need to be different. Dave and I also agree that Lund Plastics must change or the bigger competitors will crush us. We have seen your early work with Chen and his R & D organization and Project Skywalker and are impressed. We also think new products are key for the future."

"What will Dirk and Larry think?" Derek asked.

"They'll be pissed off."

"Not encouraging."

"No offense, Derek, but they're older and much more experienced in the industry, and they always thought they'd take over."

"Won't that be a problem?"

"Probably, but you have Dave Lund's support. You'll just have to win them over."

"Thanks for your confidence. When will it be announced?"

"Tomorrow morning at my staff meeting, followed by a memo to all of Lund Plastics in the afternoon."

That night, Derek announced the news to Carol.

"Wow, Derek, that's really great. I'm so happy for you!"

"I'm still stunned."

"My parents will be, too."

"They have such confidence in me."

"Well, Derek, this is a day of big news. Guess what?"

"President Bush invaded Jamaica?"

"No, silly. I went to the doctor today, and you're going to be a daddy."

Derek's glow tarnished rapidly the following day. Jack's announcement shocked his staff. Out of politeness, no one said anything to Derek in the meeting. But their looks made it clear. Larry's face turned red. Dirk just shook his head. Bobby smiled, but due to political instincts, he did it on the sly.

After the organization-wide announcement, Chen called. "Derek, this is some goods news; now we can do new product developments."

"Deal, Chen, but no more fires, okay?"

"Scout honors."

When Bev heard, she hugged Derek and asked to be his executive assistant.

Weeks later, Derek moved into Jack's spacious office and focused on implementing the new product strategy and tending to Carol's pregnancy. The pregnancy had turned into a bigger deal than initially thought: Carol was having twins, a boy and a girl. Derek referred to them as "Bonnie and Clyde;" he was completely unaware of the office nicknames for Trophy's physique.

During evenings, Derek and Carol attended a Lamaze program at the Nashville YWCA. The most notable part of Lamaze was *the movie*, which contained scenes from birth. *The movie* was the most frightening, goriest thing Derek had ever seen. He thought couples should see it before cavorting without protection. After seeing it, he said to Carol, "If the Chinese used it, they wouldn't need their one-child policy."

"No kidding, Derek. It could lead to human extinction. By the way, you're never touching me again."

The new product strategy was even more difficult to deal with than Bonnie and Clyde, because Chen and Bobby were the only ones who believed in it. Everyone else didn't think it possible, and in any event, the business was doing well without new products.

Then one day, only a few months into Derek's presidency, Lehman Brothers failed, Wall Street crashed, and economic panic hit the country. Americans severely cut spending, and sales of industrial plastics plummeted. As a result, the market for Lund products cratered, and prices fell 50 percent within a few weeks.

In the middle of Derek's gloom, Chen called.

"Derek, I hear that the price for Lund product is much lower."

"Unfortunately, Chen, it's true—50 percent lower."

"Some bad news. Derek, do you view the glass half-empty or half-fulls?"

"A wise man once told me it depends on what's in the glass."

"You are some good student."

"Why do you ask?"

"The situation is bad, but maybe also good."

"How so?"

"Because now, maybe everyones will want some new product."

10

MONIQUE

After Jack's retirement, Darrell felt more empowered to crank-up Lund's diversity efforts. His first opportunity came from Trophy, who came to Darrell's office one day and, after remarking on his latest "teamwork" poster, sat down and said, "Well, Darrell, Steve just gave me his notice." Steve was Trophy's head of accounting.

"Why?"

"He decided to pursue his dream of playing professional poker."

"Like those guys on TV with the sunglasses and hats?" Darrell asked.

"Yep. Apparently, he's been playing online and making a killing."

"Does he wear sunglasses when he plays online?"

"No, the players online can't see each others'—oh, never mind."

Darrell put his hands together in deep thought. "B'linda, this may be an opportunity to up our game."

"Steve is my best accountant. How can we up our game?"

"By hiring a woman, preferably one of color."

Darrell and Trophy agreed on a recruiter, and after a few weeks, they interviewed several candidates, all women. Due to the recession, there were many good choices. They chose Monique D'Estaing, an African-American woman originally from New Orleans.

The morning of Monique's first day of work, Darrell said to Trophy, "Tro—I mean, B'linda, this is a great hire. Monique increases our diversity along two dimensions. She's a woman, and she's African-American."

"Not that it's relevant to you, Darrell, but she's also an excellent accountant."

"I didn't realize that. Did that come out in the reference checks?"

"Yes, and she may increase diversity along a third dimension."

"Is she Hindu?"

"How many black, Cajun Hindus do you know? No, it's something else. See if you can pick it up."

Thirty minutes later, Monique arrived for her first day of work, carrying her motorcycle helmet into the office. Trophy greeted her, and after showing Monique her new office, she gave her a walking tour and introduced her to everyone. First stop was Derek's office, where Bev and Bobby had gathered for coffee.

Trophy walked in with her signature spiked heels, wild frock of blonde hair, and a tight dress that accentuated her impressive figure. Derek had trouble keeping his eyes off Trophy's famous twins. As a result, he failed to notice Monique immediately, but Bev and Bobby did.

Monique was an obvious change from the usual male, white culture of Lund Plastics. Notably, she was African-American, the first in the Nashville office. But her distinction went far beyond race. Monique stood six feet tall, and both sides of her head were shaved. From the top of her forehead to the back of her head, however, she had a stripe of thick, kinky hair that stood at least four inches tall. Very large, silver loop earrings accentuated Monique's hair. She wore an outfit of slacks and a long-sleeve shirt that displayed a high degree of fitness, along with pumps that made her seem about six foot three.

"Derek, Bev, and Bobby, I'm pleased to introduce you to our new director of accounting, Monique D'Estaing."

Everyone shook hands. Bobby was speechless. Derek said, "Monique, it's great to have you on board. We hope you enjoy it here."

Monique spoke with a pronounced Southern accent with a hint of Cajun. "I'm happy to be here, Derek. I look forward to working with all y'all."

Immediately after Monique left, Darrell came to the office.

"Well, what do y'all think of Monique?" he asked.

"She's really tall, y'all!" Bev said.

"I've never seen anything like her," Bobby said.

"How so?" Darrell asked.

"She's a giant, and what's with the hair?"

"It's her culture, Bobby," Darrell added stupidly.

Derek spoke up. "You know, I've never seen a haircut like that either, not even in Boston. It's like a hybrid between an Afro—if I'm allowed to say that—and a Mohawk."

Darrell said, "You really shouldn't say either of—"

Bobby interrupted and jumped to his feet. "It's a 'FroHawk!"

Derek and Bev could hardly stop laughing.

Later that day, Trophy visited Darrell.

"Well, Darrell, have you figured out an additional way Monique may help us with diversity?"

"Hairstyles aren't a protected class, B'linda."

"No, but her 'FroHawk is the talk of the office."

"I don't know. Can you give me a hint?"

"I think she plays for the other team."

"Monique's a corporate spy?"

"No, she bats from the other side of the plate."

"She's a lefty?"

"She prefers women, Darrell."

"Oh. Well, that's great. Corporate HR will be really happy about this."

11

BONNIE AND CLYDE

Months later, Monique had settled in, the recession continued to crush the industrial-plastics industry, and Carol's Bonnie and Clyde had grown to enormous proportions.

One morning, Derek was sitting in his office responding to e-mails, and the phone rang. It was Carol.

"Derek, Bonnie and Clyde are making their getaway."

"Seriously? What's happening?"

"I just had my first contractions."

"How far apart are they?"

"About forty-five minutes. The doctor said to hang tight at home. It'll still be awhile."

"I'll rush home right away."

"You don't need to come home yet, but you better clear your schedule for the next couple days."

"Okay, Carol. Hang in there. I love you."

"Love you, too."

Shortly after the call, Bev stuck her head in Derek's office.

"Derek, B'linda stopped by to see you. I told her to come back at ten thirty."

"That's fine; thanks, Bev."

When Bev announced B'linda's arrival, she almost referred to her as Trophy. Before Trophy sat down, she said, "Derek, excuse me, but Bev said you had time to talk."

"Sure, Tr—B'linda. How are you?"

"I've been better."

"What's wrong?"

"You know how prices have tumbled since you became president."

"Hopefully not cause and effect."

"Well, the accounting team has been updating our profit forecast for the year. It looks very grim."

"How bad?"

"We originally budgeted about $30 million in profit this year, but things have gone south—far south."

"How far?"

"Antarctica. I hate to say this, Derek, but we expect to *lose* $3 million a month for the rest of the year."

"Are you kidding?"

"Unfortunately, no, and next year looks worse—losses of maybe $50 million."

"B'linda, that's really bad. I don't know how we can recover from such huge losses."

"Derek, I hate to say this, but we may have to shut down one of the plants, which would be Maine, because their costs are the highest."

"Shit. A hundred and fifty employees with no other job prospects in the area."

"I know, Derek; we have to find a way to recover."

The phone rang. It was Bev.

"Excuse me, Derek, but our equipment supplier from Germany is on the line. He would like to have dinner with you on Thursday when he's in the United States."

B'linda sat patiently, waiting to resume the conversation.

"Sorry, Bev, but I can't do it—I will have my hands full with Bonnie and Clyde."

Trophy gave Derek a surprised look, which he acknowledged with a wink and a smile.

12

THE TROUBLE WITH XY

Trophy broke into tears and stormed out of the office, slamming the door behind her. Bev immediately came in.

"What happened?"

"I don't know. One minute, I was on the phone with you, the next, she was in tears and running out."

"Derek, when you mentioned Bonnie and Clyde over the phone, did she hear you?"

"Of course. She was sitting five feet from me. I even looked at her and winked."

"You winked?"

"What?"

"Oh, boy. Bonnie and Clyde are also the nicknames for B'linda's breasts."

"It can't be—those are the nicknames for our twins," Derek pleaded.

"I thought you knew."

In the middle of Derek's sincere apology to B'linda a few minutes later, Carol called again. "Derek, the contractions are coming much faster and harder now. I think it's time to come home."

"I'll be right there."

After checking into the hospital, Derek and Carol settled into a birthing room. It was beautifully decorated, like a bedroom. There was also a television on the wall. While Carol got hooked up to the heart monitor, Derek took inventory of the channels. Carol was relatively coherent, so Derek chose more women-friendly channels, like The Lifetime Movie Channel and Oxygen.

As day turned to night, the contractions got severe; there was a parade of nurses and doctors in the room. Derek fed Carol ice chips to keep her hydrated. But in the freezer, he found all kinds of ice cream, which he enjoyed secretly between contractions.

Around 10:30 p.m., things got ugly, and Carol started to lose it. Derek's efforts to comfort her were increasingly futile. During one set of violent contractions, Carol caught Derek eating ice cream.

"Derek, you fricking asshole! I'm dying here and you're eating ice cream."

Derek was relieved Carol hadn't dropped the "f-bomb." At eleven p.m., he made a critical error by changing to channel to ESPN to catch *Sports Center*. Derek was particularly interested in an important Red Sox-Yankee series. Unfortunately for Derek (and Carol), Bonnie and Clyde inflicted a particularly painful series of contractions during the show. At first, Carol was in too much pain to notice Derek enjoying ESPN. She had two nurses helping, one on each hand. The nurse on Carol's right blocked her view of Derek, but when the nurse moved, Carol saw Derek watching television.

"Derek, you fricking jerk! Are you watching baseball?"

"It's just *Sports Center*."

"Just *Sports Center*? You did this to me, and now you—ow! —you're eating ice cream and watching sports! When this is over, I swear I'm gonna cut off your —ow! Ow! *Ooowww!*"

Carol was now fully dilated and started pushing. Minutes later, Bonnie arrived. She was pink, slimy, and had a stripe of dark hair over the center of her head—a baby Mohawk. Perhaps inspired by her mother, Bonnie let out a huge cry. A short while later, Clyde made the scene. He was smaller and less pink. Instead of screaming, he looked around the room in great wonder, particularly at the younger blonde nurse. Clyde had big, round eyes, and as he stared at the blonde, his little hands had already found his boy parts.

Derek chuckled and said to himself, "That settles it—it's nature over nurture."

13

CHEN AND HIS SIDE EFFECTS

Bonnie and Clyde came home with Carol two days after their birth, triggering negotiations over names. For Bonnie, Derek and Carol agreed on Charlotte. Clyde's name was a hard-fought battle. Derek lobbied for masculine, tough names like Achilles, Maximus, or Patton. Carol, in league with their women neighbors, was horrified by his choices. In the end, they compromised on Everest.

A few days later, the Vogels' doorbell rang. Derek was upstairs, and Carol answered. It was a large bouquet of flowers. Derek came down while Carol read the note. She said, "How odd."

"What is it?" Derek asked.

"We got these beautiful flowers as a present, but the note is a little strange."

"What does it say?"

"'Dear Derek and Carols, Congratulation on the two new baby! I hope everyone has good healths.'"

"Remember me telling you about Dr. Chen, our Chinese R & D director? It must have come from him," Derek said.

"How did you know?"

"He has issues with plurals, and I saw that line on a fortune cookie he made for Jack."

Several days later, Derek returned to the office. Several pink message slips awaited him. Miles Templeton wanted Derek to call immediately upon his return, and Bev said he was extremely unhappy. Dave left a warmer message, congratulating Derek on the twins, but also requested a call.

Derek called Miles first, who answered with a gruff, "Miles Templeton."

"Hey, Miles, it's Derek Vogel returning your call."

"Where have you been?" he barked.

"My wife just had twins. I've been home with them a few days."

"It's a piss-poor time to be away. I received your grim new financial forecast. What the hell are you guys doing? How can you possibly submit a forecast going from $30 million in profit for the year to big losses?"

"It's all price drops from the Great Recession, Miles."

"And you didn't see this coming?"

"No, I don't think anyone saw the Lehman failure and bank meltdown—" Derek tried to explain.

"What a joke, Vogel. Not only does this screw us this year, but we are investing $100 million on a new plant in your very shitty business."

"I know, Miles. I'm sorry."

"Sorry doesn't begin to cut it. Dave Lund should have listened to me about you," Miles said tersely. "I want your team to have profit-improvement ideas worth $10 million on my desk by next month. Got it?"

"Loud and clear."

After being excoriated by Miles, Derek called Dave Lund.

"Derek, congratulations to you and Carol about the twins, but about your forecast—it's a gigantic turnaround. Do you know what this means to Lund?"

"Dave, I'm really sorry, but B'linda and I thought we should get all the bad news out at once."

"I appreciate that, but what do you plan to do about it?"

"Of course, we will have a hiring freeze and stop all travel, except for visiting customers," Derek explained.

"No offense, Derek, but we're talking more than $30 million. That's a lot of plane flights, not to mention, most of your travel and entertainment budget is already spent on customers. Bob Davis is an entertaining legend."

"I know, Dave. It won't begin to move the dial."

"Derek, this is what we were afraid of. Prices fall, and our competitive position becomes very weak."

"I think we need to accelerate our move into new products."

"That's why we promoted you, Derek. You need to change our strategy and find a competitive angle that works for a smaller player like Lund. It won't happen overnight, but you've got to approach this with a sense of urgency."

New products were the best hope, so Derek called Chen.

"Hello, this is Chen."

"Chen, this is Derek. Thank you for the beautiful flowers. Carol loved them."

"You're welcome. I hope the two baby are good."

"They're great, thanks. How are things with the foo dogs and Chinatown?"

"Still hot, humids, and full of smoke."

"Well, I hope it doesn't make you homesick for Beijing. Hey, listen, I would like to talk to you about the antimicrobial plastics."

"Okay. We are making some goods progress. I can update my MUFFARTs form."

"Chen, forget about MOFMARTs for now; just don't tell Darrell. We need to jump-start this project and make it happen."

"Great, but what about some issue with Manufacturings and Sale?"

"I have an idea. What if we make a team with members from all functions and give the team authority to make it happen?"

"Sound interesting. Who?"

"Well, you should lead the team, and Travis needs to be on it."

"Okay."

"How about getting Bob Davis from Sales? Larry La Croix trusts him. Also, I hear the buyers for American Siding like to be entertained. That's right in Bob's wheelhouse."

"Wheelmouse?"

"Wheelhouse. A sweet spot. Something he would be good at. It's an American sports term."

"Okay, I see," Chen said. "We also need someones from the Dalton plants with a wheelhouse."

"Huh? Oh, yeah, I understand. Who do you recommend?"

"How about some Croatian guy in Qualities, Sergej?"

"Is he good?" Derek asked.

"Yeah, and he also has some wheelhouse. His English is not so good, but I can help him."

"That's really funny, Chen. We need a finance person to help with costs and pricing."

"Gerry Sanders from Accountings would have some good wheelhouse," offered Chen.

"Great. Do we need someone from Human Resources?"

"I can ask Sophie Garibaldi, the HRs manager here in Dalton. She has some MBAs from the University of Georgias and does not like MOFMARTS or sensitivity trainings."

"Perfect."

Two days later, Team Antimicrobial met at the Dalton plant for the kickoff. The team was made up of Chen and Travis from

R & D, Bob Davis from Sales, Sergej from Manufacturing, Gerry from Accounting, and Sophie from Human Resources. Everyone was energized by the exciting project and sugar from Mountain Dew and copious glazed doughnuts served at the meeting. The sugar buzz from this room was ideal for creativity.

Travis wore his white lab coat and sported his usual three-day stubble. Chen also wore a lab coat and had safety shields on the sides of his glasses. Bob was puffier and redder than usual. Sophie, with her wavy, dark hair and tight jeans, was a particularly great addition, in Bob's mind. He hadn't met Sophie before, and his gaze was glued to her.

Sergej was a big fellow with thick glasses and a heavy Slavic accent. He looked about thirty years old and was thrilled to be on the team. Gerry was an accountant in his thirties with neat hair and a blue short-sleeve, button-down shirt.

After small talk about the Atlanta Braves and University of Georgia football, two of Chen's new American interests, Derek addressed the group.

"Good morning, Team Antimicrobial. I am thrilled that you all agreed to be on this important team. As you know, Lund is facing a severe downturn from the great recession. We need to do something different, and you are the cutting edge. Dave Lund and I believe that the future of Lund Plastics will be the creation of new products that have higher prices and more profits. In fact, I would like us to strive for new products to be 50 percent of our revenue within five years. It's a big, hairy goal, but we can do it. Your job is to create the first major product: antimicrobial coating for home siding. Each of you has different skills that will be helpful in getting this done. I would like you to work as a team to do this better and faster than we ever imagined.

"To make your job easier, I have a surprise for you, something very different. From now on, you are your own company. For now, we'll call you The Antimicrobial Company, but you can develop a different name. Chen is your president, and he is in charge.

Your job is to develop the product, manufacture it, and sell it to American Siding—and maybe others. That's all I have for this morning. I now turn it over to President Chen. Good luck with this important and exciting task, and thank you."

The team clapped and cheered. Chen stood and spoke to his team.

"Thanks, Derek, and thank you teammate. This is the first times I am presidents of some company. I know it is difficults, and I try not to make so many big mistake of other first presidents."

The team stole furtive glances at Derek.

Chen continued. "Before we print some new business card, I would like to brainstorms about our company names."

The room was immediately abuzz. Chen beamed, and the group immediately went to work. For the next hour, the group brainstormed about company names. They developed several possibilities, including Chen's suggestion of "The Wheelhouses," but the finalists were "Chen and His Side Effects" and "Bug Off."

The team chose Bug Off. Sophie became Bug Off's chief people officer, and she volunteered to order business cards. Chen assigned titles to everyone else. Over lunch, they designed a logo and decided to order team polo shirts with the new name and logo. Gerry created a new Bug Off profit-and-loss spreadsheet.

For the next several weeks, Bug Off worked full time on antimicrobial siding. Bob Davis, Bug Off's senior executive vice president of sales and marketing, stayed in Dalton the whole time, which caused a dramatic drop in Lund's travel and entertainment spending. There were also rumors that gentlemen's clubs in Nashville were suffering financially.

Travis continued his polymer and silver ion experiments from months earlier, while Sergej and Gerry estimated manufacturing costs. Chen and Bob spoke regularly with American Siding's chief buyer in southern Alabama, Billy Headland. American was eager to have another plastic-coating supplier and gave Bug Off detailed product requirements.

In three weeks, Bug Off had successfully developed product prototypes. To ensure that the team thoroughly understood the customer's needs, Chen organized a road trip to their plant. He rented a van, and one afternoon, they set out for Alabama. When Travis asked about dinner, Chen said, "Don't worry; I loaded up some bucket of Kentucky Fried Chickens and Mountain Dews for our roads trip."

Team Bug Off met Billy Headland the next morning. Billy was in his early fifties, had thin, blonde hair, and looked permanently sunburned. He had a normal build, except for his stupendous gut. For the first hour of the visit, Team Bug Off got to know Billy over cinnamon rolls, coffee, and Coca-Cola. The conversation centered on golf and fishing. Billy was a diehard bass fisherman who traveled to fishing tournaments throughout the South in a camper filled with beer and pork rinds.

The team toured the plant with Billy and the plant manager. They watched workers apply plastic coating to siding. Billy asked Chen when the Lund coating would be available. Chen said it would probably be a couple months. At the end of the tour, Billy said to the team, "Y'all, if your coatings meet our specifications and the price is right, we could ramp up to about half your Dalton plant capacity."

On the way back to Dalton, Gerry sat in the front with Chen, and they estimated the annual revenue of Bug Off. Excitement gripped the team.

A few weeks later, Team Bug Off convinced the Dalton plant to try manufacturing the new polymer coating. The process worked, and there were no fires. The team shipped a batch of product to

American Siding for qualification. Three days later, Billy called Chen and Bob.

"Hey, y'all, we tested your coating, and it worked just fine."

"That's great news, Billy. Maybe now it's some good time to talk prices," Chen replied.

"Hey, do y'all play golf?" asked Billy.

Bob jumped at the opportunity. "Sure do, Billy. What do you have in mind?"

"Why don't y'all come down in a few weeks? We'll play golf, have a beer, and talk bidness."

The prospect of customer golf frightened Chen. Communist China regarded golf as bourgeois decadence, and Chen was far from athletic. But as the president of Bug Off, he'd take up the game. For the next three weeks, Chen and Travis devoted their lunch and after-work time to take lessons at the Dalton Driving Range. Golf dominated conversation at team meetings, mostly to strategize about playing with Billy. The team agreed on Bob as the lead golfer because he was in Sales and was a good player. Chen also needed to play because he was the president. Chen asked Travis to be his caddie. Gerry volunteered to play if Sergej caddied for him. Sophie offered to drive the beer cart, promising to keep Billy fully lubricated.

Three Fridays later, Team Bug Off arrived at the Lower Alabama ("L. A.") Riviera Country Club. They parked the van, and out popped Chen wearing corduroy golf knickers, knee socks, saddle-shoe golf spikes, a new Bug Off-logo golf shirt, and a plaid Scottish golf cap. Beneath the cap, Chen wore large sunglasses that fit over his normal glasses. If China and Scotland ever had unprotected sex, the result would have looked like this.

Travis followed, wearing a white full bodysuit with a sign on his back that said "Chen." He looked like the caddies at The Masters Tournament, except he wore boots, had a mouth full of Red Man Chewing Tobacco, and donned an old, stained John

Deere hat. A large bottle of Mountain Dew protruded from his back right pocket.

Gerry followed Travis and wore pink-and-blue checked pants with a wide, pink belt and new, white golf shoes. He also donned a Bug Off golf shirt and a Bug Off hat. His caddie, Sergej, had the same white bodysuit as Travis. Sergej was a big man, and his suit was too short, exposing half of his calves. He wore black socks and enormous Converse high-top basketball shoes, along with a worn and faded Atlanta Braves baseball hat.

Bob exited the van after Sergej, dressed like Gerry. Sophie emerged last. She wore a very short, tight plaid skirt that matched Chen's hat, exposing her shapely and tan legs, a very tight Bug Off polo shirt, designer sunglasses, and no hat.

The team members stared at her. "If I'm going to be the beer girl," Sophie explained, "I need to play the part. Just don't tell Darrell—he thinks I should be gender-neutral."

Billy Headland watched Team Bug Off approach the first tee, thinking he would win money on golf and prevail in price negotiations. He was particularly intrigued by Chen's equipment: for head covers on his woods, Chen had Chinese foo dogs, a takeoff on Tiger Woods's head covers.

Billy spied the foo dogs as Chen approached the first tee and asked, "Chen, what in God's name are those head covers?"

"These are some foo dog, Billy."

"Scary-lookin' things. What're they for?"

"They keep away the evil spirit, and hopefully, the three-putt," Chen answered.

"What d'ya know. Well, fire away, Chen ol' buddy—you're up."

Chen stood between the tee markers of the first hole, a par-four, and Travis positioned himself about ten feet away.

"Travis, please give me my 3-drivers," Chen said.

"Yes, Mr. President," responded Travis as he handed Chen a 3-wood.

Travis pulled a large, laminated card out of his back left pocket. It was Chen's golf checklist.

"Okay, Travis, let's start."

"Grab the club, left hand above the right," Travis read from the list.

"Checks."

"Point the club head away from your body."

"Checks."

"Line up with your feet towards the target."

"Checks."

And so on. It took about five minutes to go through the list, but finally, Chen was ready. He took a swing with the grace of a grand mal seizure and hit the ground a foot behind the ball. The resulting divot was so large, it folded over the ball.

"Practice swing," announced Billy graciously.

Chen abbreviated his pre-shot routine and tried again. After a few efforts, he made contact, sending the ball fifty yards into the right rough.

"You got alla that one, Mr. President," commented Travis.

Gerry and Bob followed Chen, with much greater success. In the meantime, Sophie had worked with Billy to stock a golf cart with two cases of beer and peanut butter crackers. Billy cracked his first beer before he hit his drive. It was 10:15 a.m. Sophie noticed and gave Chen a knowing smile.

It took forty-five minutes to play the first hole, due to Chen's checklist and very high score. Billy finished two beers before two-putting for par. Billy was a ringer and a prodigious beer drinker, which accounted for his impressive gut. After the first hole, the group agreed on a "mercy rule," where no score could be more than twice par (e.g., an 8 on a par-four). Chen was the primary beneficiary of the rule, and he reached his limit well before reaching most greens.

Sophie was a brilliant beer girl, keeping Billy with an active beer continually and flirting with him shamelessly. Chen drank sparingly and focused on getting a large order from Billy, not to mention making contact with the ball.

After the front nine, the group stopped for refreshments and tallied the score. Billy was only one over par, and he had consumed ten beers. Chen's score required a computer. Bob and Gerry were in-between Billy and Chen.

During play on the back nine, Billy easily maintained his pace of one beer per hole. Chen enjoyed the golf and asked Bob whether he was country-club material. Travis had switched to beer and was going *mano a mano* with Billy.

Just shy of the eighteenth green, Billy finished his nineteenth beer. He birdied the hole to shoot a three-over-par 75. While everyone shook hands, Billy invited the group into the bar to talk business. Billy ordered a beer while walking to the table. Travis, Bob, Chen, and Gerry ordered beers, and Sophie asked for the house chardonnay. Billy ordered three baskets of French fries, two orders of supreme nachos, and a couple orders of hush puppies. Bob was delighted by the caloric orgy to come.

The group regaled over the round. Chen's score was 144, exactly 72 over par. Looking at the card, Chen said, "If only a few of those putt hadn't had lips."

After the second round of drinks, the discussion turned to business. Billy said the quality of Lund's coatings was satisfactory, and American Siding was ready to order. But he said his current suppliers had cut prices, so he couldn't offer what Lund was expecting.

"What prices are you offerings?" Chen asked.

Billy didn't respond. Instead, he grabbed a small white sugar packet and, using a golf pencil, wrote a number on it. He slid it across the table to Chen.

Chen picked it up and said, "We can't make some monies at that price."

Chen grabbed a small blue pack of Equal, wrote a number on it, and slid it over to Billy. The sugar and Equal packets slid back and forth for fifteen minutes until finally, Chen shook Billy's hand and said, "Billy, you have some deal."

The long drive back to Dalton was like a carnival. Chen was giddy. The negotiated price was 5 percent higher than expected, and the volumes were also quite better. Bug Off was off to a great start.

After a dinner stop at Chick-fil-A, Chen turned to Gerry in the passenger seat.

"Gerry, do you think Bug Off should go publics?"

14

$10 MILLION

The next day, Derek was responding to e-mails when his phone rang.

"Hello," he answered.

"Derek, this is Chen."

"Mr. President. How is Bug Off?"

"I have goods news. Team Bug Offs met with Americans Siding yesterday, and we got some first orders for the anti-bugger coating."

Derek chuckled. "Chen, that is outstanding. Nice work."

"There's mores. Their orders for the next two month are 10 percent of the Dalton plant productions. And after two month, they increase to 25 percent of productions."

"Mr. President, congratulations!"

"Derek, there's mores."

"More?"

"The price is 40 percent higher than some other products. We will make good profit."

"Chen, this will make a big difference to Lund and shows how the new strategy can work. Nice job. What else is new?"

"Derek, can ask some personal favors?"

"You name it."

"Could you please write some recommendations for my applications to join Dalton Hills Country Club?"

While Derek laughed about Chen at a country club, a new e-mail arrived from Miles Templeton. He opened it with dread.

Vogel,

    I trust you have been working on my request to find $10 million in profit improvement for this year. We are working on profit recovery plans across Lund (made necessary because of Plastics' enormous decline), and I need your list of ideas by next week. Use the attached format to capture and quantify your ideas.

                            Miles Templeton

The note scored low on subtlety and politeness. It was an insane request, designed for failure. The entire business had $200 million in revenue. There was no possible way to find $10 million in incremental profits in six months. All Derek could think was, *what a complete douche bag; no offense to hard-working douche bags everywhere.*

He immediately composed an e-mail to his direct reports, Dirk, Larry, B'linda, Bobby, Darrell, and Chen:

Dear Team,

    As you all know, the sudden drop in prices has erased our expected profits for the year, which has caused issues for Lund overall. Miles Templeton has ordered us to develop profit improvement ideas worth $10 million for the remainder of the year. Obviously, this will not be easy.

    I have asked Bev to arrange a half-day meeting this Friday for us to brainstorm profit-improvement ideas, evaluate them, and finalize a list to be submitted to Miles early next week. Please come prepared with improvement ideas, large and small. I will ask each of you to present your ideas for consideration. Everything must be considered, and nothing is sacred.

Sorry this is such short notice. Thanks in advance for your efforts.

Derek

The team took it well. Dirk responded within five minutes.

Derek,

ARE YOU FRICKING NUTS? THIS IS OUTRAGEOUS!

Dirk

Though Dirk's use of all-caps violated the communication protocol against "e-mail shouting" that had been approved at the strategy off-site, Derek thought he had a fair point.

For the next couple days, the team feverishly developed profit-improvement ideas, breaking regularly to bitch about Derek's leadership. On Friday morning, the team met in the main conference room, which Bev had stocked with flip charts, coffee, cookies, and the usual caffeinated soft drinks.

Derek's opening remarks fell flat, even after he laid blame squarely on Miles Templeton's shoulders. After he finished, Chen asked, "Derek, who is Mile Templeton?"

Dirk McAllister answered. "Chen, he is the number-two guy at Lund, only he thinks he's more important and knowledgeable than Dave Lund. He has powerful supporters on the board of directors and constantly tries to outshine Dave. Everyone is afraid of him, even Dave."

"What if we can't find the ten million dollar?" Chen asked.

"He will make life miserable, but let's do the best we can," Derek explained. "We have to find improvement ideas anyway."

He continued. "Okay, everyone. We'll go around the table, with each of us presenting improvement ideas. Bev will record the ideas on flip charts; Tr—I mean, B'linda will make sure the calculations are correct; and we will decide as a group whether the idea is a 'go' or a 'no-go.' Let's start with Darrell."

Darrell examined his notes on a yellow legal pad and said, "My first idea is to stop all business-class flights to Europe."

"Do we have any business-class trips to Europe?" Derek asked.

Larry La Croix interrupted. "We send three or four people every fall to the International Plastics Show in Germany, and they fly business class."

"B'linda, how much would we save?" Derek asked.

"$18,000 or so."

"Okay, can we all agree to this one?" Derek asked the group, who all nodded yes. "$18,000, that's a good start. Darrell, what's your next idea?"

"Postpone Dr. Dave's strategy training until next year, which would save about $10,000—"

"Deal!" interrupted Bobby. Everyone laughed except Darrell.

After Darrell added a few more ideas, including a hiring freeze and reusing discarded paper, the total was $93,000, just $9.9 million short of Darth Vader's goal.

Larry La Croix was next. "First, no travel without the advance signature of Derek and one of his direct reports."

"Even to drive to a plant?" Dirk responded.

"Well, it would cut down on expenses," Larry added.

"Yeah, but we'd spend all our time signing off on travel-request forms," Trophy added.

"What's wrong with signing off on forms?" Darrell interjected.

"Darrell," Trophy responded, "can't we trust our folks to make good decisions about visiting our plants by car?"

"What if we require signatures only for air travel?" Bobby offered.

"Good ideas, Bobby," Chen added.

"Okay, can we agree on this?" Derek asked.

Just like that, they had saved another $50,000.

Larry resumed reading his list. "Second, every employee must pay for his or her own coffee."

"Seriously?" Bobby interjected. "Larry, have you considered the potential loss of productivity due to low energy?"

"Yeah, but people also waste time going back and forth to the kitchen. Plus, they do a lotta chitchattin' there."

"How much would that save?" Derek asked.

"Maybe $500," Trophy answered.

Bobby shook his head, and Derek made an executive decision. "Let's not punish folks for such small savings. What else do you have?"

"The holiday party. We should have it at someone's house instead of a restaurant, which would save at least $3,000."

"Whose home?" Darrell asked.

"It probably should be Derek's, since he's the president and lives in that swanky part of town," Dirk suggested.

"It's not that swanky, but that's fine. I'll warn the neighbors to keep their children and pets inside."

Larry continued. "We'd save a ton on food, and we could have a cash bar, too."

"How much would that save?" Derek asked.

Trophy interjected. "It depends on Bob Davis. If he comes, it could save hundreds more, as well as reduce butt-groping incidents."

"I'd like to see Bob try to grope Monique's butt," Dirk joked.

"It might could get him killed," Bobby said, laughing.

Derek picked up the conversation. "So you want Carol and me to host the party, but charge for drinks?"

"Yep."

"Won't that look pretty bad?"

"We can tell everyone you're only breaking even," Bobby added.

While Derek laughed, Dirk jumped in. "Well, everyone works hard all year, so I hope we wouldn't skimp on the kind of drinks we have."

"What do you suggest, Dirk?" Derek asked.

"We've got to have Miller Lite and maybe one other premium beer."

"One other premium beer?"

"Definitely."

"So you want Carol and me to charge everyone for Miller Lite?"

"They'd understand—for quality."

Trophy came to the rescue. "I have an idea—let's forget the cash bar and have beer and wine only, even Miller Lite, but make it a potluck dinner. It would be fun, and we'd save lots."

Trophy calculated savings of about $6,000, and everyone agreed.

Derek continued. "Okay, everyone. We've tallied ideas from Darrell and Larry and have about $150,000. Only $9.85 million to go." Bobby laughed.

Chen was next. Because R & D had two members and small expenses, no one expected much.

"The antimicrobial coating sales will add more than one million dollar to the bottoms line this year. Maybe more if Americans really like our product."

Everyone stopped and looked at Chen. "One million dollars. Seriously?" Trophy said.

"Americans already give us order for coatings of 10 percent of Dalton productions and 25 percent after two month. At the new price negotiated with Billy Headlands over beer and sugars, we make good profit."

"Over beer and sugar?" Trophy asked and met eyes with Derek, who just shrugged.

Chen reviewed the math. Sure enough, the coatings would add $1.2 million in profits for the year, possibly even $1.5 million.

"Chen, you're an unbelievable sandbagger," Derek said.

"What is some sandbagger?"

"Someone who sets low expectations and then beats them by a mile."

"I did not know these word."

"It's really great news, Chen," Derek said.

"Next year, we may add $6-8 millions to the profit," Chen added.

"Really?"

"No sandbaggers, Derek. That should make Mile Templetoes happy."

"Did you say Templetoes?" Dirk asked.

"Yes, the mean guys from Corporate."

This lifted the mood considerably. Trophy reported that they now had about $1.4-1.7 million of profit improvement, more than anyone realistically expected.

Dirk was next, and his expression betrayed his intense dislike of the exercise.

"I have two ideas, all quite large but controversial."

"Let's hear them," Derek said.

"First, close down our Caribou, Maine, plant and layoff all the workers."

Darrell jumped in. "What? I can't believe you would do such a thing, Dirk."

"I wouldn't," Dirk snapped, looking at Derek, "but Derek and 'Templetoes' asked for $10 million."

"Just for sake of completeness, how much would this save if we did it, Dirk?" Derek asked.

"Three million or so this year, Derek, before netting out guilt and being hung in effigy in the community."

"Okay, okay, Dirk, I get it. What do you all think?" Derek asked the group.

"It's our only plant serving northeastern customers," Larry chimed in.

"We would really hurt 150 families, and northern Maine has no other jobs," Darrell added.

After discussion, the team unanimously voted against the idea.

"What's your other idea, Dirk?" Derek asked.

Dirk said they could save $2-4 million by putting cheaper polymers into products, though it would damage quality and increase customer claims. Larry vehemently rejected this idea, to everyone's relief.

Bobby followed and suggested postponing environmental consulting projects to save $320,000.

As Bev brought lunch into the room, Trophy summarized the profit-improvement ideas.

"Well, we have $2 million in ideas, $8 million short of Templetoes's goal. What do y'all want to do?"

Larry said, "Maybe 'Toes' won't notice." Everyone laughed.

Bobby spoke up. "If you ask me, we can't reasonably do more, and $2 million is pretty good. We should just put lipstick on this pig—you know, dress it up—and e-mail it to Corporate."

"Then what?" Trophy asked.

"Hide."

15

HIGH BEAMS

"The pig" now had lipstick, mascara, and a colorful sundress. But regardless, "Toes" would view the glass as 80 percent empty. Derek awaited his response with fear. Darth Vader is a notoriously poor sport.

A week after the meeting, Derek's phone rang. Derek noticed a Memphis number and answered in fear.

"Hello. This is Derek."

"Vogel, this is Miles Templeton. I'm looking at Plastic's pathetic response to my $10 million request. It took you a month to come up with this crap?"

"Well—"

"This is incredible, Vogel! Do you know what you're doing to Lund this year? We're working our asses off here in Memphis, and in less than a year on the job, you've screwed it all up. Plastics has single-handedly wiped out our bonuses."

"Bonuses?"

"Of course! All the work I've done for Lund will get recognized with a big goose egg come bonus time, thanks to you. I told Dave you were a complete screw-up."

"But isn't the new antimicrobial coating development encouraging?"

"It doesn't begin to move the dial, Vogel. Profits are what count, not some piddling project of some amateur scientist from Chungking."

"He's from Beijing—"

"Same difference, Vogel."

"Sorry, Miles."

"You should be. I'll be meeting with Dave Lund today about this. It's unacceptable!"

The phone went dead.

As Derek sat in his office thinking about his dim Lund career prospects, Trophy entered with Monique D'Estaing and Darrell in tow. Monique appeared even more Amazonian than usual, with giant earrings and a freshly shaved head (except for the 'FroHawk).

"Hey, B'linda; hi, Monique; hello, Darrell. Have a seat. How can I help you?"

They sat down with solemn looks, and Trophy said, "Derek, Corporate Compliance has been auditing expense reports of everyone for the past year. They didn't leave any stone unturned, and worse yet, they reported several rules violations."

"With my expense reports?"

"Yes, but that's not why we're here."

"I'm sorry. What are they?"

"We don't have time to go over all your issues. I'll set something up with Bev," Trophy responded.

"Can you give me an example?" Derek asked.

"You expensed a bottle of water from the hotel minibar."

"That was only about two dollars for bottled water in my room when I arrived late at night."

"I know it doesn't make sense, but it's a clear corporate rule. If you went to the bar, you can expense it, but you can't expense drinks in your room."

"But the bar would be far more expensive, wouldn't it?" Derek protested.

"I tried to explain that. This is about following the rules. Anyway, my advice is simply to label the water as 'dinner' on your report," Trophy explained. "Anyway, we're here to talk about something much more serious that came up in the audit."

"Like what?" Derek asked.

"The kind of thing that needs human resource consultation, which is why Darrell is here," Trophy added with a nod to Darrell.

"Okay. Go ahead."

"Bob Davis is the big problem. As you know, he has the largest T & E budget in Lund Plastics, if not all of Lund."

"He's apparently big on customer entertainment," Derek added.

"Bigger than Texas on steroids," Darrell chimed in. "Almost all his monthly expense reports have large entries for drinks and entertainment at High Beams—you know, the gentlemen's club on the south side of town."

Monique suddenly weighed in. "This obvious display of male perversion and sexism is highly offensive to me, as well as to other women in the office. More than that, his documentation is extremely suspect." Monique was clearly agitated.

"I'm really sorry you got offended, Monique. Can you give some examples?" Derek asked.

"Last February 14 was a classic."

"He went to High Beams on Valentine's Day? Isn't he married?" Derek asked.

"Yes, he did, but I think he's divorced, probably because he's a male pig," Monique hissed.

"So, what did he do?"

"Well, Bob and two guys from a major customer from South Carolina started at the Mexican restaurant Tequila Mockingbird. According to the receipt, they had twelve margaritas, two orders of supreme nachos, and three burritos *grandes*."

"Wow."

"He's a pig in multiple ways," Monique said. "The receipt was stamped 10:38 p.m., and there was hot sauce all over it, plus a smudge of refried beans. He used the original."

"Well, except for health reasons, there's nothing wrong with the night so far."

"It gets revolting after eleven p.m.," Monique sneered.

"What happened?" Derek asked.

"Bob claimed $400 in expenses at High Beams."

"$400? What kind of expenses?"

"Fifty dollars in drinks and $350 in customer entertainment," Monique explained, barely able to contain herself.

"What kind of customer entertainment?"

Darrell started squirming in his seat, getting ready to pounce. Before Monique could continue, he leaned forward and said, "Derek, let me interrupt to spare Monique. Have you ever been to one of these places?"

"No, sorry," Derek lied, trying to forget the bachelor party in San Francisco. "Why?"

"It's a strip joint. They serve drinks and food, but most of the activity centers on topless women and lap dances. The women dance topless in front of individual customers for cash, usually twenty dollars per dance."

"Male pigs," Monique uttered.

"You don't say," Derek said. "So, you think Bob spent $350 on lap dances?"

"Except that it isn't divisible by twenty, yes."

"Monique, did he submit receipts?" Derek asked.

"There's a corporate policy that all charges greater than twenty-five dollars must be supported by receipts—you violate this rule fairly often, I might add—so Bob used flimsy documentation."

"Like what?"

"Signed cocktail napkins."

"Cocktail napkins? Signed by who or, um, whom?"

"He submitted two cocktail napkins, both with the High Beams logo, with different female handwriting on each, indicating the amount he spent."

"Did they mention these lap dances?"

"Not directly. One, however, had an extra note at the bottom: 'Bob, you and your friends are so fun!!! Write me at lapdance4U@ hotmail.com. Love, Melody.' She used a heart to make the letter *o*. What a frickin' disgrace."

"It was Valentine's Day," Derek said.

Derek had no idea how to handle this situation. Bob Davis was loved by Lund's customers and was doing well as senior executive vice president of sales for Bug Off.

Finally, Derek looked at Trophy and asked, "Have you talked to Bob about this?"

"During the investigation, more than a month ago, we met with him and asked about the documentation," Trophy explained, "but we haven't seen him since."

"You haven't seen Bob in more than a month?"

"His desk hasn't been touched in weeks. We think the investigation spooked him, and he's on the lam."

"On the lam? Did you try phone or e-mail?"

"We tried e-mail a few weeks ago," Monique interjected, "but we got a cryptic response."

"What was it?" Derek asked.

"He told Troph—I mean, B'linda—and me that he would be working out of the office for several weeks," Monique said, "on an important, top-secret project."

Trophy interrupted. "Bob said he was working as senior executive vice president of sales and marketing for some company called ... um—"

"Bug Off," Monique finished. "We don't find this credible. Who would hire that chauvinist slob as a senior executive vice president?"

Darrell pounced. "And that's another example of egregious behavior, Derek. Bob is working for another company at the same time as working for Lund. This is a significant conflict of interest expressly prohibited by Article III, paragraph 3(b) of the employee manual, which addresses moonlighting. Do I need to show you the provision?"

Darrell had a large manual with Post-it Notes saving certain pages.

"No, thanks, I believe you," Derek replied and then asked, "Darrell, have you by any chance talked to Sophie Garibaldi, your HR manager in Dalton, about this moonlighting issue?"

"No, why?" Darrell responded.

"Because from what I understand, she's the chief people officer at Bug Off."

Darrell looked crushed. "What? So you're saying that not only is she violating Article III, paragraph 3(b) by moonlighting, like Bob, but she's also hiring Lund employees away, in violation of Article IV, paragraph 2 (a)(ii)? No wonder she's behind on processing MOFMARTs."

"Darrell, um, there's something I need to tell you."

"Derek, I know you like everyone, and Bob and Sophie are nice and all, but there's no excuse for this."

"Darrell, there may be—"

"Not this time, Derek. No more 'I'm just a new, completely unprepared, slightly slow, but nice president.' No, sir. This time, we need to take action."

Slightly slow? Derek wondered.

"Darrell, I can explain—"

"With all due respect, Derek, no explanation is necessary. Tomorrow, I'm going to Dalton to meet with them and give an ultimatum."

"Darrell, I don't think you need to—"

"If you don't support me on this, I will go to Dave Lund directly, or maybe even Toes."

"Darrell, Bug Off is part of Lund. It was set up as an experiment to build an empowered team to develop new products. Bob and Sophie are on it, along with Chen, Travis, and a couple others. That's how Chen got all those extra profits we discussed at our meeting."

"Huh?"

"Yea, maybe it was a crazy idea, but it got people really excited."

"When did you hear about it?" Darrell asked.

"When did I, what? No, sorry, I was involved from the beginning. I worked with Chen to start it a few months ago when we had to get something going. I'm really sorry you didn't know."

"Derek, do you remember our talk in the truck on the way to Dalton?"

"About MOFMARTs and the Carpenters?"

"The other part of the talk. Do you remember what I said was our single biggest problem at Lund?"

"Can you remind me?"

"Communications."

"Sorry, I guess it went in one ear and out the other."

16

HuRTS

A few days after Derek heard from Toes, Dave Lund called him.

"Derek, this is Dave Lund."

"Hey, Dave, how are things?"

"Not as bad here as with you, I bet."

"That's good, I suppose. We are still getting hammered, but there are encouraging signs."

"Yeah, Miles talked to me about Plastics and you. He's not too pleased, as you probably know."

"Yes, that was apparent during our call a few days ago. I'm sorry about things, Dave."

"Derek, I don't think you can do anything about the recession. Everyone is surprised."

"That's for sure."

"Anyway, I looked over your profit-improvement list and was very pleased to see the impact of the new-products strategy."

"It's exciting, isn't it?"

"I'm impressed with the progress. In fact—and don't advertise this to Miles—I think you should hire more R & D scientists right away."

"Really? But that would reduce our savings."

"Derek, we're a family company and need to think long-term, and long-term, this is the way to go."

"Geez, Dave, I'm a little surprised. Thanks. Do you mind putting that in writing, in case Miles sends in his auditors?"

Dave chuckled as he hung up the phone.

The day after receiving Dave's blessing, Darrell and Derek met in Derek's office to call Chen about the new R & D hires. They used the speakerphone on the table. Bev insisted on dialing Chen, which required several tries.

Bev started the call. Loudly, she said, "Dr. Chen, hello? This is Beverly Stroup. Mr. Vogel and Mr. Hartman would like to speak with you."

"Is this about MOFMARTs?" Chen asked.

"I don't think so, but I'll put you right through." Bev was unfamiliar with speakerphone technology and examined it for a transfer button. Derek quietly told her that they were all set.

"Chen, this is Derek. How are things, Mr. President?"

"Great, Derek. Americans keeps increasing their order of coatings. We will make even more monies this year."

"Excellent. I talked with Dave Lund yesterday, and he was really impressed with Bug Off."

"That's very nice, thank you. Is Darrell there in your rooms?"

"Yea, but it's not about MOFMARTs—don't worry. He's here to help deliver some good news: Dave Lund will let us hire two new R & D scientists."

"Cross your hearts?"

"I promise. So, Chen, what will you look for in these new hires?"

"This would be ideals. I would like some Chinese man with the PhDs in plastics science. He can be marrieds or single, but I prefer singles so he can work harder at the jobs."

"Chen, just to be clear, you want a male, who is Chinese and preferably not married, right?"

"Yes."

Darrell went from relaxed to full Human Resource battle stations.

"Chen," Derek continued, playing with Darrell, "could he be any religion, like Catholic, Jewish, or Hindu?"

Darrell went nearly spasmodic as he sat on his hands and turned red.

"I guess any religions is fine, unless you think Catholics work betters?"

"It may depend on his sexual orientation."

Just then, Darrell interrupted forcefully.

"Dr. Chen, Derek, do you know it's illegal to base hiring decisions on a person's gender, nationality, marital status, or religion, not to mention sexual orientation?"

"So sorry, Darrell, I do not know this new laws," Chen explained.

Darrell angrily lectured Derek and Chen about employment laws and Lund's nondiscrimination policies. It lasted about thirty minutes, and for Chen, it was all news; employment discrimination was not a priority in China.

Chen and Derek received their comeuppance in no time. Immediately after the meeting, Darrell called Lund's corporate attorney and chief people officer, sounding the HR alarm. Lawyers and HR professionals live for these things, and the response was swift. Derek's little joke would cost dearly: a full-day seminar of HR laws and hiring practices for Chen, Derek, and dozens of innocents in the organization.

Within days, a memo from Corporate Human Resources asked twenty to attend Human Resource Sensitivity Training ("HuRST") at the Marriott in Nashville. Attendance was mandatory. The topics would be sensitivity, discrimination, and hiring. No one was implicated directly, but the team quickly learned of Chen's and Derek's *faux pas*. Derek's stock fell with everyone but the Marriott catering manager.

A week later, the lucky twenty arrived at the Marriott for training. Dr. Dave was standing outside the conference room talking to Darrell when Derek arrived.

"Dr. Dave, hello. What are you doing here?" Derek asked.

"I'm helping the Human Resource and Legal people with HuRST."

"Isn't strategy your cup of tea?"

"Strategy is clearly my specialty, as you know, but I also work a lot with communications, which naturally flows into sensitivity and discrimination."

"Of course."

"Derek, tell me, how is the Lund Plastics strategy going?"

"Well, Dr. Dave, despite experiencing a tough time, we are seeing some really bright spots. We have had a big new-product success, and it is selling quite well."

"That's great. I knew you all were onto something when we did the Strategy Off-site."

"I thought we were all on something too," Derek added.

"Your vision statement was one of the best I've seen in my career," Dr. Dave added.

"Yes, our CEO also thought it was unusual."

Two new people sat at the front of the Marriott's large conference room: Connie Schmidt, the corporate director of employee relations, and Paul Gozzi, the corporate labor attorney. They looked angry, especially Connie. According to company legend, a visit from Connie was more terrifying than the Gestapo visiting a French Resistance wine tasting. Her zeal in ferreting out inequalities was so notorious that her nickname was "Commie Connie," or "Commie" for short.

The training-session participants included Chen and Derek—the instigators—along with lecherous Bob Davis and several poor innocents from Nashville and Dalton. Nashville attendees were Trophy, Monique, Bev, and several women from accounting and inside sales, and on the male side, Larry La Croix, Dirk McAllister, Bobby, and a few others. Travis and Sophie accompanied Chen from Dalton. As usual, there were flip charts, sticky notes in different colors, pens, and copious amounts of coffee, tea, Cokes, Diet Cokes, and cookies.

Dr. Dave, Darrell, Commie, and Paul Gozzi faced their class like parents about to scold their children. Dr. Dave opened the proceedings without his usual warmth.

"Good morning. Welcome to the Lund Human Resource Sensitivity Training, or HuRST, which has been tailored specifically for Lund Plastics."

"Connie, Paul, and I are happy to be with you for this session," Dr. Dave said, despite considerable evidence otherwise.

"Today, we will learn how to listen to each other better, how to become more sensitive, how to spot discrimination, and how to interview and hire without violating either the law or Lund policies. This is all critically important. I understand you have had some issues in the Nashville office and Dalton with discrimination around hiring."

Everyone looked directly at Derek. Chen was unaware of his role in this and was busy taking notes.

"Our first exercise will be listening. There are twenty of you here, including nine women and one Chinese man. I would like the women and Dr. Chen to line up on one side of the room. The other half of you, all white males, will be on the other side. I would like each of you to pair up with someone from the other group. Sit across from each other. When I say 'go,' the woman or Chinese man in the pairings will have five minutes to describe what it's like to be a minority employee at Lund. The role of the other person will be to listen actively, ask for clarification, and take notes. At the end of the five minutes, the listener will report out to the entire group. I will take notes. Okay, any questions?"

The next few minutes were chaos as people tried desperately to avoid awkward pairings. Bob Davis almost knocked Chen over to get paired with Trophy but ended up with Monique.

Chen chose Bobby, and Sophie got stuck with Derek. Dr. Dave started the clock. For the next five minutes, the women and Chen shared their thoughts while the opposing white males nodded and took notes.

After five minutes, each white male reported back to the group. Dr. Dave noted highlights on the flip charts, constantly making self-deprecating remarks about handwriting or spelling. He often nodded like he'd heard this many times before. With each new comment, Commie scowled with intensifying disdain.

Bob Davis then reported on his talk with Monique. "When you take customers to strip clubs, it shows your sexist, imperialistic, pig ways." Bob was embarrassed as he recited Monique's exact words.

Commie suddenly interrupted.

"Does that really happen?" she shouted.

"Absolutely," Monique hissed. "It's pig-like behavior typical of males!"

"That is unacceptable. It's a miracle we haven't been sued for this already. Were there any terminations because of it?" She sat down, red-faced, and wrote furiously on her notepad. Bob Davis lost all color in his generally pink face.

After each report, the team switched partners and repeated the process. At each switch, there would be several groans and complaints, accompanied by angry looks at Derek.

After several rounds, Dr. Dave, Commie, and Paul organized the feedback into themes, which soured their dark moods. They divided the group into five breakout teams to develop ideas on how to avoid discrimination at Lund.

Each breakout group grabbed a flip chart and went to their assigned area. Sophie, Bobby, Larry La Croix, and Derek went down the hall and sat, stunned, for a few minutes before Sophie spoke.

"Derek, this is a colossal downer. It should be called HuRTS instead of HuRST. Can you stop it?"

"I don't think so. Apparently, not even Dave Lund can control Commie and the HR police. They report to a higher power."

"The board?"

"Higher."

Sophie looked confused but continued. "Then we should play along with the game."

"What do you mean?" Larry asked.

"We tell them what they want: very politically correct ideas for improvement."

"Like mandatory sterilization of Bob?" Bobby suggested.

"That's an excellent start," Sophie said.

After an hour, the groups returned. For such a grim exercise, the group seemed amused and almost energized. The first group set its flip chart down, and Trophy presented.

"First suggestion: every new employee must attend HuRST on his or her first day of employment. That will set the tone."

"Excellent idea," commented Commie sternly, taking notes. Darrell and Dr. Dave clapped. No one else followed their lead.

"And every existing employee must take it, too. Also, it should be an annual training requirement for everyone in the company, including Dave Lund."

"I like it," Commie added, completely taking over the meeting. Again, Darrell and Dr. Dave clapped, but much quieter this time. And again, no one else followed.

Trophy continued: "Second: every employee must make an annual verbal loyalty pledge to follow the Lund policy on discrimination, followed by signing a document."

"To whom would they make this pledge?" Commie asked.

"We didn't get that far, but you would be the most appropriate, Comm—I mean, Connie."

Group One avoided all eye contact with each other and the rest. Several stared at the floor.

"Third: we should play *The Oprah Winfrey Show* on the TV in the office kitchen during lunch, especially when she has Ellen DeGeneres as a guest, instead of Fox News."

"Fourth: we should change the name of our main conference room to the Gloria Steinem Room."

Sophie whispered to Derek, "They're really good at this—pro caliber."

And so went the reports, with each group vying for the most political correctness. The strongest innovative suggestion was to give women a tour of the men's bathroom.

"Really good idea," Commie commented, "it would take the mystery out of it."

In the afternoon, Commie and Paul hit full stride as the agenda moved to interview training. They presented federal and state laws on hiring discrimination, which wasn't news to anyone, except Chen. After taking copious notes, he raised his hand and asked, "Connie, is it trues I cannot hires some Chinese scientist?"

"No, Dr. Chen, you can hire a Chinese scientist, but you can't ask him, or her, if he's Chinese."

"But what if he has some Chinese name?"

"You can't ask about his name."

"But I will knows because it's on his resumes. Also, if I interviews him, I will know he's Chinese. He will sit in my offices, and I will see him."

"You should not take notice that he is Chinese."

"Even if we are speaking some Mandarins together?"

"Why would you speak Mandarin?"

"Because he is Chinese."

Near day's end, Commie delved into military discharges.

"Question: if an applicant lists the United States Marine Corps on his or her resume, can you ask about his or her discharge?" Commie asked the group.

Derek raised his hand and said, "Yes, of course."

"Why?" Commie responded with a deep scowl.

"I would like to know how he or she did in the military, like in any past job."

"Derek, what if I told you that minorities and women have a disproportionately higher rate of dishonorable discharge from the military?"

"I had never heard that, but why does it matter?"

"By asking an applicant about this, you explore whether he or she is a minority or a woman."

"Connie, no offense, but if an applicant is sitting in front of me for an interview, won't I figure out if he or she is a she or a he?"

"Derek, that's the kind of arrogant management attitude around here which makes this course necessary."

Finally, HuRTS ended to a smattering of applause, mostly out of habit. On the way out, Derek walked with Chen and spoke very quietly.

"So Chen, after what you learned today, do you still want to hire a Chinese man?"

"Yes, of course. I just won't ask hims if he's some Chinese mans."

17

Makin' Bacon

The next morning, Derek hadn't finished half his coffee when Bobby rushed into his office.

"Derek, we got 'im!"

"Who?"

"Fred Thompson for the Jackson Hill opening celebration!"

"*The* Fred Thompson?"

"*The* Fred Thompson," Bobby confirmed.

"From the reverse-mortgage commercials?"

"Yes, sir."

"How'd you get him?"

"He used to be a senator from Tennessee."

"Seriously, Bobby, do you think I'm that gullible?"

The construction of the Jackson Hill Plant was nearly complete, a $100 million monstrosity that transformed Milton Place. Bobby was in charge of the opening celebration, which he wanted to rival the Olympics. He wanted superb speakers, outstanding local cuisine, fiddle music, and a perfect plant tour.

In the weeks before the celebration, Lund rented a huge white tent with seating for three hundred guests to be placed outside the plant. For food, Bobby decided on a pig roast; he ordered five large pigs and prepared roasting pits behind the plant. This job was far too important for caterers.

The day before the event, the tent was up, the pits had been dug, and the plant was running smoothly. Pig roasting takes a long time to do right, and Bobby planned a twenty-four-hour cook. He solicited volunteers to watch the pigs in four-hour shifts throughout the night. Bobby anticipated everything, except entertainment for the pig cookers, but they overcame his oversight and brought boom boxes and cases and cases of Bud Light. They brought steaks to cook over the fire. They brought beans. They brought Ding Dongs for dessert.

And they brought moonshine, one of Tennessee's most famous products. Despite its reputation in the North, moonshine was generally safe for human consumption.

Except during all-night cookouts.

Moonshine, beer, music, steak, beans, and Ding Dongs were a powerful combination, and as the night wore on, the party grew. Bobby returned to his hotel at midnight, and by three a.m., everyone had left except the four volunteers from the 2:00-6:00 a.m. shift.

The key to pig roasting is simple: turn the pigs regularly and make sure they don't get too close to the fire. Copious moonshine, however, complicates the simplest of tasks. As moonshine consumption increased, the volunteers got distracted and quit turning the pigs. Worse, they added more wood to the fire and passed out around 4:30 a.m. When the next shift arrived at the plant at 6:00 a.m., they enjoyed the delicious smell of roast pork. As they got closer, they noticed an unusual amount of smoke. Upon arrival at their posts, they found empty mason jars, beer cans, steak bones, and dirty paper plates. A raccoon blissfully gnawed a steak bone within five feet of a snoring volunteer. All four volunteers slept peacefully while burning pig fat crackled around them. Three pigs had collapsed into the fire, and the two others were overdone on the bottom side.

Roused from his sleep by a panicked call, Bobby arrived around seven. He saved most of the fallen pigs by cutting off the outer layer. All Bobby could say was, "If something bad had to happen today, I'm glad it happened before Senator Thompson and Dave Lund arrived."

At eleven a.m., guests crowded the big tent, including Johnny Ray, Chen's car buddy. Bobby had arranged for fiddlers to play while the crowd mingled. Senator Thompson stood near the elevated head table with Dave Lund, several members of the Lund family, and members of the Lund Board of Directors. A buzz filled the air, along with the strong smell of cooked pig. Around eleven thirty, Bobby went to the podium and welcomed everyone to the Jackson Hill opening. He introduced the dignitaries, including Senator Thompson, and thanked them for their support and attendance. Bobby, Chen, and Derek sat in the front row and watched as speaker after speaker rose to praise the project.

Dave Lund was impressive. Raised in Tennessee, he could eliminate all traces of Harvard from his speech, which he did for the crowd. He spoke glowingly about support from the town of Jackson Hill, the State of Tennessee and the US Federal Government. He talked about Lund's desire to improve its communities and how this plant would employ 150 people directly and many more indirectly. He emphasized Lund's passion for safety and how the plant had been meticulously planned to be safe and clean. When he finished, the crowd gave a standing ovation.

Senator Thompson followed, and everyone was enthralled. His voice and presence had no equal. A few minutes into Senator Thompson's speech, however, something went wrong. It started with the crackling of plant walkie-talkies. Derek became concerned when saw four or five Jackson Hill employees hastily heading for the plant. Chen continued to listen to Senator Thompson, enthralled.

A few minutes later, the plant manager rushed out to get Dirk McAllister.

Fortunately, the crowd was too engrossed in the speech to notice any problems at first. Then the fire trucks arrived. The speakers had their backs to the plant, so they couldn't see the trucks, nor could they hear them; the town had instructed all emergency vehicles not to use their sirens during the plant ceremony.

As Senator Thompson spoke, the fire trucks stopped outside the plant, and firemen jumped out. They madly hooked up hoses to the water system and dashed into the building.

Senator Thompson continued, oblivious to the government heroics behind him. Dave Lund was equally unaware—a condition Derek feared would change momentarily. He reflected that a plant fire during a public ceremony would not be a good addition to his dismal profit record as president. To complicate matters, Dave Lund had just spoken eloquently about Lund's commitment to safety in the new plant.

While figuring out a plan of action, Derek also mentally updated his resume, most likely for immediate utilization.

As the senator's speech ended, the crowd roared, and Derek, Chen, and Bobby rushed into the plant. Fortunately, the fire-suppression systems had worked perfectly, but the plant was flooded and would not be operating for a couple days. The tour proceeded anyway. Bobby was the guide for Senator Thompson's group, and his most common comment was, "If the plant was running, you would see …"

Dave Lund finally located Derek. He wasn't happy.

"Derek, this was not good timing."

"The worst."

"Was anyone hurt?"

"Fortunately, no."

"Thank God. Was the plant damaged?"

"Not too bad. The new fire-suppression system worked well. We have to clean up, but everything will be fine."

"Tell the team they did a good job. The timing was terrible, obviously, but many people said how impressed they were with our safety and fire systems. Senator Thompson was particularly complimentary. If nothing else, it showed we are serious about what I spoke about today."

"Well, um, thanks."

"Now let's go get some of that pork I smelled all morning. That's one thing I'm sure you couldn't fuck up."

18

MIAMI VICES

Three months after the Jackson Hill fires, business remained depressed, and Jackson Hill made it worse for Lund. The only bright side was Bug Off. President Chen and his Side Effects were hitting their stride, and American Siding sales were now half of Dalton's production. American's chief rival, Lone Pine Siding of New Hampshire, had even asked Lund to develop antimicrobial siding for them.

President Chen was giddy over Bug Off's success and took his chief executive role seriously: he joined Dalton Hills Country Club and bought a new, white Cadillac. According to Chen, "Americans executives like some Cadillac." It was odd for a Chinese scientist to drive a Caddy, but Chen desperately needed new wheels. His old, white Toyota was rusted out and insufferably hot in the summer. During one ride, Chen had said to Derek, "I hope you don't mind no air conditionings."

Meanwhile, Chen had hired two new PhDs, one of whom was Chinese.

"Chen, did you hire a Chinese scientist?" Derek asked.

"Yes, Dr. Miao."

"Meow?"

"Yes, Miao, like kitty cat, but Dr. Miao is not some veterinarian."

"That's funny, Chen."

"Derek, I follow the rule and did not ask Dr. Miao if he was some Chinese."

"You're learning."

"His Mandarin is very good."

Fortunately, Darrell did not alert Corporate HR about Dr. Miao—even he feared Commie. In any event, she was fully occupied investigating allegations that some women at the Lund Electronics Division had smaller cubicles than the men. This was a major controversy requiring swift and severe action from Human Resources.

With double the R & D staff, Lund was primed to develop more new products, which were a desperate need. Derek decided that Chen could manage another presidency and called him.

"Hello, this is Chen."

"Chen, it's Derek. How is Dalton Hills Country Club?"

"Very good, thank you for some recommendations. I play some golf twice each week."

"How's your handicap?"

"Down to 40."

"You've become a big-shot."

"What's some big-shot?"

"Sorry, it's an American expression, meaning someone successful and important."

"Oh, like Dave Lunds?"

"Exactly. How is Dr. Miao doing?"

"Mostly goods."

"Mostly?"

"Yeah, Travis has been teaching him Americans cultures. Travis talked him into trying Red Mans Chewing Tobaccos and Mountain Dew at the same times."

"Uh oh."

"It was his first times. Big problems. He was sweatings and pacings around the labs all day, got no works done. The doctor said his hearts rate was too fast, but he'll be okay."

"Chen, I appreciate Travis giving Dr. Miao cultural training, but maybe he should go slower."

"I already talks to him. All set."

"Good, thanks. Chen, I am calling about creating another company, like Bug Off."

"That would be greats. We need to find some other new product."

"Could you use your trick with polymers and heat to make other things more microbial-resistant?"

"Maybe some toilet seat."

"Could that work?"

"Maybe, if Dirk lets us use some new polysmer with silver ion inthesides."

"Do you have enough time to be another president?"

"Yes, I already promoted Travis to chief operatings officer of Bugger Off so I can do mores."

"That's great."

"Yes, he is very happy. Travis is the first chief operatings officer ever in his families. His parents are very proud and want to have celebrations, like some barbecue, maybe next months. Maybe you could come."

"Huh? Good, um, but I meant it's great that you can be president of another business. Who would you like on your team?"

"Let me think. Dr. Miao—once he get better—Sophie and Gerry would be good again, maybe Larry La Croix from Sale and Marketings—I think he has some big shot—and Billy Lansing, the Dalton plant managers. We should have Bob Davis again, too, for customer entertainments."

"How about Bobby Ray Petry?"

"He also has some big shots. Very good."

After some discussion, Derek suggested adding Monique D'Estaing, to help her develop and help keep Bob Davis in check. This gave Chen eight people for his new team.

"Okay. You have a new company. Let's organize a kickoff meeting."

"Derek, this could be big projects, very important to Lund, right?" Chen asked.

"Yes, the toilet-seat market is huge. This could be important."

"Since I am the presidents, can I arrange the kickoffs meeting?"

"Of course. What do you have in mind?"

"Miami Beaches."

Chen threw himself into his new role and organized a pre-kickoff meeting to prepare for Miami. At the meeting, they agreed to dress in Miami Vice-style for the trip. They also worked on a company name and decided on "Moon Landing." Moon Landing had a double entendre, meaning both success through technological innovation and a clean landing spot for the buttocks.

Monique was a worry at first, but Chen disarmed her with his linguistic skills and complete lack of chauvinism/racism/imperialism. They quickly became kindred spirits, and Monique integrated into Moon Landings well.

Two weeks later, the Moonies, as they quickly became known, flew to Miami. Chen, Dr. Miao, Bobby, Larry La Croix, Sophie, Gerry, Bob Davis, Monique, and Billy Lansing all traveled in varying degrees of Miami Vice attire. Monique had dyed the outer edge of her 'FroHawk purple and donned matching earrings and large, purple-framed sunglasses. She was fired-up about the outing. Chen and Dr. Miao wore sunglasses, colorful Hawaiian shirts, shorts, and sandals with white knee socks. It was not a good look for Dr. Miao, whose legs lacked muscle, had never been exposed to sun, and had only a few unsightly leg hairs. Dr. Miao also sported a stained Red Man Chewing Tobacco hat, thanks to Travis's cultural coaching. He looked like a Chinese redneck.

Chen rented two Ford Mustang convertibles. He and Dr. Miao grabbed one, and Monique joined them. The other Moonies were happy to ride separately. On the way to the South Beach Marriott, Chen stopped at a cigar store and bought several boxes. He, Dr. Miao, and Monique lit up immediately and trailed blue cigar smoke the rest of the way.

As the caravan pulled into the Marriott, the valet and bell staff stared in awe. South Miami Beach hotel workers see all kinds, but apparently nothing like this. Chen, Monique, and Dr. Miao got out of their Mustang, smiled, and said hello to the head valet. The valet asked about their outfits, and Chen explained: "We're Miami Vices."

The Moonies' opening festivities featured mojitos with Cuban rum, plantains, and a Cuban dinner of rice, beans, and various meats. Everyone changed for the party, except Chen, Dr. Miao, and Monique. Why mess with a good thing? Bobby wore a white fedora he had bought from a local vendor. Sophie opted for makeup, a short, red dress, and spiked heels. All heads turned as she passed. The other Moonies wore Hawaiian shirts and blue jeans.

The sweet mojitos were deceptively strong and caught Dr. Miao unawares. He taught the Chinese custom of *ganbei* to fellow Moonies. *Ganbei* is a practice far better in moderation—with weaker drinks. Dr. Miao was initially unfazed by the mojitos and clinked glasses with anyone near him, even strangers. When he added Cuban cigars to his repertoire, he got the spins and wobbled to his room, gone for the night.

During dinner, Chen gave a rousing speech about the Moonie project.

"My dreams is to make Moonies more successfuls even than our Bugger Off coatings. Because we have some big-shots team, we will create a new microbial-resistant product. Our stretch goals should be to sell enough new product to use more than half of the new Jackson Hill plants, now that it has recovered from the fires." The team cheered and toasted each other.

The next morning, The Moonies met in the Presidential Conference Suite, thanks to Chen's connections and title. Thirty minutes into the meeting, Dr. Miao arrived, looking very sick. His skin was pale, his eyes were glassy and red, and he wore the same Hawaiian shirt, which had clearly been slept in. He smelled of cigars and rum, only slightly disguised by hotel mouthwash.

Chen urged the Moonies to work diligently through lunch to make time for team building at 3:00 p.m. The team got really excited.

By 2:00 p.m., the Moonies had listed the key issues to resolve in their work and assigned responsibilities and schedules. Using flip charts, Chen created tables and timelines. At 3:00 p.m., the meeting was over, and it was time for team building.

Chen stood and addressed the group.

"For our team-buildings, you will each find some bag with costumes in your rooms. Please change into some costumes and meet at the walkways by the beaches in front of the hotels in thirty minute."

When the team arrived at the meeting spot, they found Chen on roller blades dressed like Don Johnson in *Miami Vice*. He wore an off-white suit with a tan crewneck shirt. Chen was talking with Cher, who also wore roller blades. Bobby was thrilled about meeting Cher until he got close and realized that Cher had done a poor job shaving his legs and showed a five o'clock shadow. What Cher lacked in shaving, however, she made up with mascara, eyeliner, and lipstick.

Chen explained the event, which was called The Celebrity Roller Blading Scavenger Hunt. Everyone had to dress as celebrities and collect items on a scavenger hunt list while on roller blades, which were provided by Cher. Before starting the hunt, Cher gave roller-blading lessons to the group.

After thirty minutes of practice, Chen divided the Moonies into two groups. The celebrities all lived around or frequented South Beach. Sophie became Sophia Loren, which took little work; she already had the figure and dark, curly hair. Chen had given her a tight dress, fake eyelashes, and makeup, and she was a dead ringer for the Italian star. Dr. Miao became Sylvester Stallone as *Rambo* by wearing a pullover black T-shirt with muscular arm sleeves, black pants, and a wig of long, straight hair with a bandanna headband. He had a bow over his shoulder. Bobby was Dolly Parton with a wig of thick, long, curly blonde hair, and large breasts protruding from a violet dress. For the first time ever, Bobby wore false eyelashes and makeup. Blatantly ignoring HuRTS training, Bob Davis compared Bobby's knockers with Trophy's Bonnie and Clyde. Monique howled.

Gerry became Spiderman and wore the full bodysuit. Billy Lansing became Hulk Hogan, complete with a bald skullcap with stringy, long, blond hair. He also had a sleeveless T-shirt with fake chest muscles and bicep enhancers. Monique was Tom Cruise dressed as Maverick from *Top Gun*. She wore a navy flight suit and flight helmet, as well as aviator glasses. Bob Davis became former President Bill Clinton and wore a full facemask, complete with the president's thick, curly hair. He also wore a blue suit with white shirt and red tie, along with a pocket square. Larry La Croix transformed himself into Cameron Diaz in the tight red dress from *There's Something About Mary*. He had trouble keeping his boxer shorts from showing below the hemline. Larry also wore a blond Diaz wig.

Cher gave each team a list of items to collect. The rules were to stay in costume and only use roller blades for transportation. The list included a Cuban cigar, an autograph from an actual celebrity, a yacht, a freshly opened coconut, a picture of the team with a topless sunbather, an article of Armani clothing, and a sample of ocean water in an unusual container. Cher gave each team a cloth bag to hold the items, a camera, and two drink tickets per team member for one of the hotel beach bars. The finish line was the Marriott patio bar, where Cher and Don Johnson would judge each team's speed, completeness, and creativity. Cher warned the team of significant penalties for finishing after 7:00 p.m.

At 4:00 p.m., the race started. Sophia Loren (Sophie), Sly Stallone (Dr. Miao), Tom Cruise (Monique), and Spiderman (Gerry) took off along the beach walkway in one direction. The other team of Cameron Diaz (Larry La Croix), Dolly Parton (Bobby), President Clinton (Bob Davis), and Hulk Hogan (Billy Lansing) went the other way. Within ten minutes, each team had found a Cuban cigar, and the race was on.

Team Clinton had better roller-blade skills and ran circles around Team Rambo. Dolly Parton was a natural with her long, curly blonde hair flying in the breeze. President Clinton was a surprisingly good skater, even in a suit. Team Rambo, however, attracted more attention because Sophie resembled a young Sophia Loren. Tourists stared and took pictures. The team had no trouble getting an autograph from the real Sophia Loren, who was flattered by Sophie's rendition. The Clinton squad had more difficulty getting autographs—Hulk Hogan scared everyone in his path.

Neither team had trouble getting a picture with a topless sunbather; there were dozens around. Bob Davis vowed to move to South Beach. For a yacht, Dolly Parton (Bobby) bought a keychain yacht at a tourist shop, while Team Rambo took a picture of a yacht in the harbor.

Through it all, Don Johnson (Chen) and Cher roamed around South Beach on roller blades enforcing the rules.

Halfway through the event, Team Rambo took a break at a sidewalk café. They sat at an outdoor table: Tom Cruise, Sophia Loren, Spiderman, and Sylvester Stallone. As they ordered drinks, the waitress was thrilled to serve such an important collection of celebrities. She didn't notice that Sly Stallone was Chinese and Tom Cruise was a black woman with a purple 'FroHawk. After a few minutes, she couldn't help herself and asked, "So, I'm just curious, how do you all know each other?"

On and on, the race went. As time grew short, the teams grew desperate. At six forty-five, the Clinton squad only needed a sample of ocean water in an unusual container. They decided that the best container, considering South Beach's fleshpot reputation, would be a condom. Hulk (Billy) and President Clinton (Bob Davis) volunteered to buy a condom, fill it with ocean water, and meet Dolly (Bobby) and Cameron Diaz (Larry La Croix) at the hotel patio for the finish. Unfortunately, the closest pharmacy was a mile away—too far to skate there and back on roller blades in time for the finish. So they violated the rules and hailed a taxi.

The taxi driver, a middle-aged Cuban immigrant named Gonzalez, gave Hulk and President Clinton a double look when he stopped. Gonzalez looked again when Hulk asked to go to the Rite Aid Pharmacy down the road. The whole way, he stared at them in the rearview mirror. When they arrived at the Rite Aid, Hulk said to the driver, "Can you wait here a minute? We just have to pick up a condom."

Hulk and the popular former president got out of the cab, laughing, and skated into the pharmacy. Minutes later, they were back in the taxi, panting heavily and fiddling with the condom. Driving back to the Marriott, Gonzales sensed his passengers' hurry. Finally, he pulled up to the Marriott. Hulk and President Clinton had planned to skate to the beach, fill the condom, and then rush to the patio for the finish.

But they realized there wasn't time. As Gonzales looked in the rearview mirror, Hulk turned and said to President Clinton, "We have to hurry, Mr. President. Let's grab the condom and go to my room."

19

TRYING TO SCORE

While the Moonies were at work, Derek traveled to Memphis to keep Toes at bay. It didn't work. When he returned to Nashville, an odd present awaited him: a large, framed picture of Sophia Loren, Don Johnson, Cher, former President Clinton, Spiderman, Dolly Parton, Cameron Diaz, Hulk Hogan, Sylvester Stallone, and Tom Cruise. They were on a patio next to a beach, with grins all around. The matting around the photo had autographs from each celebrity. After studying the curious photo carefully, he realized it was the Moonies dressed as celebrities, plus someone with hairy legs who looked like Cher.

Derek's phone rang.

"Derek, this is Chen. Did you get our presents?"

"The picture?"

"Yes, it's some photo from our team buildings event: Celebrity Roller Blades Scavenger Hunts."

"You and the Moonies actually rollerbladed around South Beach dressed as celebrities?"

"Yes. Chers organized it. She's very talented."

"Yes, and she needs to shave her legs. Did anyone get arrested?"

"Only troubles was President Clintons and Hulk Hogans taking the taxi to buy some condom."

"Careful or we'll have to do HuRTS again. This is really great, Chen. We need to find a place to hang this picture."

"Derek, we could take some photo of Bug Offs too, start some collections."

Chen's suggestion got Derek thinking about having cool offices. The office would have an awards wall with pictures and awards Lund had won.

Later that day, Trophy and Derek went to the diner to discuss the company's financial situation. Kim greeted Derek with a warm smile but turned chilly when introduced to Trophy. She disdainfully studied Trophy's impressive figure, nice clothes, and spiked heels.

Derek and Trophy sat down and ordered. Trophy clearly was not used to such a place and tried to order a Cobb salad with raspberry vinaigrette dressing on the side and tea. Kim looked at her like she was deranged and said their only salad was one with buffalo chicken and ranch dressing. Trophy settled on a tuna sandwich without the bread.

As they sipped sweet teas, Derek broached the idea of new, cooler offices to inspire the team and reinforce Lund's innovation efforts. She listened attentively and then responded.

"Derek, great idea, except you'll never get it past Toes."

"He doesn't need to know."

"Won't he find out eventually?"

While Derek sat thinking, Kim brought the orders. She smiled as she placed Derek's usual open-faced turkey sandwich with gravy and fries and Trophy's tuna salad without bread on the table. It had two scoops of tuna side by side. Kim gave Derek a devilish smile and winked.

Sensing trouble, Derek studied Trophy's plate. The scoops had been sculpted to resemble two large breasts with olive bits placed as nipples. Presumably for realism, both breasts sagged slightly downward to simulate the effects of gravity.

Bonnie and Clyde under the sea, Derek thought with alarm.

"B'linda," Derek said, pointing at the retreating figure of Kim behind her, "have you ever seen a waitress with an exposed belly-button ring?"

When Trophy turned, Derek knocked over Bonnie with his fork and cut the nipple off Clyde. She didn't notice and turned back to Derek and said, "No, but if my woman's radar is working right, I'd say she has a thing for you."

"If I wasn't happily married ..."

Crisis averted, Derek steered the conversation to the new office and asked Trophy to work with Bev to find a good one. Two weeks later, Bev and Trophy recommended an office in a new five-story building. The owner thought Lund Plastics would be perfect, especially after a personal meeting with Trophy. Trophy negotiated favorable rent, especially for the first two years, to get Lund past the Great Recession and avoid the wrath of Toes.

Trophy and Bev created a team to work with architects to design the office. The team hired the architectural firm of Brock & Associates, a midsize outfit in downtown Nashville. Brock's account manager for Lund was Robbie Vaughn.

A week later, Robbie returned with a Brock architect, and Bev invited Derek to join them. Robbie showed many design possibilities, from ornate wood to modern cube-farms. None appealed to the team, who had their hearts set on something really different.

Robbie asked what was missing. Everyone on the team responded.

"We need to be really cool."

"Let's show wood, but not be dark."

"We should have a foosball table."

"How about a place to hang bicycles from the ceiling?"

"Let's have open offices, even for Derek."

"How about a loft?"

"We need a totally cool main conference room where we can hang pictures of teams and awards and stuff."

"Let's have open ceilings, like that cool Italian restaurant on Johnny Cash Boulevard. You know, the one with the great risotto."

"Hey, what about a coffee bar with espresso machines?"

"You know what would be cool? A gym with mirrors all around, a stereo, a shower, and maybe one of those Bowflex exercise machines that makes you look really buff."

"We should have team rooms named after rock bands."

"What we need are really cool bathrooms, maybe with TV screens in the stalls."

After hearing the feedback and ideas, Robbie and his architect recruited Brock's secret radical architect for the job. Two weeks later, they returned with stunningly radical and brilliant designs. The interior walls were unfinished wood. The ceilings were high, open, and painted black. All lighting was modern and indirect, avoiding stark brightness. Every color was earth tone. The kitchen featured a coffee bar with espresso machines, a large, flat-screen TV, and a foosball table. Offices along the outside of the space had glass interior walls, giving a feeling of light and openness. The office cubicles had low walls to facilitate communication. The main conference room had a stunning table and a prominent award wall. Everything was cool, except the bathrooms, which had no TVs in the stalls.

The team enthusiastically blessed the design, and within a month, construction began. Bev proudly advertised the design to the entire office through posted drawings. She was wildly enthused. The team assigned offices and cubicles and ordered new, cool furniture.

The office move happened over a weekend. By Monday morning, the move had been completed, and the new offices were stunning. The new lobby displayed a large Lund corporate logo. The lights were on; name plates were on every office and cube; the espresso machines were operating; the phones and computers were hooked up; and the conference rooms were all labeled with names of cool American cities: San Francisco, Seattle, Boston and Miami. The picture of the Moonies in South Beach, as well as a photo of Team Bug Off, hung on the main conference room walls.

Bev had banners made for the lobby that read: "Welcome to the New Lund Plastics!" Each member of her team had signed the banner.

As Derek walked down the hallway, he was thrilled with the new office. He noticed a surprise addition: two Chinese foo dogs guarding the entrance to the main conference room. When Bev saw Derek's smile, she exclaimed, "It's to keep away the evil spirits, Derek. Chen's idea. Aren't they great?"

"Let's hope they work on Toes," Derek chuckled.

At 10:00 a.m., there was a new office celebration in the coffee bar/kitchen. Bobby made espresso for everyone, and Bev unveiled a giant cake with the Lund logo on top. The mixture of strong coffee and sugar juiced the group's energy level. The foosball table had its inaugural game, with Trophy and Monique playing Bob Davis and Larry La Croix. The new television had music videos blaring, and the mood was high.

By around ten thirty, the espresso had kicked in fully, the music was loud, and the foosball table was rocking, with loud cheers for each goal. Just then, the receptionist, Gail Schwarz, opened the door. Her concerned look contrasted sharply with the festive mood. She searched the room, found Derek, and said, "Derek, excuse me, but there's someone here from Corporate to see you."

Before Gail turned around, Commie stormed into the room. Somehow she had caught wind of the new office, including its location, and timed her strike to coincide with the opening festivities. She was not pleased.

Not everyone noticed Commie immediately. Just as she entered the room, Bob Davis scored a powerful goal against Trophy on the foosball table.

"Take that, bean-counting beahtches!" Bob yelled, to the delight of the spectators who hadn't noticed Commie yet.

Trophy and Monique laughed at Bob's abuse—until they caught sight of Commie. The mood in the room went from joy to quivering fear in less than a second.

Commie struck first. "Derek, can I see you outside, please?"

Derek walked out, his head hung low. In the hallway, Commie confronted him. "Derek, I see Lund Plastics has a new office."

Refraining from a snide comment about Commie's powers of observation, Derek meekly said, "Today's the opening. How do you like them?"

"I'll let you know after my audit."

"Audit?"

"I'm here to check offices and cubes to make sure they comply." Commie's look of disgust was unnerving.

"Comply with what?"

"With our corporate worldwide standards for spaces, of course. Several months ago, we received complaints about office and cubicle sizes. To ensure fairness and nondiscrimination, we issued standards on sizes and materials, as well as office rules. You received the memo."

"Office rules? A memo?"

"Rules of behavior in the office."

"That was serious? We all thought it was a gag."

Commie didn't appreciate Derek's humor. "Very serious. We need rules and norms: what can be hung on office or cubicle walls, minimum height of cube walls, meetings in cubes, use of excessive cologne in cubes, prohibition against 'prairie dogging,' etc."

"What's prairie dogging?"

"It's when people in cubes pop up and down to talk to their neighbors, like prairie dogs."

"But don't we want our employees to communicate with each other?"

"Not at work."

For the rest of the day, Commie audited the office and bathrooms using a tape measure and camera, and took copious notes. Around midafternoon, she ordered a post-audit review in the main conference room with Darrell, Bev, Trophy, and Derek.

The main conference room was an unfortunate venue choice for the home team. When they entered the room, Commie was already there, carefully examining the South Beach photo of the Moonies on the award wall. She looked extremely peeved at what could be perceived as dozens of HR and political-correctness violations.

Commie said, "Was this picture taken after our HuRST session?"

"Yes. It's from The Celebrity Roller Blading Scavenger Hunt in Miami, a team-building event for a new product team. That's why it's up there," Derek answered.

"It's patently offensive to women, not to mention former presidents. This will go in my report, along with the fact that you're displaying it openly in the office."

"Your report?"

"Yes, I will write up my audit for Miles Templeton and Dave Lund, copy to the Board Compliance Committee."

Commie continued, "This new office has several violations of the Corporate Policy on Real Estate and Offices."

Foo dogs are worthless, Derek thought.

"This policy is a bit, um, new to us. Can you describe the issues?" Darrell asked.

"For starters, you failed to have Corporate Human Resources review the designs."

"Is that required?" Derek inquired.

"Yes; in fact, if you had, the other issues would not have appeared, except maybe the picture and Bob Davis abusing B'linda and Monique while playing foosball."

"Bob was just trying to score. What are the other issues?"

Commie opened her notebook and read her list: the rent per square foot was above Lund standard; Bev's cubicle was smaller than some of the men's cubes; Derek's office was too big; Monique was caught "prairie dogging" twice; no other Lund location had a foosball table and it was unfair for Plastics to have one; Monique's motorcycle helmet was on top of her cube wall; Lund locations could not have free espresso because everyone in Lund would want it, and it would hurt productivity for people to leave their desks to go to the coffee bar ("Connie, have you seen these people move after a couple of espressos?" Derek asked.); Bob Davis had a "Girls of the Atlantic Coast Conference" calendar tacked to his cube with a picture of a Duke co-ed in a bikini on a beer keg; the cube walls in Sales were too low, making it too easy for them to talk to each other ("But that's the point," Derek meekly argued); the foo dogs showed cultural insensitivity; and there was gender toilet inequality—the men had two urinals and two stalls, while the women had three stalls.

"Wow," Trophy answered. "We're sorry and will look at this."

"You must address all the issues. It's required under corporate policy," Commie stated emphatically.

"Some will be quite difficult to change," Trophy stated, "like the number of toilets."

"You could just shut down one or build others," Commie explained.

"Connie," Derek asked, "I am a little confused—who is underserved, the men or women?"

"The women, as always," Commie explained. "The men have two urinals and two toilets, giving them one more outlet."

Darrell spoke up. "Do you equate urinals with toilets?"

"Of course, Darrell," she barked. "The men's room can accommodate four men at a time, while the women's can only take three. Clearly, this favors the men."

Darrell elaborated on his point. "There is much faster turnover at urinals, Connie, but at certain times of day, more toilets are needed in the men's room."

"What do you mean, Darrell?" Commie asked, sensing fault in her logic.

"Well, toilets can be used as urinals, but not the other way around. There are times first thing in the morning when there's high demand in the men's room. Some of the guys have to go to another floor or, if they have the luxury of time, back to their offices."

"Our policy doesn't address this," Commie said.

"Why don't we conduct an occupancy study?" Darrell suggested. "We could make any needed changes based on the study."

"Would you be open to that, Comm—I mean, Connie?" Trophy interjected.

"Yes, though it would require a change in corporate policy."

"How would we measure occupancy?" Trophy asked.

"Video surveillance would be out of the question," Darrell explained. He paused for several moments, deep in thought, and continued. "Come to think of it, maybe there's another solution. We could have a sign-up sheet for the bathrooms."

"Do you mean a reservation system?" Derek asked.

"That's what I was thinking," Darrell responded.

"Advanced reservations might be difficult for the more spontaneous user," Trophy added.

"Good points," Derek said.

"Chen is wearing off on you, Derek," Trophy commented with a laugh.

Darrell continued pondering and then had an epiphany. "Hey, I got it! Why don't we have lighted signs in the hallways, one for men and another for women? It would show green when stalls are available and red when they're occupied."

Commie responded immediately. "We would have to change corporate policy to allow toilet-occupancy lights, of course, but it might be worth a try. Great idea, Darrell."

Darrell just modestly said, "It's really nothing. I got the idea from airplanes."

As Commie was packing up to leave, Gail Schwarz entered the room and asked, "Ms. Schmidt, would you like an espresso for the road? They're free!"

20

PILGRIM'S PRIDE

After the toilet controversy, Derek found new respect for Darrell and decided to make peace. He also resolved to stop fighting the powers of HR at Lund.

The Tuesday before Thanksgiving, Derek wandered into Darrell's office for the peace conference. Darrell's office walls were full of standard motivational posters. On his credenza was an autographed picture of Darrell with Barry Manilow.

"Darrell, do you have a minute?" Derek asked.

"To what do I owe an honor of a visit to?" Darrell asked, unable to stop himself before adding the improper preposition.

"There's something that's been bugging me for a long time, and I just wanted to clear the air."

Darrell got very serious and said, "Sure, Derek; do you need to shut the door?"

"No, that's okay."

"What is it?"

"Do you remember the ride to Dalton in your Volvo when I was new?"

"Like it was yesterday."

"Well, when you asked me about music, I wasn't entirely honest."

"Oh, how so?"

"It's hard for me to admit."

"It can't be that bad. What is it?" Darrell asked.

"I really like ABBA and have seen *Mama Mia* five times."

"I knew you weren't just a hard rocker!" Darrell cheered. Then he started singing a famous ABBA tune with customized lyrics:

"If you change your mind, I'll be first in line;

Derek, I'm still free, take a chance on me."

"Darrell, really, that's okay—"

He resumed singing even louder.

"If you need me, let me know, gonna be around

If you need a place to go, if you're feeling down ..."

"Darrell—"

"Take a chance on me ..."

"Darrell ..."

"Take a chance on me."

"Darrell, the lighting here just isn't romantic. And not to nitpick, but your proposition probably constitutes sexual harassment."

"Only if it's unwanted," Darrell added with a wink.

This constituted a fully signed peace treaty, and they celebrated with talk about ABBA and all their hits. The conversation progressed from ABBA to Thanksgiving.

"What are your plans, Derek?"

"My parents are coming down from Minnesota. How about you?"

"We're going to The Smoky Mountains to get away."

Derek stood up and started out the door. "That sounds nice, Darrell. I hope you and your family have a wonderful Thanksgiving."

Darrell shouted out, "Happy Holidays to you and yours, Derek!"

"Did you just say 'Happy Holidays?'"

"Yep. Corporate HR has instructed us to discourage using the word *Thanksgiving*."

"Because it discriminates against turkeys?"

"No. It glorifies the European exploitation of Native Americans."

"By a band of starving Pilgrims?"

21

WHITE ZINFANDEL

During a break in his market research for the Moonies, Bob Davis invited Derek and Chen to dinner with one of Lund's largest customers, Talladega Industries, who were in Nashville for a Shania Twain concert. Talladega was owned by Dom and Dave Perry, the great-grandsons of the founder, Colonel Dominicus Perry. Dom and Dave had spent their whole lives in rural Alabama and little time in cities. For them, Nashville was a cosmopolitan jewel and center of the country-music universe.

The fivesome went to Morton's Steakhouse in the center of downtown, which was famous for huge, succulent steaks and presented its menu by having servers display a cart of uncooked meats. Chen wore his new blue suit from Jos. A Bank—("Derek, I got three suit for the prices of one.")—with a white shirt and red tie. Derek wore a dark-gray suit with a pink shirt and blue tie. Bob wore a blue sport coat with salsa stains on the sleeve, a tie, and khaki pants. The Perrys each wore blue seersucker suits and blue ties.

When they entered Morton's at seven, the sights and smells were tantalizing. The Perrys had never seen such a place; they gawked at dishes as they passed and pointed enthusiastically at the meat carts. Bob knew the maître d' and had arranged for the center table.

Soon after the group sat down, the waiter asked for their drink order. The Perrys ordered double margaritas with no salt, and Bob joined them enthusiastically, saying he was trying to watch his health. Chen and Derek ordered Heinekens.

For the next thirty minutes, the group talked about Talladega and Shania Twain.

Dom asked Chen, "Hey, Dr. Chen, do y'all have Shania Twain in China?"

"No, Dom, we have no Twains."

"Too bad. She's a great singer and one helluva looker."

"What's some looker?"

"A fox, Chen, a real fox."

As Chen pondered the meaning of *fox*, more rounds came. The waiter returned with Morton's wine menu. While he stood by, Derek turned to Dom and Dave and asked, "Hey, guys, what kind of wine would y'all like? Morton's has a great wine list. Maybe a good cabernet? They go great with their steaks, I hear."

Dave said, "How 'bout a white zinfandel?"

Derek panicked and desperately searched the menu for their choice. The waiter sensed the problem and pointed out Morton's only bottle of white zinfandel, while whispering that no one had ever ordered it before.

To complicate matters, from Derek's point of view, Dom said, "Derek, you might want to get two bottles. Dave and I usually polish off at least one by ourselves. That ol' boy's got a hollow leg, if you know what I mean."

Bob grabbed the opening gracefully. "Why don't we order a bottle of cabernet so we can all try some variety?"

After the wine was poured, the group turned its attention to dinner. The waiter brought the famous meat cart with enormous steaks and side dishes. But Dave had trouble imagining the finished product and ignored the cart. He stood straight up and examined the dishes on neighboring tables. After a 360-degree turn, Dave spied a steaming plate in front of a woman at another table.

He took a step forward, pointed at the woman's plate, and shouted, "I'll have that one!" The woman flinched in terror. Bob and Derek laughed while Chen sipped his white zinfandel calmly.

True to their word, the Perrys finished the bottle of white zinfandel. When the waiter grabbed the empty bottle, Dom asked, "Could we please have another?" The waiter's face went pale—the Perry Brothers, with an assist from Chen, had drunk Morton's only bottle of white zinfandel. But he kept his composure and went to the kitchen. Ten minutes later, he returned with a bottle of white zinfandel of a different brand. As he poured out of the new bottle, he smiled at Derek and winked. When he turned to walk away, Derek noticed a plastic 7-Eleven bag in his back pocket.

As the waiter brought dessert, Dave turned to Bob and said, "So, Bob, are we going to the 'ballet,' like last time?"

"What is the ballet?" asked Chen.

"Well, doctor," Dave replied, "you're in for a real treat. It's a gentlemen's club. You know, High Beams."

Bob jumped in. "It's all set. I even hired a van to take us there, so we can have more margaritas."

Derek turned to Bob and said, "Bob, we talked about this. You know we can't—"

"Nonsense, Derek!" Dave said. "We're your customers, and we insist. It'll be a ball."

"The customer is always right, Derek," Bob added. "Don't worry, no more napkin receipts."

"Atta boy, Bobby," Dave said, a slight slur already creeping into his voice.

So immediately after dinner, the group piled into a waiting van. The driver was an Ethiopian named Ashenafi who preferred to be called Ash. As they rode to High Beams, Dave wondered aloud, "I wonder if Jessica will be dancing tonight?"

"She's usually there on Thursdays," Dom added.

Derek got the impression the Perrys and Bob were long on experience at High Beams.

The club was on the south side of Nashville, in a large building with bright signs. The parking lot was jammed with cars, taxis, and limousines. As the van pulled up to the front door, Bob said, "Ash, can you wait for us? We'll be a couple hours. We'll pay you for the time."

Ash enthusiastically agreed and pulled out an Ethiopian sports magazine, and the five men piled out of the van.

Inside a small lobby stood a pretty woman behind a podium in front of a large door. She collected hefty cover charges and kept out the riffraff. Interestingly, she knew Bob by name and waived his group along at no charge. The Perry brothers were excited as they passed through two sets of doors, walked past tough-looking bouncers, and entered a bar area. Past the bar was a large lounge with tables and topless women walking about or dancing provocatively.

A very attractive woman escorted the group to a table near a small stage. It had a "Reserved" sign on it, which she removed. Moments later, a waitress arrived to take orders. The Perrys and Bob opted for more margaritas, while Chen and Derek reverted to beer. Chen had not spoken for several minutes.

Soon after the drinks arrived, three topless dancers came over. At first, they made small talk, asked about jobs, etc. Chen answered earnestly, and they giggled at his speech. He seemed unaware that they were topless and beautiful. Derek marveled at Chen's discipline.

"Dr. Chen," Bob asked, "Do you have strip clubs in China?"

"No, Bob, just some foot massage with the pretty lady."

"Feet?"

"Yes, Bob."

"Wow. That's kinda weird, isn't it?"

"No, it's relaxing time."

"But isn't it strange, especially if the gals have had their feet shrunk, like they do down there?"

"No, Bob, the lady massage the man foots."

"With their clothes on?"

"Yes, Bob."

"What's the point? I'm glad I live in the good ol' U. S. of A."

The Perrys passed small talk in a blur and progressed to major lap dancing, funded by Bob's colossal roll of twenty-dollar bills. They had done this before. Chen sipped his beer and watched. Bob quickly hired the third dancer for his own lap dance, grinning from ear to ear and trying to fondle the girl's nearly perfect breasts. Derek drank beer faster and faster, worried that he couldn't afford another infraction on his HR rap sheet.

"Chen," Derek said without looking away from the nakedness in front of him, "if Commie finds out about this, you know what happens?"

"We get some PhD from HuRT?"

"Exactly."

"You know, Derek, I think Bob is having some good times," Chen said.

"How do you know?"

"He is having drool on his chins."

Derek finally broke down after Bob arranged a dance for him from a girl named Carly, a twenty-five-year-old stunner. She had light-brown, shoulder-length hair, medium-sized breasts, and a gorgeous smile.

"Are you the boss, Derek?" Carly asked, rubbing his arm.

"Um, yes; how did you know?"

"Because you look like a successful executive—you have that aura," Carly said as she oriented her breasts within inches of his face. Carly got closer and closer, nibbling Derek's ear and then pressing her breasts against him. Derek quickly lost all consciousness of being the boss and enjoyed himself thoroughly.

Chen drank beer and sat without expression.

Bob had Derek firmly in his HR criminal enterprise. He kept feeding Carly twenties, and she stayed in Derek's lap. After another hour and more drinks, they decided to leave. Carly wrote her name and a personal note on a High Beams napkin and tucked it in Derek's front coat pocket. She said Derek should ask for her specifically whenever he came back and then kissed his cheek.

The bar bill was a whopper. Beers were fifteen dollars each, and margaritas were twenty dollars. The waitress placed the bill in front of Bob, who, without looking, slid it in front of Derek. Derek looked at him incredulously, and Bob said, "Lund expense policy, Derek—the most senior person at the table pays."

Being a master of expense-account manipulation, Bob knew his stuff. The policy was there to prevent bosses from forcing their underlings to pay for shady items, like strip clubs, and then approve their expense reports.

Holy shit, Derek thought, *how will I explain this to Monique?*

Chen said to Derek, "I think Bob is pro calibers at not paying his bills."

With trepidation, Derek gave the waitress his Lund American Express card. She sensed his worry. "Don't worry, Mr. Vogel," she said after reading the name on the card, "the receipt will only say ABC Entertainment, not High Beams."

Derek added a tip, signed the bill, and took a receipt. He was far too preoccupied to remember to grab his American Express card.

On the ride home, Bob rode in the front seat of Ash's van and played loud music on the radio. Everyone talked and laughed about the whole evening. Infused with many beers, Chen giggled at his newest cultural indoctrination and looked forward to telling Travis about it. The Perrys professed their deep love of Lund, Bob, Derek, and Chen. With margarita salt still on his chin, Dom vowed to make Morton's and High Beams an annual, if not quarterly, tradition.

It was 2:00 a.m. when the van pulled into Derek's driveway, the first stop. He exited the van and staggered to the front door, only then realizing that his keys remained with the Morton's valet. As the van pulled away roaring with loud music and laughter, Derek considered his options. The most obvious, ringing the doorbell, was not attractive due to the late hour, his extreme tipsiness, and the lingering smell of Carly's perfume.

He pursued his backup plan: finding an unlocked window on the first floor. Still substantially impaired by a night of drinking, Derek was over-confident in his plan, forgetting important details like the burglar alarm. He found an unlocked bathroom window, seemingly a big break. When he shoved the window open, he heard the initial warning of the alarm, which—unfortunately for Derek—pierced the night's quiet throughout the house.

Derek pulled himself through the window and fell on the floor before getting up and running to the alarm keypad to enter the security code. As he raced down the hall, he heard footsteps on the second floor. From the sound of them, he gathered them to be adult steps, confirming his fears that he had awakened Carol. A few moments passed, and he heard Charlotte yell, "Mommy, what is it? Where's Daddy?"

The answer to Charlotte's very reasonable question would not be favorable to Derek, he figured in his alcoholic haze. Nonetheless, he remained focused on the mission of turning off the alarm before the full screech went off. He was a tad too late, and all hell broke loose. On his third try, Derek successfully entered the security code, and the alarm finally shut down. By then, he could distinctly hear both Charlotte and Everest crying hysterically upstairs.

The phone rang.

That would be the security company, Derek surmised.

He ran to the kitchen to answer the call. When Carol heard him answer the phone, she started down the stairs. From the frequency of her steps, Derek gathered Carol was not approaching at a casual speed. Through somewhat slurry speech, he recited the emergency code to the security company and explained the incident.

Derek didn't get off the phone in time to straighten out before Carol arrived. When Carol turned on the kitchen light, Derek figured his disheveled appearance betrayed a long night of customer entertainment. One look at Carol confirmed his fears.

Cleverly, he said, "Hi, Honey."

"Derek, it's two a.m. The lights were out. You're completely shitfaced and woke up the twins and me."

"Sorry, Honey. I left my keys at Morton's and had to come through the bathroom window, like that song by the Beatles," he explained, trying to interject a little humor, a strategy he would not have pursued if given a second chance. "We had to entertain the Perry Brothers from Talladega Industries tonight."

"What the hell's that smell?" Carol asked.

"Probably beer, (*hiccup*), we had a few."

"No, something else." She moved closer. "Darrell, you fucking jerk, it's perfume!"

She pulled the napkin from his front coat pocket, and then noticed it was from High Beams and included the handwritten note from Carly. Carol put one and one together and came up with two.

Customer entertainment is an oft-cited excuse for bad behavior and can be effective if used correctly. In Derek's case, it was less than effective, and he faced Carol's fury for several minutes. Fortunately for Derek, the twins distracted her, and he was temporarily off the hook.

Derek didn't get to sleep until after 3:00 a.m. and had to rise by seven for a meeting at work. Four hours of sleep was not nearly enough, especially with a hangover. Carol noticed his pain and enjoyed it thoroughly, placing a bottle of Advil next to his coffee, along with an empty Heineken bottle. Little Charlotte looked up from her cereal bowl, surveyed the scene, and asked, "Mommy, is Daddy sick?"

"Yes, Charlotte, in so many ways."

"Poor Daddy," Charlotte said, "he doesn't look very good."

Carol drove Derek to get his car, barely speaking to him. All she could say was, "How's the hangover?"

"Really bad."

"Good. Have a nice day."

It was Friday, the day when Lund Plastics was very casual. Derek's Friday tradition was to wear blue jeans and a black button-down shirt with a Lund Plastics logo on the left breast pocket. It was a cool shirt and everyone noticed it. On that particular Friday, the morning meetings were challenging, and Derek made full use of the espresso machine. He even drank a Coke around ten a.m. to settle his stomach. Bev sensed something was off.

Around eleven a.m., he gathered his receipts from the previous night, wondering how to handle them without offending Monique. He noticed an empty slot in his wallet and realized he had left his Lund American Express card at High Beams, a realization that created great anxiety. Derek didn't want anyone from High Beams calling the office or Lund Corporate Headquarters to report finding it.

Around noon, he left the office, telling Bev he would be back in an hour. He drove across town to High Beams, hoping it was open during the day. Fortunately for Derek, the world of male entertainment was not solely nocturnal, and High Beams was bustling.

He walked into the lobby and approached an attractive woman behind the podium.

"Welcome to High Beams," she said.

"Hi," Derek responded. "I was here last night and forgot my credit card. It's an American Express. My name is Derek Vogel."

"Okay," she said, "I'll call security to get it for you. You can wait right here."

Derek was being low-key, trying to remain anonymous. As she called security, she kept looking at his shirt, particularly the Lund logo. After hanging up, she said, "Mr. Vogel, do you work for Lund Plastics?"

"Um … uh … yes," he said sheepishly.

"My friend Diana works as a temp there—in Sales."

Shit, Derek thought in a panic.

"Oh, yes, she's very nice."

"By the way, you have really cool offices. I love the unfinished wood walls and glass offices."

"You've been to our offices?" he asked, his voice rising an octave or two.

"A couple times. When I'm not working, I sometimes go meet Diana for lunch."

"Well, I'm glad you like the offices."

"Where's your office?" she asked.

"Well, um, at reception, if you turn right and go down the hall with the exposed wood, it's down there."

"Yes, I've walked down that hall. You pass two conference rooms on the way—the San Francisco and Seattle conference rooms. Is your office past those?"

"Yes, a little bit."

"How far?"

This is not going well, Derek thought.

"Um, kind of all the way down on the left."

"You mean the big corner office? Diana showed it to me. It's cool."

"Um, yes, that's the one."

"You're the president of Lund?"

Suddenly, a variation of a quote from an old American Express commercial popped into Derek's head: "American Express, Don't Leave High Beams Without It."

22

L. Beans

All the fuss about Jackson Hill and Dalton's exciting new products made Lund's other two plants feel neglected. This was particularly true of the plant in Caribou, Maine, which was tucked into the far northeastern corner of the United States.

The Caribou plant was old, had inefficient technology, and was much further from industrial-plastics markets. Caribou's inefficiencies, coupled with a prolonged slump in business, created an extremely insecure workforce. Caribou employed 150 workers, and their other job opportunities were slim. Anxiety was persistently high.

Contributing to this anxiety was the fact that Caribou received little attention from the rest of Lund Plastics. The management team rarely visited. Distance was a major factor, as was brutally cold and snowy weather. Winter began in October and was brutal. Temperatures well below zero were common, and snowdrifts reached telephone wires. Winter entertainment included snowmobiling, eating, drinking, and watching northern Maine high school basketball on television.

None of these pursuits—except eating and drinking—appealed to Derek's senior team, but they decided to hold a February meeting at the Caribou plant nonetheless. The plan was to travel Tuesday, meet at the plant on Wednesday and Thursday, and have an outdoor team-building event Friday. The whole trip was a frightening prospect because nearly everyone was either from the South or China. Trophy asked about wearing spiked heels at the Caribou plant. Chen wanted to visit the mammoth L. L. Bean store in Freeport, Maine, a five-hour drive from Caribou. Darrell and Larry asked if the hotel TV had anything other than the high school basketball playoffs. Bev was excited to go north of the Mason-Dixon line for the first time.

Larry, Dirk, Bobby and Darrell flew through Boston and took a puddle jumper into Presque Isle, a small airport near Caribou. The rest flew to Portland and rented a car. Chen talked the group into shopping at L. L. Bean, his lifelong dream. Trophy and Bev acquiesced because they needed snowsuits and mittens for the team-building event.

They landed at the Portland International Jetport around 1:00 p.m. It was snowing hard and very cold. Trophy had a huge, stylish suitcase with lavender trim and a colorful bow tied to the handle. She could barely lift it off the belt.

"B'linda, only one little bag?" Derek.

"I had to really scrunch things up, Derek, but I might get another bag at L. L. Bean."

Chen pulled two large bags from the belt. Derek asked, "Chen, did you bring Travis and Dr. Miao in those?"

"No, they are workings on some experiment for the Moonie this week—making the new microbial-resistant toilet-seat coating, so they couldn't come. The bags are for L. Beans."

They picked a Grand Marquis at Avis and drove to Freeport, thirty minutes north. Despite having a Grand Marquis, they barely had room for their suitcases. As they pulled into Freeport in the blowing snow, they noticed the town was uncharacteristically empty. Freeport was a famous outlet-store center that attracted visitors from far and wide. As they drove past the gigantic L. L.

Bean store, Chen stared in awe. Trophy, meanwhile, noticed some women's designer outlet stores across the street.

Dr. Chen moved through the L. L. Bean doors like a cheetah. Trophy and Bev went for women's jackets, and Derek stayed with Chen. For the next two hours, Chen led Derek on an inspirational tour of the giant L. L. Bean store. The first stop was men's footwear, where Chen bought two pairs of L. L. Bean's signature boots.

"Chen, why are you getting two pairs?" Derek asked out of mild curiosity.

"One pairs is for me this weeks, and the others is for my brother."

"I didn't know you had a brother. Where does he live?"

"Hong Kong."

"Chen, isn't Hong Kong tropical?"

"Yes. The boots are just for the styles."

"What's his name?"

"Chen."

"Isn't that a little confusing?"

"Yes, so he has some nicksname, Cleveland."

"Why Cleveland?"

"He like the Cleveland Indian baseball teams—from the movie *Major Leagues*. He likes Charlie Sheens."

Chen graduated from boots to long underwear, flannel shirts, and thick, wool socks. He even wore the long underwear in the store. For Chen, so much winter clothing at bargain prices trumped the fact that he lived in Georgia.

After Chen bought winter clothes for every part of his body, the excursion started winding down. On the way out, however, Chen noticed a sign for the hunting and fishing department and changed direction in midstride.

The first selection was an insulated, bright-orange hunting cap with side flaps. Chen got two, the second for Cleveland. Derek imagined a Chinese businessman in sweltering Hong Kong wearing a fashionable suit accessorized with L. L. Bean boots and orange hunting hat. From hats, Chen moved to camouflaged vests and wore one in the store. He also got matching pants and gloves. Just when Derek thought he was finally done, Chen noticed an archery display.

After two hours, Chen and Derek left the store with bags of clothing. It was snowing hard, and the day's light was fading. Trophy and Bev had just arrived at the car, carrying bags from L. L. Bean, Ralph Lauren, and J. Crew. They gazed toward Chen and Derek, then stared and blinked repeatedly, unable to see them clearly. They saw Chen's hat first, cutting through the snowy haze. Then they noticed Chen's ensemble of a fully strung hunting bow over his shoulder and quiver of arrows attached to his back.

It took twenty minutes to pack Chen's purchases into his suitcases and arrange the luggage, shopping bags, hunting bow, quiver, and arrows. They left Freeport at 4:00 p.m. for the long drive to Caribou, stocking up on Tostitos, peanuts, beef jerky, Diet Cokes, and Mountain Dews.

Around 9:00 p.m., the Grand Marquis entered Caribou and pulled into the hotel, The Governor, the largest hotel in Caribou. They parked, grabbed their bags, and entered. Chen brought his new bow and quiver and still wore his orange hat and camouflage vest. The Governor's lobby was only a reception area with a transparent door to the bar. While checking in, Chen saw Darrell, Larry, Dirk, and Bobby in the bar, watching high school basketball playoffs. He immediately joined them.

In many parts of the world, even America, a camouflaged stranger entering a bar with a hunting bow and full quiver would cause panic. But no one flinched, except a guy who asked Chen not to block the TV—it was a crucial moment in the second girls' regional semifinal game. Bobby ordered a beer for Chen and invited him to sit down. Chen raved for an hour about Freeport and "L. Beans." The group was fascinated. Trophy and Bev ordered the house chardonnay—a colossal judgment error in such a place—and joined the group. After a couple drinks, everyone went to bed.

At 6:00 a.m., the outside temperature was minus 15 degrees. The group met in the bar for breakfast at six thirty, the smell of stale beer mixing with scrambled eggs and bacon. The TV played highlights of the two girls' semifinal regional games, the leading story.

They arrived at the Caribou plant at seven thirty. Most wore casual attire, but Trophy wore spiked heels and a fashionable pants suit that showed her figure, to the great delight of the male plant workers.

The plant manager, Jake Theriault, greeted the team and gave them a tour. The Caribou team was thrilled to have visitors, which was a rarity. Derek's team smiled, shook hands, and made small talk, mostly asking if it was always this cold.

Derek's primary mission in Caribou was to be visible and ease anxieties. With this mission firmly in mind, he and his team sequestered themselves in the plant conference room and shut the door.

To start the meeting, Derek used a Dr. Dave technique called "Good 'n New." The idea was to create a positive atmosphere by reporting on good things. Derek started with Bev.

"There's just so much good to report," she beamed. "This is my first trip to Caribou."

"We're pleased to have you with us, Bev," Derek added.

"Actually, it's my first time in the North. Good Lord, it's cold!"

"Great. Okay, let's—"

"And The Governor Hotel is really nice."

"Okay—"

"And Derek, B'linda, Chen, and I had a great visit to Freeport and L. L. Bean, and—"

"Great, thanks, Bev," Derek interrupted. "Who's next? Larry?"

"I have really great news I've been dying to share with you all. We had a record for American Siding sales last month."

"How much, Larry?" Derek asked.

"We sold nearly 70 percent of Dalton's capacity to American, and as Chen can tell you, we finished development of a new antimicrobial coating for Lone Pine Siding. We'll start selling that next month."

Chen interrupted. "Travis is doing some great jobs as the chief operatings officer of Bugger Offs."

Darrell jumped in. "Chen, we can't give titles that weren't approved by Corporate HR. Everyone will want to be a chief operating officer."

Trophy raised her hand to go next. "Gerry from Dalton told me that as a result of American Siding sales, Dalton had by far its best month since the Great Recession. It hit breakeven."

"That's outstanding. Our strategy is starting to make a difference," Derek said.

Darrell went next. "Sophie and I attended a really good seminar at Corporate last month about ways to improve MOFMARTS forms. We had great, productive discussions, and everyone left with a better understanding and a positive attitude."

"That's remarkable, Darrell, on so many levels," Derek said.

After Bobby and Dirk went, it was Chen's turn. "Well, Larry already stole my thunders and lightnings about Bugger Offs, but it's okay. I have other good news about new product developments. For the last few weeks, Dr. Miao and Travis have been doing the experiments to make microbial-resistant coatings for the toilet. The initial results are positives. I will check with them on Mondays when I return."

"That's great, Chen."

"And they are also experimenting with making the toilet-seating coating glow in the dark."

"Glow in the dark?" Trophy interrupted. "Why?"

"So the mans know the seat is down when they visit in the midnights, and the lady also know it is some safe landing."

"Oh, I get it. That's very clever."

"Thanks, but it was Darrell's idea."

"It was nothing," Darrell commented. "My wife complains all the time."

"Darrell," Dirk added, "you really missed your calling."

From there, the group conducted a typical meeting that included reviewing poor financial results, discussing Bob Davis's entertainment spending, and speculating on the turnaround of the economy. The highlight was Darrell's report on a program to improve communications, including a new e-mail etiquette course. All eyes rolled. His presentation cover had a stock photo of a group of people diverse in ethnicity, age, and gender with their arms interlocked, smiling.

Jake Theriault joined for lunch and explained plans for their stay.

"At shift change this afternoon, around four, we will have a cookout supper with you and shifts one and two."

"Cookout?" Trophy asked.

"Yes. Then on Thursday, we will have three town hall meetings to talk about our new strategy and how Lund is doing. The first will be at 6:00 a.m."

"Wait, 6:00 *a.m.*?" Derek interjected incredulously.

"Yes, we need to get the night shift before they go home. Don't worry—we'll have coffee and doughnuts."

"That wasn't my worry."

The next morning, the team's five a.m. wake-up recording reported it was minus 20 degrees. They arrived at the plant cafeteria, an open room with tables and vending machines, at six a.m. for the meeting. Awaiting them were about thirty employees, mostly male, looking tired and dirty after a night's work. Two events perked them up considerably: Jake brought doughnuts and coffee, and Trophy wore a shapely pants suit and spiked heels.

Jake introduced Derek, who discussed the current state of Lund Plastics, including its poor economics. Someone asked about losses in the Caribou plant. Derek dreaded the question but spoke the truth.

Another man raised his hand.

"Yes, sir," Derek said as he pointed to him.

He was in his mid-fifties with a heavy plaid shirt, large, weathered hands, and thick glasses with safety side shields. His face was a bit dirty. He spoke with a heavy Maine accent.

"Mistah Vogel, I'm Larry Lemieux. All us employees have worked hahd here for twenty yeahrs or more. It's hahd work, but we Mainahs like to work hahd."

The senior team frantically asked each other for a translation.

"Larry, please call me Derek. Thank you—and thank all of you—for your dedication and working so, um, hahd."

Larry continued. "The point is, Mistah Vogel, we want to keep working hahd, but we hear rumahs about Lund closin' this plahnt."

"Larry, we are losing money here, as you know. However, we have a new strategy that is working. If it takes hold, it would make a big difference here and for all of Lund." Derek continued, "The best person to explain our strategy is our director of R & D, Dr. Chen."

Chen rose, wearing the camouflaged hunting vest. No one in Caribou had seen anyone like Chen. They stared in silence.

He introduced himself. "Thank you, Derek. My name is Chen, and if you have some troubles understanding me, it's because I'm from Beijing."

The group fixated on him like he was an alien.

"In Beijing, the weathers is almost this colds, but we don't have some snowmobile or the high schools basketball playoff on televisions."

Everyone laughed. Chen was the strangest person they had ever seen, yet he had somehow become one of them. He described his team and told how Travis gave Dr. Miao Mountain Dew and Red Man Chewing Tobacco. A guy in the front row roared and pointed at a colleague in the back, which led to several knowing guffaws.

Chen then described Chinatown and how it was smokier than the Caribou plant and way too hot. Finally, he talked about Bug Off siding coating, how it was created, and how it had changed the economics of Dalton. He said other new products were coming— and some for Caribou, too.

Near the end of the talk, a guy raised his hand and asked about Chen's camouflaged vest.

"I got it at L. Beans on my ways here," Chen explained, "along with some new huntings bow, arrow, and long underwears." The group roared with laughter.

Chen was a big hit, and a few employees talked to him afterward about his bow. One asked him to go deer hunting in the fall.

The other town hall meetings were similar; everyone loved Chen and felt more confident in their jobs at the end.

The next day was team building. After breakfast, the team met in the lobby in full winter gear. Trophy had ditched her heels for fur-lined purple boots that matched the snowsuit she had bought at L. L. Bean. Chen had his new orange hat and all his gear. The rest had more normal winter attire. At 9:00 a.m., the temperature had climbed to a balmy minus 10 degrees.

A van from Aroostook Snow Tours drove the group to a spot near Ashland, a very small town west of Caribou. Five snowmobiles awaited them. Bobby, Dirk, Larry, and Derek were the Lund designated drivers. The rest rode tandem. The guide trained the team and cautioned many times about excessive speed on turns.

After forty-five minutes of single-file driving through trails with huge snowdrifts, the caravan arrived at a clearing, where the guide distributed snowshoes and explained that they would be hiking around the woods until lunch.

Larry, Dirk, Darrell, and Bobby had no trouble with snowshoes. They walked in large circles to stay warm while Derek stayed with Chen, Trophy, and Bev. Bev picked it up reasonably well, but Chen and Trophy had issues. Chen was an eager, albeit poor student. As he watched the others, he turned and said to Derek, "Derek, maybe we should do the Snow Shoe Celebrity Scavengers Hunts."

"It might be hard to find a topless photo."

"Good points."

Chen had trouble and fell repeatedly. He and Trophy finally got the hang of it, and, along with Derek and Bev, they followed the guide. After several minutes, the group got strung out, with Larry and company well in front of Bev and Derek, who were far ahead of Chen and Trophy. Another ten minutes passed, and the stragglers fell further behind. Derek urged Bev to continue and turned back to find Chen and Trophy.

After several minutes, he spied Chen's orange hat a few feet from a pine tree. It appeared to be abandoned and lying upright in the snow, but as he got closer, he realized Chen was still under his hat. He had fallen through a snowdrift and sunk slightly past ear level. Near him was highly churned snow with flailing snowshoes at one end. Derek heard Trophy's voice, muffled by the snow.

"Chen, honey, can you feel my hand? I think it's by your stomach."

"Not yet. The snows is packed around me. I can't moves my arm."

"Okay, hang tight, darlin'. I'm still digging."

"B'linda, do you thinks we can get out of this deep snows?" Chen asked.

"I tried to lie down to stay on the surface, like in movies with quicksand, but I fell through. Everything's buried, except my snowshoes. I can't see anything,"

Derek offered to help, and after five minutes of digging, he freed Trophy, whose fur-lined hood was filled with snow. The two then dug a trench to Chen. When they finally cleared the snow from his face, he looked at Derek and said, "Good thing I am wearing my new long underwears from L. Beans."

"The orange cap came in handy, too," Derek said.

They caught up with the group on a break: they were only slightly worried about their disappearance. After a short rest, they snow shoed back to the snowmobiles, stopping only to show the crater where Chen had gotten stuck.

After an outdoor picnic lunch complete with hot chocolate, they took turns driving snowmobiles. For Chen, it was another dream come true. He put on his helmet and took off. The group watched as he flew down the trail, tilting perilously to one side.

"I hope he remembers to slow down on turns," Bobby commented.

Trophy, Bev, and Darrell put on their helmets and took off in another direction. After fifteen minutes, everyone had returned but Chen. Their adrenaline was high from snowmobiling, and they enthusiastically traded stories about their drives.

Suddenly, Trophy said, "Uh, oh, where's Chen?"

"He went another direction," Darrell explained. "I haven't seen him since we left."

Everyone stopped talking and listened.

"I can't hear him," Derek said. "I hope he's okay."

After ten minutes, the team sent a search party of two snowmobiles. Derek drove one with Trophy riding behind him, and Bobby drove another with Dirk.

A few miles down the trail, they found Chen's snowmobile overturned next to a huge snowdrift. There was a long skid mark between the snowmobile and snowdrift. They followed the skid mark and found Chen's legs sticking out of the drift.

Trophy gasped and said, "There he is! Oh, my God, Derek, he's hurt and not moving!"

Chen's legs started thrashing.

"Chen, are you okay?" Bobby called out.

He kept thrashing and appeared stuck.

Chen didn't hear Bobby. He finally pulled out of the snowdrift, and the cause of his deafness was revealed: his facemask had been open, and snow had completely stuffed his helmet and filled his ears, nostrils, mouth, and eye sockets. His glasses were still on, and snow was packed behind them. He couldn't hear or see and was madly flailing his arms to remove the helmet and clear his face.

Derek laughed and said, "Buried alive twice in one day—a new world record."

23

GETTING FRAMED

For weeks before the L. L. Bean road trip, the Moonies technical team had conducted several lab experiments to increase microbial resistance in plastics for toilet seats. Their goal was to develop a product that would coat toilet seats to kill microbes, eliminating the need for plastic toilet covers, as well as generally improving sanitation. Dr. Miao was the technical leader, with Travis in support. The two had built a relationship around technical competence, Mountain Dew, and Red Man, the trinity of Lund Plastics R & D.

Dr. Miao and Travis produced dozens of different lab samples. After initial testing, they selected five finalists for testing in a high-humidity and -temperature chamber, perfect for bug growth. The chamber was a converted storage room in the warehouse of the Dalton plant. Travis installed toilets for each sample seat. He assigned each finalist a number from one to five, but over lunch one day, he and Dr. Miao decided this approach lacked pizazz. They wanted a contest that got the whole Dalton plant involved, like the NCAA Men's Basketball Tournament betting pool.

During an initial inspection, it hit Travis—why not make the contest like NASCAR? Dr. Miao loved the idea. He followed NASCAR for cultural indoctrination; it was American and very cool. Travis and Dr. Miao chose five drivers and cars: Dale

Earnhardt Jr. (number 88, sponsored by the National Guard); Jeff Gordon (number 24, sponsor: DuPont); Rusty Wallace (number 2, sponsor: Miller Lite); Jeff Burton (number 31, sponsor: Caterpillar); and John Andretti (number 34, sponsor: Red Man Chewing Tobacco).

When President Chen left for Maine, the Moonies went to work on the samples and coated a toilet seat with each and later added bacterial contaminants. They wanted to surprise him and hoped he would approve. Travis built makeshift car bodies around each toilet and decorated each with its appropriate color, number, and sponsor decals. The plant personnel, all huge NASCAR fans, were energized by the idea. The maintenance crew built a large scoreboard in the cafeteria to display bacteria counts over time. They decorated the scoreboard with pictures of each NASCAR vehicle and driver, as well as sponsorship ads.

The NASCAR approach immediately led to a betting pool managed by Gerry from Accounting. Gerry posted odds and projected payouts as bets came in. Sophie suggested having a captain for each car who dressed like the driver. Dr. Miao desperately wanted to be Jeff Gordon, his hero, but the team nixed the idea because of the need for Dr. Miao's impartiality. Sophie conducted a raffle to select drivers and ordered uniforms for them at the official NASCAR store.

The plant was abuzz when the employees donned their NASCAR racing suits, all completely covered with sponsor advertisements. Sophie photographed each in front of his or her "car" to post on the scoreboard.

Dr. Miao and Travis planned to measure bacteria growth daily and post results on the scoreboard. Sophie convinced Billy Lansing, Dalton plant manager and fellow Moonie, to have a NASCAR party on Friday afternoon to announce the results. Billy thought it would help morale and support Lund's new product strategy (he'd come a long way since the fire). On that day, Gerry would pay out the winning bets at an employee barbecue.

The Moonies' biggest concern was Commie. If she found out about the contest, she would undoubtedly stage a preemptive strike. Sophie anticipated that Commie would frown on gambling and consider the event an unfair preference to Dalton. She wasn't sure if NASCAR uniforms would somehow offend. After careful consideration, the Moonies decided it was all worth the risk.

Chen was due to return from Maine the following Monday, so Sophie and The Moonies prepared a surprise. At 8:00 a.m., all five drivers were dressed in uniform and stood at attention beside their "cars" in the testing area, holding their helmets under their arms NASCAR-style. When Chen arrived, Sophie escorted him to the testing chamber. After Chen entered, no one said a word; the drivers remained at attention, looking forward. Chen walked the line, like a general inspecting his troops, and examined each car and driver. Sophie, Dr. Miao, and Travis stood to the side, trying to assess Chen's reaction.

Chen remained serious throughout the inspection. At the end of the line, he turned, flashed a big smile, and said, "What about Bobby Labonte and his 47s car?"

Travis guffawed and everyone huddled around Chen, who complimented them on the creative NASCAR idea. He was eager to see the scoreboard and "place some bet."

Day after day, Jeff Gordon and the 24 car built a lead. Most of the samples had little bacteria, but the 24 car had virtually none. On the last day, Dr. Miao and Travis made the final bacterial measurements. The excitement was palpable. Dale Earnhardt Jr. and his 88 car fought valiantly, but Jeff Gordon took the checkered flag.

The victory party was a big hit, complete with burgers, dogs, coleslaw, baked beans, and sweet tea. There was even country music. Jeff Gordon, played by a mechanic, made a heartfelt winner's speech while standing on a cafeteria table with sweet tea in one hand and his helmet in the other.

"I would like to thank Dr. Miao, Travis, and the R & D team for their excellent work, and thank all y'all for your support. I love y'all!" He then chugged his tea, spilling it all over his uniform.

At the Moonie meeting days later, Dr. Miao reported on the successful prototype development, with pictures of the NASCAR contest and Jeff Gordon. Gerry and Monique presented the estimated cost of the product. Monique demonstrated that Moonies would cost 30 percent more than the cost of Lund's current industrial-grade plastic coatings, due to the more complex structure and added silver ions. This fact worried the Moonies.

"We have to find some ways to charge the higher prices," Chen commented, and then he asked Larry La Croix and Bob Davis to present their market research.

They started by showing charts of survey data about toilet seats. The vast majority of respondents believed toilet seats were contaminated and that the only way around this issue was to use the plastic or paper covers provided. The respondents indicated, however, that these measures took time, were not comfortable, were not "green," and sometimes got messed up. They showed pictures of how the plastic and paper coverings got tangled or bunched up. The sanitation process was a major contributor to long lines at public women's bathrooms, especially at sports events and concerts.

According to research, schools, sports stadiums, and rest stops were the areas of biggest concern, but many were also concerned about sanitation in the home. The research also indicated a latent demand for glowing toilet seats at home. Many women respondents reported a problem with occasionally falling into the toilet at night after their husbands or boyfriends failed to lower the seat after use.

"This research shows the problem," Larry explained. "It costs money for alternative sanitation methods, wastes time and materials, and causes delays."

Monique chimed in, "This looks like an opportunity. You can't believe how annoying the long lines are for the women's room at sporting events. I had to wait fifteen minutes in line at a Tennessee Titans football game last year."

"No kidding," Sophie added. "Plus, those plastic and paper covers are not environmentally friendly."

"Stadiums might be able to sell more beer if lines were shorter," Bob interjected.

"Bob, you have a one-track mind," Larry chuckled.

"Actually, two tracks," Monique noted.

Chen said, "This research is some good sign. We can offer some good value to the toilet market, which should allow much higher prices."

Heads nodded all around. The next step was a field trial. Bob said he had contacted a large toilet company, National Porcelain, about running a test in a sports stadium. He and National Porcelain had arranged for the Moonies to apply the new antimicrobial coating to existing toilets at River Dogs Stadium in Charleston, South Carolina. River Dogs Stadium was a good place because it was a minor-league venue and had high temperatures and humidity, perfect for bacterial growth. Bob was also familiar with many bars and strip clubs in the area. Chen, Dr. Miao, and Sophie eagerly volunteered to help Bob, but Monique quietly warned Sophie about Bob's nocturnal tendencies.

"Be really careful, Honey, I've seen his expense reports."

To add credibility to the team, Chen went to the Dalton Home Depot to buy plumbing supplies and tool belts. He stocked them with wrenches, hammers, pliers, metal shears, and tape measures. Home Depot impressed Chen almost as much as "L. Beans;" he picked up some extras for home: a large table saw, a gas grill, and a new umbrella for his deck.

Bob had containers of the new coating delivered to River Dogs Stadium. He also arranged to meet with National Porcelain's contractor in Charleston and arrived before the Dalton group. There he met the lead contractor, Johnny Husk, who looked about sixty with weathered features; he wore jeans, a worn baseball hat from a local hardware supplier, and had a pack of Marlboros in his shirt pocket. Johnny had a melodious Low Country accent. He referred to his crew as "his boys." His truck had a Confederate flag decal on the rear window and a gun rack in the back.

Bob and Johnny hit it off immediately as they discussed deer hunting, golf, Krispy Kreme doughnuts, beer, and gentlemen's clubs in Charleston. Conversation eventually turned to toilets, and Bob enthusiastically explained the new product's microbial-resistant benefits and how it had a distinct color that would distinguish it from traditional seats. While they were discussing the product, Chen's white Cadillac pulled up. Bob realized, too late, that he had not prepped Johnny for having two Chinese scientists and a pretty woman on his job site. As Johnny turned, three doors of the Caddy opened simultaneously and out popped Chen, Dr. Miao, and Sophie in nearly identical outfits of blue Lund Plastics polo shirts and new plumber tool belts. Chen and Dr. Miao wore khaki pants, and Sophie had a short, tight khaki skirt. All had sunglasses; Chen wore new aviator shades.

Johnny stared as the three approached and waited for an explanation. Bob noticed and said, "Johnny, I'd like to introduce you to my Lund colleagues who are working on this new product."

The three Moonies faced Johnny Husk with Chen on the left, Sophie on the right, and Dr. Miao in the middle. Turning to Chen, Bob continued. "This is Dr. Chen, our director of R & D. Chen, this is Johnny Husk."

Johnny stuck out his hand. "Pleased to meet you, Dr. Chen."

As they shook hands, Bob said, "You can call him Chen; you'll end up calling him that anyway."

"Well, Chen, you can call me Husk."

"Okay, Husker," Chen said.

Bob continued with introductions. "This is one of Chen's scientists, Dr. Miao."

"Dr. Miao?" Husker asked in surprise. "Are you a veterinarian?"

"No, Mr. Husker. I am a plastics doctor."

Husker asked Chen and Dr. Miao, "Are y'all from China?"

"Yes, Husker. We're boths from Beijing, the capitols."

"Are you Commies?" Husker asked.

"No, we are not in HRs," Chen explained.

"Huh?" Husker asked.

Bob explained how both Chen and Dr. Miao were die-hard capitalists and that Chen was a member of Dalton Hills Country Club, a golfer and bow hunter, and Dr. Miao was a die-hard NASCAR and Jeff Gordon fan. He even drank Mountain Dew and chewed Red Man.

Johnny smiled and said, "I like your style, Dr. Miao."

Bob finally turned to Sophie, who wore makeup and looked stunning.

Before Bob could speak, Husker said, "Well, lookee here."

Bob said, "This is Sophie Garibaldi. She's from HR, but we don't hold that against her."

Husker was instantly smitten. "I don't blame you boys. Welcome to River Dogs Stadium, young lady. It's a true honor for us to have you. Would you like a personal tour?"

Sophie smiled, nodded, and followed Husker around the stadium. Husker thoroughly enjoyed the tour and gave Sophie a detailed explanation of everything, including how the beautiful, green field was maintained.

In the meantime, Bob, Chen, and Dr. Miao started coating toilet seats, beginning with the women's bathroom on the ground level. Working with Husker's boys, they put the coating container on wheels and rolled it into the room. Using special paintbrushes, they began carefully coating toilet seats. The work was time-consuming due to the stickiness of the coating. It took an hour to complete the women's room, and they moved to the men's room on the same level.

While the crew was finishing the men's stalls, nature urgently called for Dr. Miao. He quietly reported the predicament to Chen, who replied, "Miao, the coatings are too wet in the men's rooms now. Just go to the lady room—it's dry there, and nobodies is in the stadiums."

Dr. Miao walked to the women's room, knocked on the door, and entered. No one was inside. He sat down for business and took the opportunity to check his phone for messages. (Chen discouraged looking at phones in the presence of customers, a request the team took seriously). Not surprisingly, there was a text message from Travis. Travis was younger and strongly preferred texts over e-mails.

"Dr. Miao, have you heard the NASCAR news today?"

Dr. Miao quickly responded. *"No, what is the new?"*

"Jeff Gordon got caught with illegal tires and got suspended for three races."

Dr. Miao was crushed and sat with his head low.

A minute later, his phone pinged. A new text from Travis arrived. *"Just kidding, buddy."*

"What relief. I almost had some hearts attack."

"Sorry, but I wanted you to know I heard from our patent lawyer, and it looks good for our patent on our antimicrobial coating."

"Great news, Travis."

"Yes, it's awesome. How's the toilet-seat coating going?"

"Pretty goods, Trav. We finished the first lady room about 1 hour ago, and it looks great. In facts, I'm in a stall right now."

"In the women's room?"

"Yes, we were working in the man's room, and Mother Nature sent me some message."

"You mean nature called?" Travis texted in response.

"Yes, she gave me some call."

"Are you sitting on the seat now?" Travis asked.

"Yes. It's the only way I can do the textings. Chen does not like the phones when we are doing the jobs."

"Uh oh. Dr. Miao, the coating is very sticky and takes more than an hour to cure at room temperature."

In a panic, Dr. Miao realized he had been sitting for several minutes. He tried to stand up and found himself firmly stuck to the seat. He tried again and again, without success. After weighing his options, he decided not to shout for help, and he couldn't reach Chen and Bob because their phones were off. He would have to find a solution on his own.

Because Dr. Miao was thin and flexible, he could turn and reach the back of the toilet seat. So he unbuckled his tool belt around his ankles, grabbed a wrench and screwdriver, and went to work. In five minutes, he had unfastened the seat from the toilet and tried to stand up, a difficult task with the seat glued to the bottom of his thighs and the top of his buttocks. Dr. Miao could only move by bending over, but when he moved forward, he tripped on his pants. So he took off his pants and shuffled out of the stall. After washing his hands, he waddled out the door into the massive hallway, heading towards the men's room and likely help from Chen.

As Dr. Miao moved slowly to the men's room, bent over and naked below the waist, Johnny Husk was finishing the stadium tour with Sophie. They were also heading for the men's room to check on the team's progress. When they rounded the turn before the men's room, they spied a very skinny man's pale, hairless bottom framed perfectly by a toilet seat.

"Oh, my God!" Sophie screamed.

Johnny jumped to block her view. "Sophie, don't look!"

Just then, Chen and Bob emerged from the men's room and turned toward the commotion. They saw the top of Dr. Miao's bent-over head, his tool belt in his right hand and pants in the left.

Directly behind him, Sophie had transitioned from screaming to laughing hysterically.

Bob turned to Chen and said, "Maybe the coating doesn't repel bugs after all."

Dr. Miao was a very good sport about the whole incident. Fortunately, Husker's paint removal dissolved the coating, and Dr. Miao was liberated from his seat in no time.

The group worked together the rest of the day. By the end of the afternoon, they had coated every toilet seat in the stadium. During cleanup, Bob invited Husker and his boys for a celebration dinner in downtown Charleston. Husker enthusiastically agreed and suggested a restaurant called Secession, known for great boiled shrimp and murals depicting Confederate cannons firing on Fort Sumter in 1861.

The Moonies checked into a Holiday Inn, showered, changed, and piled into Chen's Cadillac for the trip downtown. When they arrived at Secession, Husker and his boys were at the bar, framed by painted cannons behind them. They cheered at the Moonies' arrival. Dr. Miao received high-fives while the boys gawked at Sophie in her black blouse, tight jeans, and heels.

Bob ordered beers for Dr. Miao, Chen, and himself, and chardonnay for Sophie. They clinked glasses with Husker and boys and said, "Cheers." Dr. Miao said, "*Ganbei*" and chugged his beer, which delighted Husker and his team. Chen turned to Husker to explain.

"In China, they clinks the glasses and drink bottom-ups."

"Even the Commies?" Husker asked.

"Yes. Chairman Mao was some very strong drinker."

They ordered more drinks and regaled bystanders with the tale of Dr. Miao "getting framed." After more than an hour, they sat down for dinner of boiled shrimp, fried fish, and fries. The drinks continued to flow at an impressive pace, especially for Bob.

After dinner, Bob hired two horse-drawn carriages for a Charleston tour. He bought a twelve-pack of Bud Light at a nearby 7-Eleven. The group rode the streets of Charleston, singing and laughing. The twelve-pack didn't last long, which prompted Bob to instruct the driver to visit the 7-Eleven for another round.

"This was the way our great-, great-granddaddies did beer runs," Bob said.

"Wow, I never knew that," said the driver.

"I took a lot of history in college," Bob added.

Around midnight, the Moonies said good night and took a cab back to the Holiday Inn. Bob, Husker, and his boys decided to keep going. They went to a bar called Southern Belles, a well-known hot spot with live bands and beautiful women.

At Southern Belles, Bob continued imbibing at an impressive pace and talked to several young women. One blonde from Ohio was fascinated by Southern men in general—and Bob and Husker in particular. Their stories of Fort Sumter and the start of the War Between the States captured her interest. At one point, she turned to Bob and asked, "Bob, were you scared fighting against the Yankees at Fort Sumter?"

Bob's face lost all color.

"Don't worry, Bob, ol' boy," Husker said as he patted Bob on the back, "this dim light in Southern Belles makes everyone look older."

Bob continued his merriment until last call at 2:00 a.m. By then, his eyes were red, his skin was pinker than normal, his speech was slurry, and his clothes were disheveled. Bob picked up the bar tab for Husker and his boys, plus that of several women. He hugged everyone and professed love to the women and lifelong friendship to the guys.

He stumbled out of Southern Belles and hailed a taxi. During the twenty-minute drive to the hotel, Bob befriended his Ethiopian driver and asked if he knew Ash in Nashville. They agreed to keep in touch and exchanged e-mail addresses.

Bob wobbled through the hotel lobby to the elevator. Like most modern hotels, the Holiday Inn had the same floor plan for every level. He had room 324 but mistakenly got out on the second floor.

Unaware of his mistake, Bob drunkenly zigzagged down the hall of the second floor looking for room 324. When he reached 224, Bob inserted the magnetic key into the slot by the door. The light above the slot turned red, and the door didn't unlock.

"Shit!" Bob mumbled.

He repeated the process with similar results.

"Motherfricker," Bob said again, a bit louder.

He reversed the key and pushed harder, then slower. It still didn't work.

"Sonuvabitch!" he shouted.

Then he fiercely shook the door, and it flew open violently. Standing in the doorway was a large man in a white wife-beater T-shirt, Tony Soprano-style, and boxer shorts. He had big, hairy arms full of tattoos. His chest hair poured out of his shirt. It was nearly 3:00 a.m., and he was not happy, nor was his woman companion.

"What the hell are you doing?" The wife-beater roared.

"Just tr—, trying to get into m ... my room, man. Why are you here?"

"Your room? This is *my* room, asshole; now get the hell out of here!"

"No, it's m ... m ... my room," Bob urged, with noticeable slurring. "Get lost, will ya?"

"Look, you drunken asshole, it's three a.m. You just woke my girlfriend and me up."

"Sorry, man, but she's sleeping in the wrong bed."

"Get outta here or I'll beat the shit out of you."

Bob finally relented. "Okay, okay, buddy, t ... t ... take it easy. Tell you what: just give me my clothes, and you can keep the room."

24

PEARL HARBOR

The success of the Moonies and Bug Off offered a strong ray of hope, but the business was far from healthy. The recession remained dismal. The Lund troops worried about the business and their futures. There were rumors of layoffs.

As Derek sat in his office thinking, the phone rang.

"Derek, this is Chen."

"*El presidente!*"

"Huh?"

"Mr. President, in Spanish."

"So sorry; I only know the Mandarin and Englishes."

Derek laughed. "How are things?"

"Pretty goods, thanks."

"So, Chen, how is the field trial in South Carolina going?"

"Mostly goods."

"Why only mostly?"

"We had some field trial in Charleston, South Carolinas last week. With Johnny Husker's company."

"How was it?"

"The new coatings looks great, and the stadium owners like it. We had some problem with Dr. Miao."

"Nothing serious, I hope."

"Not really. He glued himselves to some toilet seat."

"Glued?"

"Yes. The coatings was not dry while he was doing some textings with Travis."

"Huh?"

"He had to unfasten the seat and walk to the men room without his pant."

"You mean his pants?"

"Yes, his pant."

"Oh, boy. Who was there?"

"Sophie, Bob, and Husker."

"Sophie saw him?" Derek asked with concern.

"Yes. Don't worry, she laughed and did not have the times to take picture for the conference room walls."

"Chen—"

"Don't worries too much, Derek, Commie won't find out. We don't need more HuRT."

"Chen, what happens next in the field trials?"

"We wait for some couple baseball game and then test the seat for bugs."

"Then we'll know if it worked?"

"Yes," Chen explained.

"Let's cross our fingers."

"Yes, I will put my fingers crossed."

Two weeks later, Chen and several Moonies returned to River Dogs stadium and swabbed the toilet seats to test for bacteria. The results were far better than expected—the seats had virtually no bacteria, even less than toilets with the disposable plastic covers.

The Moonies tested the coating with other National Porcelain customers, from bus stations to airports to bars, and results were uniformly impressive. They decided that facilities would no longer need the disposable seat covers, provided they could visually distinguish antimicrobial seats from the normal variety. Travis and Miao invented a distinct color pattern that would appear in the curing process and would clearly show the product. The pattern would also help accentuate the brand. They also created a coating that glowed in the dark for the residential market, which they thought would be a big plus for women whose husbands failed to lower the seat at night.

Chen prepared a field trial report with data, photos, and several quotes from customers. He sent the report to the Moonies and Derek. The new coating clearly had the potential to be a winner. The next step was to develop a product name and logo.

Larry La Croix and Bob Davis, the Moonies' marketers, recommended an outside marketing firm to help with product naming. Chen agreed, and they hired Smoky Mountain Advertising of Knoxville, Tennessee.

They decided to focus on the glow-in-the-dark residential product first, and Larry gave Smoky Mountain background on the new product and arranged a joint meeting in Nashville. He invited all the Moonies and Derek. Smoky Mountain sent their account manager, Rick Mueller, and two advertising professionals, Jane Branson and Jimmy Baker. Rick Mueller was about forty-five years old, trim, and wore a blue pinstriped suit and white shirt with large cuff links. His hair was perfectly oiled. He had the air of a successful, confident business professional. Ms. Branson was a very attractive blonde in her mid-thirties who was also quite trim, and she wore a gray suit and white blouse. Bob's radar locked onto her immediately. Mr. Baker was a dapper professional in his mid-thirties and wore a double-breasted sport coat, dark slacks, white shirt, and a yellow power tie. After giving a second and third look at Monique and her 'FroHawk, they all smiled confidently with unusually white, perfect teeth.

During introductions, Team Smoky Mountain talked about themselves with lofty titles and bloviated about their experience in advertising in Manhattan before moving to Knoxville for "lifestyle reasons." In contrast, the Lund introductions were short and self-deprecating. Dr. Miao joked about not being a veterinarian.

Bobby described his background like he had been born on the dirt floor of a sharecropper's cabin. Team Smoky Mountain instantly considered him intellectually challenged, possibly moronic. The introductions got awkward when Larry introduced both Chen and Derek as president. It took a few minutes to explain the product-development team concept, the birth of the Moonies, and Chen's presidency. After the explanation, Jane looked at Chen and said the whole thing was "cute." Chen didn't consider the remark complimentary. Bob became increasingly drawn to Jane, like a lion to a wounded zebra.

The Smoky Mountain team had brought their portfolio and discussed their past work extensively, highlighted by several projects for large plastics companies. Their plastics clients were all much bigger and better known than Lund Plastics, a point made repeatedly with emphasis. The Moonies' intimidation about being a smaller outfit grew.

The Moonies finally wearied of Team Smoky Mountain's bragging and began fidgeting. Sophie spoke first.

"Mr. Mueller, Smoky Mountain has an impressive client base and has done major projects and all, but wouldn't you like to hear about our needs?"

"Well, Miss," commented Mueller, clearly forgetting Sophie's name, a mistake made only by the most self-absorbed men, "Dave made it clear on the phone that you wanted a name for your new antibiotic glowing toilet seat."

Chen interrupted. "Excuse me, Mr. Muellers, but it's antimicrobial, not antibiotic."

"Same difference, Dr. Chang—bugs are bugs," Mueller explained with a condescending smile.

Chen was not pleased at all, but he kept on mission, explaining the new product and its features. He emphasized its value as the only coating that effectively killed all bacteria on toilet seats and also glowed in the dark so women know when their husbands don't put the seat down. Chen's great pride in his R & D team was evident as he explained the technical breakthrough that killed bacteria on contact. Bob Davis emphasized the product's advanced technology and how it was unlike anything on the market. It was real and serious, Bob said, not some gimmick. The Moonies felt strongly about their new product, an observation obvious to everyone but Team Smoky Mountain.

After ten minutes of discussion, Mueller said dismissively, "I think we've got it, folks, thanks. Our next step will be to develop possible names, logos, and themes back in our office and present our top choices to you."

"How long will it take?" Larry asked.

"For this? About two to three weeks, tops. This is much easier than projects for our bigger clients."

"What will it cost?" Monique interjected.

Giving Monique a strange look, Mueller continued. "Much less than our typical projects—we know you're a small, family company, kind of new to this. Maybe $10,000."

After Team Smoky Mountain left, the Moonies commented on their cockiness and lack of client orientation. Chen was pissed off about Mueller calling his product "antibiotic." Sophie referred to Mueller as "The Slick Prick." The lone supporter was Bob, who said Jane Branson was very attractive. Monique and Sophie rolled their eyes. After further discussion, they decided to proceed due to price and rave referrals from their other clients.

For the rest of the meeting, the Moonies discussed other marketing issues, including their initial target market, pricing, product guarantees, and product appearance. Pricing was critical, and Gerry was skeptical about charging a significantly higher price than that of other coatings.

Chen replied good-naturedly, "Gerry, this is why you are not in Marketings. You are just some beans counter."

Everyone roared, even Gerry.

Three weeks later, Team Smoky Mountain returned with their recommendations. Bob was excited to see Jane again. When the Moonies and Derek arrived at the main conference room, Mueller and his team were already there, decked-out in suits and casually drinking espresso like they belonged there. They had a computer projector set up, and all three were smiling with their perfect teeth, sitting back in their chairs with their hands folded.

Mueller stood as they entered and extended his hand to Chen.

"Dr. Chang, great to see you again."

"My name is Chen."

"My mistake, Doc! So Derek, hello, how's business?"

"Not too bad, thanks," Derek said. "We're really looking forward to launching this new product. We think it's a winner."

"So do Jane, Jimmy, and me. We're quite excited to show you our work—we think you'll love it!" Jane and Jimmy nodded enthusiastically.

Everyone settled around the table and made small talk as Mueller got the projector ready. Bob asked Jane how long she was staying in Nashville.

Not now, Bob, Derek thought.

"Rick and Jimmy are going back today, but I've got a meeting at The Bank of Nashville this afternoon," Jane replied, "so I'm not going back until tomorrow morning."

Bob leaned forward. "That's great. Have you ever been to Morton's? It's a world-famous steak house, and it's near the bank."

Monique and Sophie gave each other knowing looks.

"Sorry, but I'm a vegan," Jane explained.

"What's a vegan?" Bob asked.

"We don't eat meat, chicken, fish, eggs, dairy, or food dye made from beetles."

Bob looked perplexed. "There's food dye made from beetles?"

"Afraid so. Poor little things."

"Well, none of those things are in margaritas, right, Jane?"

Jane lightened up instantly. "Margaritas are definitely on my diet, especially frozen ones."

Bob looked like a gold prospector with a nugget. "I know this great Mexican place called Tequila Mockingbird downtown. They have great margari—"

Larry cut him off abruptly. "Bob, let's get started, okay?"

Mueller stood up and turned on the projector. His cover slide had the Lund logo with the title: "Naming Ideas for Lund Glowing Antibiotic Toilet Seat Coating." He had also brought two posters on stands, which stood on both sides of the projector screen and were covered by black cloth. Jane stood by one and Jimmy the other for the grand unveiling.

Mueller started. "When Smoky Mountain Advertising does naming work, we usually develop several possibilities to present to the client, and they select their favorite."

Larry chimed in. "This is what we expected, Rick."

Mueller continued. "Well, we went about it a little differently this time, but before we go further, we'd like to play back what we heard from you. Jane?"

Jane stepped to the center and took over. Bob admired her very shapely legs as she started her explanation.

"Lund has developed what it calls glowing, bug-free toilet-seat coating It is unlike anything else on the market in that it is glows in the dark and is highly antibiotic. The glowing alerts women to typical male toilet transgressions. This is the central benefit of the product."

"Not really," Sophie interrupted, "the product's antimicrobial nature is the gist of its value."

Mueller interrupted, waving his hand dismissively. "Yes, we are aware of this fact, Miss—"

"My name is Sophie Garibaldi, Mr. Mueller."

"Yes, Miss Sophie. Marketing and value propositions happen to be my specialty; it's really not an area for HR people," said Slick, who remembered Sophie was from HR, but his condescending remark was a colossal mistake.

Slick, you just bombed Pearl Harbor, Derek thought.

Sophie turned red and was readying for a swift counter-attack when Larry stepped in and diffused the tension.

"Why don't we see what you have, Rick?"

"Thanks, Larry. Like Jane was saying, the key to this product is home safety, both from women falling into the toilet at night and bugs. Finally, a product to keep us men out of hot water at home!" Mueller and his team chuckled at this, but the Moonies remained stone-faced.

Mueller paused to work the crowd, unaware he had lost them forever, and tried to build the drama again. When he had the room's full attention, he continued.

"As I said, we normally present several choices to a client. But in this case, we found one name that stood apart from the rest—a name so strong, so fitting, so appropriate, so simple, so brilliant, so compelling—that we present it to you alone. And the name is …"

With great flair, Slick pushed the button on the projector remote and gestured to the screen as the slide changed. At the same time, Jane and Jimmy pulled the cloths off the poster stands. On the screen and both poster boards were identical pictures: a white toilet seat looking like a Life Saver superimposed on the universal symbol for women.

"Wife Saver!"

Slick and his team beamed, waiting for exultation from the Moonies.

There was stunned silence. Everyone stared in shock.

None of the Moonies dared make eye contact with each other. Slick and team kept smiling and pointing at the picture, waiting for reaction from the team. Time seemed to stop; no one made a sound. Bobby looked nervously at Derek. The quiet was interrupted by Sophie's giggling, which was under control at first, but it evolved into hysterical laughing. She laughed so hard, tears ran down her cheeks.

Derek finally said, "Sophie, what's so funny?"

"It looks a lot better with Dr. Miao's butt in it."

25

DOLLYWOOD

The Moonies fired Smoky Mountain Advertising. "Wife Saver" just wouldn't cut it for a serious brand. It was too much a gimmick and completely missed the antimicrobial gist of the product. The decision was made before Team Smoky Mountain reached the elevator. The only disagreement was over timing: everyone wanted an immediate firing but Bob. Since Bob had a margarita date that night with Jane, his ulterior motives were obvious.

After Bob left the conference room, Bobby predicted that Jane would out-duel Bob at Tequila Mockingbird. Bobby's prediction precipitated a heated debate among the Moonies. Everyone disputed his projection vehemently. Bob was social legend and could handle an uptight professional like Jane. Bobby said he would bet anyone ten dollars that he was right.

"Bobby, you know I can't condone betting in the office," Derek explained, "but I'd like some of that action."

"Let's make it twenty dollars, Derek."

"Deal."

The next morning, Bob's defeat was clear:

1. He didn't show up at the office until 9:45 a.m.

2. His skin was much puffier and pinker than normal, and his eyes were swollen and red.
3. His forehead was sweating profusely.
4. There was a faint whiff of tequila on his breath.
5. He was drinking a Coke when he entered the office.
6. He had salsa all over his shoes.
7. Bob asked Chen not to fire Smoky Mountain.
8. At around 11:00 a.m., Bob took a nap in one of the men's room stalls.

Flush from his betting victory, Bobby visited Derek's office. Derek was talking to Darrell about Jackson Hill when Bobby arrived.

"Bobby, come on in," Derek gestured, "we have an issue at Jackson Hill that could use your expertise."

"Does it concern predicting wild women?" Bobby asked with a grin.

"Try to be a gracious winner," Derek said as he handed Bobby twenty dollars. "It's about safety, your supposed area of expertise. Darrell, can you explain the situation?"

"Bobby, as you know, Jackson Hill has had several accidents over the past six months that have resulted in injury to employees," Darrell explained.

"Yes, I know. I have been working with the plant team on a new safety program."

"Well, we have new information about the accidents that is alarming."

"What's that?" Bobby asked.

"As you know, company policy requires a drug test for any employees involved in an accident."

"Yes, of course."

"We got the results back from the last three several weeks ago, and all were positive for marijuana," Darrell explained.

"Seriously? All three?"

"Yes, and the results were clear."

"Have we talked to the employees?" Bobby asked.

"Yes. One denied ever using pot. Another said he smoked a few days before the accident, and the third said it was due to her breakfast cereal."

Derek chimed in. "Breakfast cereal?"

"You got it. It was Jesse Rae Martin, and she claims to eat hemp cereal every morning, which caused her to test positive," Darrell said.

"You've got to be kidding," Derek said.

"No. I asked her to name the brand of cereal, and she couldn't."

"Interesting. So, what are we doing about it?"

"A couple things. First, we notified the sheriff of Jefferson County to alert them to a possible drug ring in the area."

"What did they say?"

"They know that drugs are being brought into the county, but they don't know how. The sheriff visited the plant to investigate and interviewed several supervisors and employees. He didn't find anything, which he said is not too surprising."

"What is the other thing you are doing?" Derek asked.

"Under our policy, every employee who tests positive is required to attend a drug rehabilitation course for thirty days, after which they can return to work. Once back, they are subject to random drug tests, and if they ever test positive again, they are immediately terminated."

"Okay, good. I sure hope we don't have a drug problem at Jackson Hill. They are having enough problems as it is; everyone is just now forgetting the pig roast incident," Derek said, looking Bobby's way.

Two months later, things had settled down. Smoky Mountain was a distant memory, except the toilet-seat picture had become a permanent addition to the sales conference room. Larry hired a local marketing firm that developed a new product name: SaniSeat, which the Moonies decided would work for both residential and commercial markets. They also designed a cool logo. Using the new name and logo, they created high-quality brochures and product packaging.

Before the launch, Derek decided to visit Jackson Hill with Bobby, Chen, and Darrell to ensure the plant was ready to produce SaniSeat, as well as to follow up on the earlier safety incidents. They took one of the large company vans.

Early one morning, they started the long drive to Jackson Hill. Chen brought biscuits, Mountain Dew, and several packages of beef jerky. As they passed Knoxville, they started seeing billboards for Dollywood, the large theme park in eastern Tennessee named after Dolly Parton.

After the second sign, Chen asked, "What is Dollywoods?"

Bobby answered. "It's a huge theme park named after Dolly Parton."

"*The* Dolly Partons?"

"Yes, the famous singer."

"The same Dolly Partons you were in Miami Beaches for the Celebrity Roller Blades Scavenger Hunts?" Chen asked.

"Big hair, dress, and all," Bobby explained.

"You were very sexy, Bobby."

"Why that's very flattering, Chen."

Unbeknownst to Chen, the other three had agreed to stop at Dollywood as a treat for Chen. When they pulled into the park, Chen said, "Are we going to Dollywood?"

Derek said, "Welcome to Dollywood, Chen. Enjoy your visit."

"Thank so much, Derek."

"Just don't tell Commie," Derek advised.

"Is Dollywood against some rules?" Chen asked.

"Probably. Let's make it our secret, okay?"

"Deals, I want to buy some camera for picture on the conferences room walls."

The concept of *secret* apparently had a different meaning in Chinese culture.

Chen stopped at a souvenir shop to buy Confederate cavalry hats from the 1860s as team uniforms. Once they donned the hats, Chen got someone to take their picture in front of a Dollywood sign. For Derek, the thought of a published picture was his worst executive nightmare, and he vowed to steal Chen's camera and toss it off the roller coaster.

And so the afternoon continued, the team going from one ride to another. They rode the Ferris wheel, and Chen photographed the park from the top. They tried the roller coaster; Chen took pictures. They rode the 1880s-style train; Chen took pictures.

As Chen continued taking pictures, Derek said, "Chen, are you sure you're not a Japanese tourist?"

"No, Derek, Japanese have the different eyes and drive the small car."

"Just checking."

After a short supper of ham and beans, Chen saw a sign for "Dolly's Family Reunion," a band of Dolly's family who played songs and recounted growing up with Dolly. Within minutes, they were inside the pavilion. Sure enough, a band was on stage led by a full-figured woman singer with long, thick, curly blonde hair, clearly Dolly's sister.

A male guitar player was with Dolly's sister. He had long, stringy hair that hung below a dingy, black cowboy hat. They told stories of Dolly's childhood with humorous anecdotes and heart-touching tales. Chen was enthralled. Darrell was too, but he had enough sense to pretend otherwise.

The show ended around 8:00 p.m., and Chen convinced the group to go backstage for autographs. Fearing discovery or pictures, Bobby and Derek kept their cavalry hats low over their eyes. Meanwhile, Chen had purchased an authentic Dollywood autograph book and was busy collecting autographs and photos from the family and band.

Around 9:00 p.m., they left and drove ninety minutes to a Holiday Inn near Jackson Hill. They checked in, drove the van to the back of the hotel, and went to bed, agreeing to meet for breakfast the next morning. The Holiday Inn had a free breakfast buffet with doughnuts, eggs, bacon, muffins, and grits. The grits were a big draw.

The next morning, Derek got up at six thirty, took a shower, dressed, checked his voice mail, and drove the van to the hotel reception. On the short drive to the reception area, he noticed police cars from different towns parked all around. Several of the police cars were from K-9 units and had dogs inside.

While getting coffee in the lobby, he greeted several police officers standing around eating doughnuts.

"Excuse me, Officer, but why are there so many K-9 cars at the hotel?" he asked cheerfully.

"We're having a convention for K-9 patrols and drug-sniffing dogs for Tennessee," the officer replied, a fit man named O'Donnell in his mid-thirties with a crew cut.

"That's cool," Derek said. "I didn't know there were so many in this area."

"We have a lot more these days," Officer O'Donnell continued, "especially in eastern Tennessee, where the drug problem has really grown."

"Interesting. I would have never known. Thank you for your service, officer."

During checkout, Derek noticed two German shepherds on leashes showing unusual interest in the van.

Must be Darrell's shoes. If a dog's sense of smell is really ten thousand times a human's, I sure feel sorry for those hounds, Derek thought.

After a few minutes, Derek grabbed his coffee and walked outside. The dogs were sniffing all around the van. As he walked to the driver's side door, he gave the dogs' handlers a hearty "Good morning!"

"Is this your vehicle?" one of the handlers asked.

"Yes, I mean, um … no, it's our company van."

"Our dogs picked up a strong scent here."

"It's probably my director of HR's dirty tennis shoes," Derek joked. "They're nasty. Those poor dogs might have to apply for workers' comp."

Neither handler cracked a smile.

"Sir, the dogs are onto something. We need to look inside your van. Would you please open the doors?"

"No problem, officer," Derek said, his mood darkening.

Derek opened the sliding doors and back tailgate. The dogs jumped in and sniffed wildly all over. A couple other cops showed up with their dogs, and there were four German shepherds in the van. A couple dogs sniffed the floor where Darrell's feet had been, but they backed off immediately.

Poor hounds, Derek thought.

After a few minutes of frantic sniffing, all four dogs settled on a spot in the back of the van. The officers and dogs practically fell over themselves searching this area. Chen, Bobby, and Darrell arrived. When Derek looked up, he saw Darrell gravely peering over an officer's shoulder. Bobby was behind him trying not to laugh. Chen was confused and looked worried.

"There's definitely been dope here," one of the officers announced. "This is a very strong scent."

"Officer, there must be some mistake. None of us are carrying drugs," Derek said.

"That's what they all say," he replied sternly.

"Officer," Derek stammered, "I don't know how it could happen. This is a company van used only by our employees to visit our plants."

"Where are you boys headed?" the officer asked.

"We're on our way to the Lund plant at Jackson Hill," Derek explained.

"In Jefferson County?"

"Yes, the big, new plant."

"The one with the drug issues?"

26

THE PERP WALK

The ride to the police station was short. Derek's defense of being important executives held little sway, especially after the cops found four Dollywood cavalry hats and Chen's autograph book in the van.

Chen and Derek were in one patrol car; Bobby and Darrell shared another. Chen's usual fascination with American culture had vanished. He was terrified. Chen's terror was understandable. In Beijing, an arrest for transporting drugs would result in an abrupt reduction in life expectancy.

The station was abuzz with excitement when the arrestees arrived. The K-9 officers had reported the bust of four Lund executives for transporting marijuana. This was a big break in the drug investigation at the Jackson Hill plant.

The two police cars unloaded their quarry and escorted them inside. When the door opened, everyone stared as they marched to the cells in the back of the station, a classic perp walk. They divided the group into two adjoining cells, where they sat on beds, stared at exposed stainless-steel toilets, and discussed their next steps.

After a few minutes, Bobby said, "Hey, any of y'all seen *The Shawshank Redemption?*"

Bobby's humor failed to cheer Chen, who sat fearing imminent execution.

Darrell spoke up. "Derek, should we call Lund headquarters for help?"

"It would probably trigger a major new HR investigation."

"Good point. Maybe jail isn't so bad after all."

After an hour, an officer asked which member of the group was the most senior. Everyone immediately pointed at Derek, who left the cell to talk to the police lieutenant. Bobby accompanied him for support. The lieutenant's name was Billy Ray Jackson, a classic good ol' boy. Derek's Yankee status was not an asset here. Fortunately, he and Bobby traded stories about Pickin' It and the dripping deer head. Billy Ray loved the stories about Genevieve London.

Eventually, they discussed the drug bust. Bobby and Derek explained that they were senior executives at Lund Plastics traveling to Jackson Hill to investigate the positive marijuana tests of a few employees. Billy Ray laughed and said his officers were slightly overzealous. He said the police had searched the van thoroughly, confirming the absence of drugs. Billy Ray said they were free to go.

"Just one last question, out of curiosity," Billy Ray said. "Did you fellas actually visit Dollywood?"

"How did you know?" Derek asked.

"We found four cavalry hats and a partially filled autograph book from Dollywood in the van."

"It's a bit embarrassing to explain," Derek said. "One of our colleagues, Dr. Chen, is a scientist from China. He's fascinated with all things American, and he's become a big fan of Dolly Parton."

"How'd he like Dollywood?"

"Chen loved it, especially the Parton Family Reunion Show."

"The one with the buxom blonde singer and the guitar player with long, stringy hair?" Billy Ray asked.

"You know it?"

"My wife forced me to watch it last summer," Billy Ray said with a chuckle.

"What a treat, huh? Anyway, Chen was so into it that he went backstage to get autographs in his official Dollywood autograph book."

"Wow, a fanatic. So, is this Dr. Chen fella actually Chinese?" Billy Ray asked.

"Yes, sir. Frankly, he's terrified right now. In China, a trip to the police station is often a one-way journey."

"I've never met anyone from China," Billy Ray said. "I might could interrogate him anyway, just for fun."

"It might kill him," Derek cautioned. "Could you give him a VIP tour instead and maybe sign his autograph book?"

"Certainly. Let's go see the good doctor."

Billy Ray walked Bobby and Derek back to the cells, where Chen's despondency had deepened. The lieutenant introduced himself to Chen, apologized for the arrest, and offered to show him around.

"Thank you, Mr. Lieutenants," Chen said, "Are we out on some bails?"

"No, Dr. Chen, ol' boy," Billy Ray laughed. "There will be no charges. You are all free to go. Want to see our guns?"

Billy Ray showed Chen shotguns, pistols, Tasers, and other gadgets. They found a common interest in bow hunting. The lieutenant was impressed by Chen's knowledge of archery.

"Did you learn to shoot a bow in China?" Billy Ray asked.

"No, L. Beans."

After a while, Billy Ray asked Chen if he wanted a mug shot as a souvenir. Billy Ray took Chen through the booking process, from fingerprinting to mug shots. Chen was fascinated and loved getting copies of his own mug shots.

"Maybe I could use this photos for some Christmas card."

"Good ideas," Derek said.

Shit, I've caught his speech virus, Derek thought.

The drive to Jackson Hill was exhilarating. The morning's events had energized the group, especially Chen. To celebrate, they stopped for barbecue for lunch, their first meal as free men.

That afternoon, Chen and Derek met with the plant staff about producing SaniSeat. Darrell and Bobby delved into the recent safety issues at the plant. They reviewed investigation reports, interviewed employees, and tested new procedures.

By day's end, they were satisfied with Jackson Hill's progress with SaniSeat manufacturing and safety. Before leaving for dinner, Darrell received a lab report on the follow-up drug tests for the three employees who had tested positive earlier. As he read the report, his face lost all color. He looked up and said, "Derek, Bobby, we have a problem."

"What is it?" Derek asked.

"We conducted random follow-up drug tests for the three employees involved in accidents earlier this year."

"Was there an issue?"

"Jesse Rae Martin tested positive for marijuana again."

"She was the one who tried the 'hemp cereal' defense," Bobby interjected.

"That's really disappointing," Derek said. "What's the next step?"

"Normally, we terminate the employee immediately, but since we are here, why don't we interview her first? She's on shift in the morning."

"That's fine with me. We're here all day tomorrow."

The next day, Bobby, Darrell, and Derek set up in the conference room again, and Darrell sent for Jesse Rae. Jesse Rae was a large woman in her mid-thirties who drove a forklift in the warehouse. She wore a dirty University of Tennessee T-shirt with jeans and entered the conference room carrying a twenty-four-ounce bottle of Mountain Dew. After brief introductions, Darrell started the interview.

"Jesse Rae, do you know why we called you in today?"

"I have no idea, y'all."

"Do you remember getting the random drug test a few days ago?" Darrell inquired.

"When I had to pee in that little cup?" Jesse Mae asked.

"Yes, that one."

"I remember," Jesse Rae said. "Why d'ya ask?"

"It came back positive for marijuana."

"That's impossible, y'all."

"These tests are very accurate, Jesse Rae."

"Well, I don't smoke no dope."

"How do you explain the positive test?" Darrell asked.

"It must be wrong, all's I can say," Jesse Rae said defiantly.

"They re-tested the sample, and it was positive a second time," Darrell explained.

"It must a been somebody else's pee."

"No, it had your name on the label, written in your handwriting."

"Well, I can't 'splain it," Jesse Rae said, "It's your damn test."

"It's the county hospital's test, and they do hundreds of these each month."

The conversation went around and around, with Jesse Rae denying again and again that she smoked pot. Darrell was relentless, countering every possible explanation of innocence. He was as good with drugs as he was with urinals.

After nearly an hour, Jesse Rae finally cracked.

"Okay, okay, maybe I smoke a little pot, but only on weekends ... and only to help me lose weight."

27

THE GAG LINE

Later that day, they hopped in the van to go home. It was the first chance Derek had had to discuss Jesse Rae privately with Darrell.

"Darrell, just out of curiosity, did you ever smoke pot?" Derek asked.

He hesitated at first and then said, "I experimented a little in college at Aiken State."

"Did you inhale?" Derek asked, referring to the President Clinton line.

"Maybe a little."

"Doesn't pot give you the munchies?" Derek asked, grateful Darrell hadn't asked about his college experience.

Bobby chuckled revealingly. Chen had no idea what they were talking about.

"Absolutely. People eat whole packages of Oreos after smoking—so I've heard."

"So, as a diet aid, it probably would not be highly recommended."

"Not unless you were trying to gain weight. Big time," Darrell added.

"I guess Jesse Rae probably shouldn't consider law school," Derek said.

For the remainder of the trip, they discussed SaniSeat. The official launch was planned for Monday, and they speculated about how much they would sell. Chen and Bobby were bullish. Derek reminded them that SaniSeat was a new product that would take time to catch on. In the middle of their debate, Chen saw the Dollywood exit.

"Don't even think about it," Derek said preemptively.

Instead of asking to stop, Chen asked, "Derek, do you think Dolly Partons would be some spokelady for SaniSeat?"

"Chen, I tell you what. If you and The Moonies sell more than one million gallons of SaniSeat, I will ask Dolly Parton to be our spokelady. Deal?"

"It's some deals. I would also like to get her autographs in my books."

An hour outside Nashville, they stopped for gas in an outlet mall area and noticed a Japanese restaurant called Fuji. They were hungry but had trouble agreeing on a restaurant. There were two choices: Applebee's and Fuji. Darrell favored Applebee's for its all-American decor, and he feared getting worms from raw fish. Chen and Derek convinced him that Fuji would have cooked food, and in any event, he wouldn't get worms from sushi. They chose Fuji, but Darrell remained highly concerned about worms.

When they entered Fuji, there were two sushi chefs with headbands and traditional Japanese garb behind the counter. They held large knives and shouted *"Irasshaimase!"* Bobby and Darrell jumped.

"What'd they say?" Darrell asked Derek.

"Watch out for worms!"

When the waitress arrived, Darrell perked up. She was a petite, beautiful young Asian woman with long, straight, jet-black hair, a slender figure, and a perfect complexion. Her eyes were almond-shaped and fetching, and her smile was inviting. She caught the group's attention immediately. Her nametag said Misako, and she greeted the foursome in Japanese, *"Konbonwa* (good evening),*"* and asked for drink orders. She spoke poor English with a heavy accent. Her terrible English and beautiful Asian looks cast a spell on Chen.

Chen was immediately taken with her and started conversation.

"*Misako*, is that some Japanese names?"

"Yes." Misako giggled; she covered her mouth with her hand when she laughed.

"Are you from Tokyos?" Chen asked.

"No, Ho Chi Minh City, Vietnam." She giggled again with her hand in front of her mouth.

"But you have the Japanese names."

"My real name is Hong Hanh. Misako is just for the jobs."

She speaks fluent Chen, Derek thought.

Derek interrupted and asked Misako if the sushi chefs were genuinely Japanese.

"No, they are froms the Phillipinos, like Imelda Marco," Misako answered.

"Is there anyone here actually from Japan?" Derek asked.

"Sometimes, we have the Japanese customers," Misako said.

Suddenly, Darrell interrupted. "Misako, do y'all check the fish for worms?"

After considerable discussion, Derek convinced Darrell and Bobby to try sushi for the first time. Bobby was more adventurous, so they focused on Darrell, who professed not to like fish. They started with California rolls since they had cooked crab. Chen taught him to mix wasabi with soy sauce for dipping. Darrell liked the spicy wasabi and didn't object to the seaweed wrap. They ordered Kirin Ichiban beers, and Bobby stuck with Japanese tea.

Darrell's next step was a tuna avocado roll with raw tuna disguised by seaweed and avocado. The Kirin helped, but the group still proceeded cautiously. Again, Darrell liked the soy and wasabi for his roll. After he had eaten several, Derek told him about the raw tuna.

"Derek, Chen, are y'all sure this tuna doesn't have worms?" Darrell asked.

Chen explained. "No, Darrell, the tunas swims in some deep oceans. The worm stay in the shallow."

This calmed Darrell temporarily.

Chen and Derek ordered more advanced sushi: *unagi* (freshwater eel), *hamachi* (yellow tail), and *tobiko* (flying fish roe). Bobby went along with no concerns.

For Darrell, the next big step was traditional sushi, starting with *maguro* (tuna). It was the least fishy-tasting and best positioned for the worm theory. Darrell hesitated—the visual protection of seaweed wrap was gone, and the tuna slices were much larger. Chen encouraged liberal use of soy and wasabi, and he took the plunge. Darrell made a funny face but said he liked it.

"Are y'all sure this doesn't have worms?" Darrell asked again.

This time, Derek picked up the conversation. "Absolutely. This is from deep water, and as Chen said, the worms like to be near land, where they spawn. Besides, Kirin beer is known to kill worms. It's one of the reasons Kirin is so popular in Japan."

Chen nodded and said, "This is some truths."

It worked.

After more thought, Darrell asked, "Do worms swim upriver to lay eggs, like salmon?"

Darrell's sagacity with urinals did not extend to biology.

Misako/Hong Hanh made several visits to the table, checking their progress and making conversation with Chen.

"So, you're some doctors?" Hong Hanh asked.

"Yes," Chen answered.

"Do you have some nurse?"

"No, I am a plastics doctor and do not have some nurse."

"Oh." She replied, and she giggled some more.

Chen was in his mid-thirties and had never been married. Except for Dolly Parton, he had never showed interest in women, even the dancers at High Beams. Now he was smitten by a Vietnamese/Japanese waitress.

After Misako/Hong Hanh left, the group progressed to *hamachi* (yellow tail), and after a generous bath of soy and wasabi, Darrell tried it. Not only did he like the *hamachi*; he asked what was next.

Chen grew up in China during the 1970s and 1980s, when people were plentiful and food scarce. The Chinese ate anything with protein, including scorpions, insects, jellyfish, lamb lung, deer placenta, fish eyes, and duck tongues. This fact should have alerted Derek to danger, but he was too busy enjoying Kirin and watching love blossom between Chen and Hong Hanh. Chen next ordered *uni* (sea urchin).

For the uninitiated, *uni* represents several challenges. The first is appearance: greenish-brown slime corralled on rice by a ring of seaweed. The second factor is smell, resembling that of the Jersey Shore at low tide. The third factor, and not a trivial one, is consistency. It's in a no-man's-land of mouth sensation and can't be chewed or drunk. Rather, it requires tongue action to break it up. The fourth and most important factor is taste. It makes rotting catfish seem mild by comparison.

Chen watched as Derek took a bite of *uni*. His gag reflex responded immediately; he grabbed his Kirin for relief. But it wasn't enough. Derek suffered through the bite, seemingly one molecule at a time. Chen thoroughly enjoyed his suffering.

"Derek, you are no mores Mr. Sushi Big Shots," Chen pointed out.

As the meal ended, Chen left the table to chat with Hong Hanh.

For the remainder of the drive home, the group focused on Hong Hanh and SaniSeat. Chen was very interested in calling Hong Hanh and asked Derek for his advice.

"Derek, do you thinks I should call Hong Hanh?"

"Chen, if you don't call her, I will send you to HuRTS for a week."

"With Commies?"

"It wouldn't HuRT without Commie."

"Okay, I will call Hong Hanh tomorrows."

"Maybe she has a friend for Dr. Miao."

"Good thinking. He has had bad lucks with ezHarmony.com."

Energized by his resolve to call Hong Hanh, Chen talked boldly about SaniSeat, which triggered a debate.

"Derek, I bet we sell ten thousand gallons of SaniSeats in the first month."

"Chen, that would be really great, but that's thirty full containers. You really want to bet on that?"

"Yes, I want some of that actions."

"Okay, what are the stakes?"

"Sushis."

"What?"

"For every container above thirty, you eat one *unis*."

"And what will you pay if you are short of thirty containers?"

"For each container shorts, I will drink six packs of Mountain Dews and use Red Mans Chewing Tobaccos for a day."

"Deal."

Chen and Derek shook hands.

The following Monday, Chen and the Moonies gathered in Nashville for the SaniSeat launch. The stakes were high. Bob Davis had heard about the bet and created a scoreboard on a huge white board in Sales. It had an empty column like the thermometers used in fund drives. On the bottom portion of the column, he had pictures of Mountain Dew and Red Man Chewing Tobacco,

Chen's payoff if sales were below thirty containers. He drew a line to indicate thirty containers, which became known as "The Gag Line." Above the line, he had multiple pictures of *uni* sushi.

Around 11:00 a.m., the first order for SaniSeat came from a distributor in South Carolina for one unit (there were ten units per container). The Moonies cheered as Dan, a young inside salesman, took the order and put a slash on the whiteboard. Shortly after lunch, Dan received another order, this time for two units. The Moonies cheered when he put two slashes on the board. By the end of the day, there were six marks on the board, which amounted to more than half a container. Chen came into Derek's office around 5:00 p.m. to chat.

"So, Chen, you sold about half a container on the first day."

"Yes, it was some good days."

"But at that rate, you won't reach thirty containers in a month," Derek pointed out.

"Derek, don't orders the Mountain Dews and Red Mans yet. The Mooners just started."

"Chen, are you staying in Nashville tonight or going back to Dalton?"

"I want to stays here to watch the SaniSeats sale tomorrows."

"Would you like to have dinner with Carol and me tonight?"

"No, but thank you, Derek. I have some meeting tonights."

"A meeting? Really?"

"Yes, it's some very important appointments."

"Does it by any chance involve a Vietnamese waitress?"

"Well, if not, I would have to attend the HuRT with Commie, right?"

"Smart man."

The next morning, the Moonies gathered in Sales again. Sophie was ecstatic about the previous day's orders. Chen looked tired, but his mood was high. He beamed, showing unmistakable signs of a successful date. When Derek asked about it, he said,

"Derek, gentlemens don't kiss and tells." Then he smiled and gave a thumbs-up sign.

At nine a.m., Dan received an order from South Carolina for six units, more than half a container. The order came from a National Porcelain distributor who wanted to coat toilet seats that it had in inventory. The distributor was working with Johnny Husk, and they told National Porcelain that they only wanted toilets with SaniSeat from then on. The Moonies roared, as Monday's total had already been reached.

Before Chen left around five, he reported sales of fifteen units for the day, about one-and-a-half containers. Bob's thermometer was rising. The two-day sales total was more than two containers.

"Have a safe drive, Chen," Derek said.

"No problems. I will go a little out of my ways to stop for the Japanese dinners."

"Hong Hanh?"

"Yes. She want to talk and practice making the *unis*, for your bets."

The next day, SaniSeat orders intensified. Lund's field sales force was in full gear, and hardware stores and distributors were requesting SaniSeat to coat their toilets. The phone kept ringing, and by noon, another fifteen units were on order. The Moonies were excited, and Bob's thermometer rose. Every time they received an order, Dan visited Derek's office to share the news. There was obvious glee in predicting how many *uni* pieces Derek would be eating. At the close of business, they had sold twenty-five units for the day. The three-day total was forty-six units, nearly five containers. The Moonies were already within twenty-five containers of The Gag Line.

Thursday was even more intense. Home Depot and Lowe's stores all over the southeast ordered SaniSeat, and Dan constantly put hash marks on the board. Late in the morning, Dan received the first order for a full container, ten units. It was a big moment, and the Moonies hollered on a speakerphone with Chen, Sophie, and Gerry back in Dalton. By day's end, the team had sold three containers, and Bob's thermometer was climbing fast. Derek started finding sushi menus, with *uni* highlighted, wherever he went—next to the espresso machine, above the urinals in the men's room, on his chair, under his car's windshield wipers.

Friday saw further increases in orders. Dan's hash marks became denser and denser on the board. The office and the whole business were abuzz about SaniSeat. Distributors received orders on top of orders. At 5:00 p.m. on Friday, Dan and Bob updated the scoreboard and summarized the totals for week one: twelve containers (40 percent of the bet, with more than three weeks to go.)

This was a surprising amount for the first week. Early signs were very encouraging for everyone, especially sushi restaurants near the office.

The following Monday morning, Chen and Sophie arrived to monitor SaniSeat sales. Chen had spent all day Sunday with Hong Hanh giving her rides in his Cadillac. By noon, Sales had sold another four containers of SaniSeat, including the first re-order. Chen, Sophie, and Derek had lunch that day, and Chen said the Moonies had already surpassed 50 percent of the target sales goal.

At the end of the week, the Moonies had sold another sixteen containers, totaling twenty-eight since launch. Bob's thermometer had almost reached The Gag Line.

Before he left to spend the weekend with Hong Hanh, Chen came to Derek's office.

"Derek, we now have some twenty-eight container of SaniSeats."

"Yes, I know. I check the scoreboard every hour. Congratulations on a really strong start, Mr. President. I'm proud of you and the Moonies."

"Only two mores to win the bets."

"Yes, Chen, thank you for pointing this out. There's a downside to everything."

At 9:30 a.m. the following Monday, the Moonies surpassed their sales goal of thirty containers—ten thousand gallons—to huge cheers in the office. Every order was a punch to Derek's stomach, and they happened again and again. Customer responses were more positive than expected. They loved how the antimicrobial seats, colored for easy identification, which made people feel more comfortable such that they no longer needed seat covers. Homeowners loved the glow-in-dark feature, too. Re-orders now happened routinely. SaniSeat orders reached four to five containers per day, and at the end of the week, Bob's thermometer was well above The Gag Line. The three-week total was forty-six containers, which meant eating sixteen pieces of *uni* that night. Chen and Derek had agreed that Derek could pay the bet in installments each Friday.

The Moonies arranged a sushi party at a nearby Japanese restaurant, Tsunami. The whole office was invited to "The Gag Fest." Derek's strategy was to drink milk before dinner, use nose plugs, and numb himself with Kirin. Unfortunately for Derek, these tools were no match for the powers of *uni*.

After a cocktail hour, the Tsunami staff brought a tray with sixteen pieces of *uni* arranged to form the number 16. Before Derek started, Chen handed him a pink message slip. It was from Carol wishing him good luck and, for good measure, it also had the address of the emergency medical clinic.

While everyone encircled Derek, some with cameras, he took the first bite. The nose plugs helped, but the smell was too strong to hold back completely. As he massaged the *uni* with his tongue, trying to swallow it, cameras flashed, and the crowd roared.

Then his gag reflex fired. He tried diluting the taste with Kirin, but it didn't work. It took several minutes to finish the first *uni*. Bob Davis summed up *uni one*: "Hey, y'all, this is a whole lot better than I expected!"

It took ninety minutes to finish the other fifteen. Derek's technique improved considerably, and the Kirin beers helped, but it was still painful. The crowd loved every minute; strangers even joined the party. By the end, everyone chanted, "Gag Fest, Gag Fest!"

Derek couldn't eat for the next twenty-four hours, which Carol found unusually funny. Chen called her to report on The Gag Fest, and Carol asked for pictures. Charlotte and Everest asked why Daddy was sick.

Carol asked Derek if he would grill dinner. After he lit the grill, she brought him a platter covered with tinfoil. When Derek removed the tinfoil, he looked in horror at what lay underneath: a very large, stinking, whole catfish.

28

Random Scum

The smell of the catfish was unbearable for Derek after so much raw sea urchin. Charlotte and Everest watched in horror as he gagged and retched next to the grill. Their mother's laughter at his expense confused them further.

Carol waited until he had recovered and then said, in perfect Chen, "Look who's Misters Sushis Big Shots now."

In the following week, SaniSeat orders soared. Lund was selling five containers per day, which was almost ten thousand gallons for the week, far beyond anyone's wildest expectations. If not for the *uni* bet, Derek would have been ecstatic. For his benefit, the Sales team nicknamed each container an *uni*. Since his office was close to Sales, he could hear each sale announced: "Another *uni!*" "Two more *unis!*" "Derek's gonna love this—three *unis!*" To make sure Derek hadn't missed the cheers, Dan came to his office to let him know.

"Got any plans for Friday night, Derek?" he said, chuckling.

Sushi menus appeared everywhere—in Derek's home refrigerator and under his pillow (Carol was clearly in league with the Moonies). Derek also found pamphlets for stomach remedies and emergency medical services.

Chen turned out to be cocky winner. He visited Derek's office and asked, "Derek, would you like to bets doubles or everythings for next month?"

"You mean double or nothing?"

"Yes, doubles or nothings."

"No, get outta my office, Chen."

I've got to do something about my gambling problem, Derek thought.

The next day, Chen returned.

"Derek, when I played golf with Billy Headlands in Alabama, we had some special rule."

"What was it?"

"He called it 'mercy rule,' and no one could shoot more than double pars."

"What's your point?"

"I think you need some mercy rule for *uni.*"

Derek immediately perked up. "You mean the bet's off?"

"No, but you don't have to eat more than the first week—sixteen."

"How generous, Chen."

"A bet is some bet, Derek."

For the next six months, sales of SaniSeat went wild. National Porcelain and other fixture companies throughout the country became hooked. The employees were highly energized by SaniSeat's success—they knew it would have a big impact on Lund's financials, and it was fun. SaniSeat orders, still called *unis,* rocketed. Dan and the Sales team constantly marked *unis* on the whiteboard. Lund averaged sales of more than one hundred thousand gallons per month, far beyond even the Moonies' expectations. Trophy was ecstatic, and she showed Derek financial reports that described SaniSeat's impact on Lund's profitability— the company was profitable for the first time since the Great Recession

Derek's next gambling issue, however, was the Dolly Parton promise to Chen. At the current pace of SaniSeat orders, Lund would surpass one million gallons in nine months. To keep his promise to Chen, he would have to call Dolly Parton and entice her to meet with the team.

While Derek wondered how Dolly would react to Chen, his phone rang.

"Hello. This is Derek."

"Derek, this is Cooper Forton, the chief innovation officer of Lund. Remember me? We met a few times in Memphis when you were here for meetings."

"Sure do, Cooper. Good to hear from you. How are things?"

"Pretty good, but there are some issues, I'm afraid."

"What kind of issues?"

"As you probably know, Dave Lund put me in charge of new-product development for all of Lund. My job is to make Lund world-class in new-product development—top 10 percent or better."

"What do you mean, 'in charge?'"

"That's one of the reasons I'm calling. Do you know that Lund has a standard new-product development process that my team and I developed a couple years ago?"

"I remember hearing something about it, but I don't know the particulars."

"Well, it's a detailed, best-in-class process with five stages and clear rules. It applies to all Lund divisions."

"All divisions?" Derek asked, his voice rising slightly.

"Yes. Plastics too. It's a corporate requirement."

Like toilet access? Derek wondered.

"Requirement?"

"Yes, it's mandatory for every new-product development effort."

"Well, to be honest, Cooper, we have done pretty well with our new—"

"You mean SaniPad?"

"It's SaniSeat."

"Right, SaniSeat. I know you're excited and all, but we have concerns about the process used to develop the product."

"Who's 'we?'"

"My team and I in Innovation, along with a few others in Corporate."

"I didn't know about a team. What are the concerns?"

"We don't believe you followed the corporate process—which is required under Lund policies and procedures and is essential for a world-class system."

"We're not trying to fool anyone, Cooper. We didn't follow this standard process or any process really—it was a more like a Chinese fire drill, starting with the Chinese leader. But it worked really well. You might actually even be interested in some of our techniques. SaniSeat is a big hit. Just last month, we sold more than—"

Cooper interrupted. "But you launched a product outside the process and without approval from my group, not to mention that of Miles Templeton, Finance, HR, Legal, and others, and you did not have sufficient documentation."

"Cooper, excuse me, but this is a little out of left field. Did I need your approval to launch SaniSeat? And Miles's too?"

"Of course you did. I am responsible for Lund product development for all divisions, and Miles oversees it all. And you need approval from Innovation, Legal, Finance, Marketing, and HR, which is now called the Corporate Oversight Board, or COB. We meet monthly to review all new products from the divisions and approve moving from one stage to another. You are supposed to make presentations according to our schedule, which is published."

"I didn't know. Dave never mentioned anything like this to me."

"Dave isn't into the details. He's a big-picture guy, and he's family."

"This seems like a pretty big-picture thing, Cooper."

"It's an implementation detail, which I am handling."

"Okay, Cooper, but don't you think it's a bit late for SaniSeat? We launched several months ago."

"Not necessarily. We need to audit the entire process of developing SaniSeat, from start to finish, to determine what action should be taken. We'll compare what happened with the corporate requirements and highlight the deficiencies."

"Deficiencies?"

"Where your team failed to follow the corporate process."

"But they didn't know about any corporate process."

"That's deficiency number one—and a big one," Cooper said. "We will draft the audit and give you two weeks to reply."

"What do you mean, reply?"

"Basically, you say how you will fix the deficiencies."

"But we already launched SaniSeat many months ago. The market loves it. We have sold about—"

"That's not relevant. Once we have your reply, the audit will be finalized and distributed to Dave Lund, Miles Templeton, the COB, and the compliance committee of the board of directors."

A week later, the Moonies and Derek gathered in Dalton for the audit. Cooper and his team were expected at 10:00 a.m., so they met at nine to prepare. To motivate the Moonies, Derek ordered copious amounts of doughnuts, Mountain Dew, Coke, and coffee. Chen and Derek decided to discuss positive things before addressing the audit. They talked about The Celebrity Roller Blading Scavenger Hunt, Dollywood, the Gag Line, and the enormous success of SaniSeat. Chen, who was still very much in love with Hong Hanh, was flying high. He beamed about SaniSeat, and for the first time, he informed the team of "the bet about Dolly Partons."

Sophie interrupted Chen, turned to Derek, and said, "Derek, you made another losing bet on SaniSeat?"

"It's a gift."

Dr. Miao chimed in. "Derek, excuse me, but maybe you have some gamblings problem."

Derek looked around the room. This team was a cross between the United Nations and patrons of the Alabama State Fair. Chen sported side shields on his glasses, wore a lab coat, and was drinking Mountain Dew. Dr. Miao had a cheek full of Red Man Chewing Tobacco. He was becoming more American every day, thanks to Travis. Bobby wore blue jeans with a large, silver belt buckle, a plaid shirt, and boots. He also sipped a Mountain Dew, his second of the morning. Sophie wore a black top with tight jeans for their corporate guests, which Derek hoped would dilute their vigor. Monique's head was freshly shaved, and she wore jeans with a huge buckle and a tight shirt that showed her ripped abdominal muscles. Bob focused on the doughnuts like a buzzard on roadkill and kept spirits high by reporting on the latest sales for SaniSeat. SaniSeat was clearly becoming a blockbuster.

Finally, Derek had to prepare them for the storm troopers.

"SaniSeat has been a great success. You all have done a wonderful job, and it's making a difference to Lund Plastics financially. Quite honestly, when I saw the picture from The Celebrity Roller Blading Scavenger Hunt, I had to wonder—even though you were a stunning Dolly Parton, Bobby."

"It was from the makeups," Chen added.

Derek continued. "Next time, it would help if he shaved his legs. Anyway, I wanted to talk to you before Cooper Forton from Corporate arrives. He's upset with the way we handled SaniSeat."

"Why would anyone be upset about SaniSeat? It's been amazing," said Sophie.

"Cooper designed a detailed new-product development process, which is apparently required for all Lund divisions. As you know, we made up our own process, starting with The Celebrity Roller Blading Scavenger Hunt."

Chen chimed in. "We used the most talented peoples in our teams and made fun things."

"Look, I know, but apparently not everyone agrees with our approach. Today will probably not be fun. I just wanted to prepare you, and I wish I could protect you from this."

"It's okay, Derek," Monique said. "It can't be worse than those *unis*." Everyone laughed.

Around 10:00 a.m., Cooper Forton arrived with one of his guys. Cooper was in his fifties and wore pressed khaki pants, tasseled loafers, and a blue, heavily starched Brooks Brothers shirt with his initials, CUF, on the cuff of his right sleeve. His sidekick was named Don Marlette, who was dressed identically as his boss.

"Cooper, Don, welcome to Plastics," Derek said, extending his hand.

Chen, Dr. Miao, Bobby, Bob, Larry, Sophie, Billy, and Monique all stood and shook hands. Except for Sophie, they were all dressed in their normal work attire, which made casual Friday look like a British royal wedding. Cooper seemed surprised over the group's sartorial informality; he stared at Monique incredulously and spied the bulge in Dr. Miao's left cheek. Dr. Miao smiled back, exposing pieces of Red Man on his teeth.

"Would y'all like something to drink?" Sophie offered with a big smile and her alluring brown eyes. Unfortunately for the Moonies, neither of the guests noticed Sophie, an ominous sign.

"I'll have a coffee, with foam, and two Splendas. Thanks, Honey."

Monique looked at Sophie and rolled her eyes.

Sophie excused herself to get the coffee. But she was mightily pissed off; her face glowed bright red. Cooper had just committed a cardinal sin, and he would pay through foam tampering.

Sophie returned with a mug of coffee loaded with foam. She handed it to Cooper, who said, "Thanks, Honey."

Sophie curtsied in a mocking way, and Monique chuckled. As she turned, she looked at Derek, smiled, and winked.

Cooper took a sip and said, "Um, that's good coffee, Honey. Great foam." Sophie grinned.

Cooper introduced himself to the Moonies, including generous, boring, and quite favorable details about his career and product-development experience. After fifteen minutes of self-promotion, he introduced his colleague, Don Marlette. Don was about forty and eager to please his boss. According to Cooper's elaborate introduction, Don had worked in new-product development programs for DuPont for ten years and was "world-class" in product-development management.

After Cooper's long introductions, it was the Moonies' turn. Derek suggested having each Moonie introduce himself or herself, describe his or her function, and explain his or her role in SaniSeat development.

"That won't be necessary," Cooper said, sipping his coffee and dismissively waving his left hand. "We will get into that in the audit."

Cooper explained the purpose of the audit, which was to correct violations of corporate policy. The Moonies felt the discordant vibe immediately; their spirits sank rapidly, like the air in the room had been replaced by a rancid dog fart. Dr. Miao doubled his Red Man in a vain attempt to energize himself. Bobby took a long pull from his Mountain Dew. Even Monique grabbed a doughnut and Dew.

Being a self-proclaimed expert on product development, Cooper insisted on leading the inquiry. Don's job was to write notes on flipcharts he brought. His first page was titled "Stage 1: Concept" and had two columns, one entitled "Lund Process" and the other "SaniSeat." The Lund Process column was already filled out with the steps required for this stage.

Cooper started. "As you all should know, the Lund New-Product Development Process, which my team and I developed two years ago as the standard for Lund, is a world-class system. It is best-practice."

Monique looked at Derek, rolled her eyes, and chuckled.

"The process has five stages, each with several detailed requirements. No project can proceed to the next stage—and especially not launch—without being reviewed and approved by the Corporate Oversight Board, or COB," Cooper said, looking directly at Derek.

"Any questions so far?"

Chen raised his hand. "Dr. Coopers, I have some question. What if a divisions did not follows the processes and has already launched some new products, and they have many sale?"

"Dr. Chen, that's why we're here. We'll get to that."

Chen and the Moonies sat, stunned, and exchanged concerned looks. Sophie had venom in her eyes leftover from the foam incident.

"But before we get to this central question," Cooper continued, "we will go step by step, comparing what you did with the process requirements. Let's start with stage one, which is called 'Concept.'

"The first step in the concept stage is 'Ideation,' which is a process to generate new product ideas. What is Plastics' ideation process?"

Chen started. "We go on the roads trip and talk about some idea."

"Road trip? Is this method of ideation described in a documented process?" Cooper inquired.

Chen continued. "There is some documentations: we have to reserve the vans before the roads trip." The Moonies nervously chuckled.

Don picked up a red marker and wrote, "No documented ideation process, except van reservations." He underlined it twice in red.

Cooper continued. "How did the concept of SaniSeat come up?"

Bobby spoke up. "Larry, Derek, Chen, and I talked about it in the van."

"Was the van reserved?" Cooper asked.

"Gee, I can't remember, but probably yes. Is that really important? We were driving from Nashville to Jackson Hill."

"Can you find a record of this, either the reservation or the conversation?" Cooper asked.

"I don't know, probably not. Does it matter?"

"If it's not documented or planned, it would be a violation of the Lund Process," Cooper explained. Don wrote "No documented record of conversation or van ride," again in red, underlined.

"Sometimes, people hide records to cover-up mistakes," Cooper continued.

Bobby was incredulous. "What in the world would we be covering up?"

"I don't know, Bobby. I wasn't the one hiding the records. Okay, we've covered Concept," Cooper said. "The next step is developing a preliminary assessment of customer needs and competitive offerings. What did you do to understand the customers' needs?"

"We talk to National Porcelain and other fixture companies and distributors all the time," Larry La Croix chimed in. "It's a regular part of our job."

"How did you assess their needs?" Cooper asked.

"We—you know—we just talk to them about their products and their customers' needs," Larry said.

"Did you document these conversations?"

"No, except maybe an e-mail or two."

"Can you find these e-mails?"

"I doubt it. Is that important?"

"Of course. Did you conduct market research of toilet users?" Cooper asked.

Bob Davis broke in. "Not initially, Mr. Cooper. We had an idea that came from years of complaints about seat covers and long lines at women's restrooms, especially at sporting events."

Don pulled out the red pen and wrote: "No market research and no documentation of customer needs."

"So, where did the idea come from?" Cooper asked.

"Gee, Cooper, I don't know. We all just talked about how it would be nice if we could have toilet seats that killed microbes. Then Derek asked Chen if it was technically possible, and when Chen said yes, Derek decided to create a team."

"Whoa, Bob, one step at a time. Who talked about it being nice?"

"It was a long time ago—"

"That's why we insist on documentation," Cooper scolded.

Bob had finished his doughnuts and was turning red. Sophie found humor in all this, as did Monique. In Monique's mind, Cooper represented the worst of the white, male, imperialist world.

Bob tried to explain. "Let's just say that Larry, our field people, Derek, Chen, and a few others talked about it."

"When you talked about it being nice to kill germs, did you specify how much they should be killed?" Cooper asked.

"Not at firsts," Chen chimed in, "but after some times, we decided on some minimums percentages of survivors, one percents, so no ones need the seat cover."

"What did he say?" Cooper asked Derek.

Derek translated, "Chen said we developed an objective for bug kill of 99 percent, which was the minimum allowed so toilet seat covers would no longer be necessary."

"So when you first said it would be nice to kill bugs, you didn't have objective requirements?" Cooper said, like he was a prosecutor cross-examining a star witness.

Don pulled out the red marker again and wrote in all-bold capitals: "NO OBJECTIVE CUSTOMER REQUIREMENTS."

After a bit more cross-examination, Cooper arrived at the topic of organization of their new-product development efforts.

"Dr. Chen, I understand you were the leader of the SaniSeat team," Cooper said in an unflattering way.

"Yes, Dr. Coopers, this is the truths."

"How did you get this authority?"

"Derek asked me by the telephones."

"Did he tell you that I was chief innovation officer for Lund?"

"No, Dr. Coopers, he just asked me if I thought we could make some toilet-seat coating that killed many microbe, and if I would be the president of some other companies to develop the products."

"Derek made you president?" Cooper asked in a surprised tone.

"Yes. Just the same ways I was president of Bugger Off, another company for some new-products development."

"Did HR know that Derek gave you this title?"

"Yes, Miss Sophie is from the HRs, and she is on both teams— chief peoples officer of boths."

"Our product-development process does not authorize assigning extra titles," Cooper explained.

Don wrote, again in red: "Unauthorized use of titles of President and Chief People Officer."

Chen read Don's notation and said, "Excuse me, Mr. Dons, we also haves the other unauthorized title: chief operatings officer, senior executives vice presidents of sale, and chief financials officer."

"Thanks, Dr. Chen, that's very helpful," Don said as he added the other unauthorized titles.

"We called the teams the Moon Landings, or Moonies, for shorts," Chen explained further.

"Whoa! Did you clear this name with Legal?" Cooper asked.

"No, Dr. Coopers, it was just for the fun."

The Moonies were now on maximum idiot alert, and they started to view this as sport. They had the unfair advantage of vastly superior intelligence, outstanding success in the development and sales of SaniSeat, and complete lack of respect for Cooper, who was obviously a fastidious moron.

"Dr. Chen, once you had your team—these 'Moons'—assembled, how did you get started?" Cooper asked.

"Excuse me, Dr. Coopers, but it's the Moon Landings, like Apollo 11 and Neil Armstrength."

"Okay, Moon Landings."

"We went to Miami Beaches and had the Celebrities Roller Blading Scavenger Hunts."

"Celebrity Roller Blading Scavenger Hunt? Am I hearing that right?"

"Yes."

"Whose idea was this Celebrity Roller Blading Scavenger Hunt?"

"Cher," Chen replied.

Derek almost spit up his drink.

"Cher? The singer?" Cooper asked.

"The sames one, except she had some hairy legs and the five p.m. shadows."

"Huh? Okay, I guess, but did Cher sign a nondisclosure agreement?"

"What's some nondisclosures agreement?"

"An agreement to keep any Lund information learned by outsiders confidential. Under our policy, it is required for any contractors involved in Lund new-product development."

"My apology, Dr. Coopers, but Cher did not sign some nondisclosure agreement."

Don already had his red marker out and wrote "Failed to Obtain Nondisclosure Agreement from Cher."

Cooper continued. "So, Cher refused to sign our nondisclosure agreement?"

"No, Dr. Coopers, I never asked Cher to sign some agreements,"

"Now we're getting somewhere," Cooper exclaimed.

He continued. "The next Stage is 'Feasibility,' where the project is shown to be possible. Before we discuss this in detail, can one of you explain how you moved from Concept to Feasibility?"

"We just did it," Bobby said, "and besides, we knew nothing about these stages."

"So," Cooper inquired, "you didn't document the work in the Concept Stage or get approval to move to Feasibility?"

"No," Bobby said, "what approval are you talking about?"

"You need to present your Stage review to the Corporate Oversight Board—the COB—and get formal approval to enter stage two."

"We did not meets with some COBs," Chen offered.

Don grabbed the red marker and wrote: "Failed to document Concept and did not obtain Stage 1 exit approval from the COB."

"Let's talk about technical feasibility," Cooper continued. "We have already established the lack of objective criteria about killing germs—you only said it would be 'nice.'"

Derek interrupted. "Cooper, let the record reflect that we had an objective criteria for killing, 99 percent, which was developed after we said it would be 'nice.'"

"Your comment is noted for the record, Derek, but it was clear the team started work because they thought it would be 'nice.'"

"Never mind," Derek said, enjoying this immensely.

Cooper continued. "How did you determine the product would work?"

"We didn't know for the truths," Chen said.

"You didn't know?"

"No, we thought it was possibles, but we were not sure."

"So, you had already spent money to meet in Miami Beach and hire Cher, but you weren't sure?"

"Cher wasn't so expensives, Dr. Coopers, and we got a president's discount at the Marriotts Hotel."

"Don will note this. Let's move on. What did you do to make sure the product would work?"

"We built the NASCARs with some sample as a fields test."

"Dr. Chen, the Lund Process specifies that field tests must be designed to mimic the actual conditions of use for the new product. You would agree that SaniSeat was not designed to be used in race cars, right?"

"Yes, the NASCARs do not have some toilet. The NASCARs was for some bets with employees."

"Employees were betting on field tests?" Cooper asked indignantly.

"Yes, but we did not let Dr. Miao race because he loves Jeff Gordons and the 24 car, who ended up winning."

"Is that true, Dr. Miao?"

Dr. Miao had so much Red Man that he could barely move his mouth or speak. "Yesshh, fhat's c'rect."

"Did anyone bet who was involved in the race—I mean, field trial?" Cooper asked.

Billy Lansing finally broke his silence. "Dr. Cooper, it was just some fun for the plant employees to get them interested in new-product development and build morale."

"Was Jeff Gordon given a nondisclosure agreement to sign?"

"What? No," Billy answered.

Don pulled out the marker again, writing "Jeff Gordon Did Not Sign Nondisclosure Agreements before NASCAR Race."

The audit lasted for hours, with a short break to order lunch. The Moonies and Derek chose sandwiches from a greasy menu. Cooper looked at the menu with disdain and asked, "Sophie, could I order a Cobb salad?"

Chen asked, "Dr. Coopers, do we also need some COB reviews of lunches?"

Around 4:00 p.m., Cooper finished a long and tortuous cross-examination of Larry over the name, "SaniSeat." He was particularly interested in the decision not to use the name "WifeSaver" and the betting around Bob's margarita night with Jane. By the end, Don had several flip charts of notes, mostly written in red and underlined or in bold.

Finally, Cooper said, "Well, that about does it. This has been enlightening."

Chen then spoke up. "What will happens now, Dr. Coopers?"

"Don and I will write up the audit report and give it to Derek to respond within two weeks."

"Will there be anything other than a report?" Bobby asked.

"We have to analyze all the information before deciding what to do with SaniSeat."

Larry interrupted. "Cooper, just so you know, we have sold more than five hundred thousand gallons of SaniSeat. It is by far the most successful new product in the history of Lund Plastics, if not all of Lund. SaniSeat's financial impact has made Plastics profitable, even in the Great Recession. Furthermore, the product has been installed in stadiums, theaters, rest stops, and thousands of homes across America; everyone loves it."

"That's not relevant to the inquiry," Cooper said.

After Cooper and Don left the plant, the Moonies stayed to debrief. Derek started.

"Sophie, did you put something in Cooper's foam?"

"Just some random scum from the kitchen."

"What?"

"Assorted scum. I scraped under the sink and picked up a few mouse hairs from the trap in the cupboard."

"He deserved worse," Monique interjected. "He's a white male pig."

"Well," Derek said, "that was very interesting. What did you all think?"

After a short pause, Chen spoke. "Dr. Coopers is a total bummers. He is some soggy sheet."

"Do you mean wet blanket?"

"Yes, the sames."

29

THE AUDIT REPORT

A few weeks later, Derek received the draft SaniSeat New-Product Development Process Audit from Cooper. It was twenty pages long and was organized around the five stages of the new-product development process. The audit findings were rated as Level 1 (extremely serious), Level 2 (major), and Level 3 (minor).

In the "Concept" section, there was only one Level-1 finding: "Failure to Obtain Nondisclosure Agreement from Cher." Derek needed to draft the management response to each finding, ideally to be constructive and responsive, even if he considered it to be total bullshit. He responded with:

> Plastics agrees with this finding and admits that we failed to obtain a nondisclosure agreement from Cher. We mitigated this risk, however, by confining our conversations around Cher to less sensitive matters and having her escorted by Don Johnson from Miami Vice. In all future new-product development activities, we will get Cher to sign nondisclosure agreements.

Derek thought the board would take comfort in this response. There were also two Level-2 findings in this section. The first was:

"No Documented Ideation Process Except Van Reservations." Derek's response was:

Plastics agrees with this finding. We will develop a cross-functional team and conduct ideation brainstorming sessions to develop a manual describing our ideation methodology, in addition to van reservations.

The second Level-2 finding was: "No Documentation of SaniSeat Idea from Road Trip." Derek's response:

Plastics agrees with this finding. From this point forward, each company van will have a notebook for logging all conversations during road trips. Participants in each road trip will be required to document, date, and sign their conversations.

The Feasibility section's Level-1 finding was especially choice: "Jeff Gordon Did Not Sign Nondisclosure Agreements before NASCAR."

Trying not to be obviously derisive, Derek settled on the following response:

Plastics agrees with this finding. We are making every attempt to contact Jeff Gordon to obtain a backdated nondisclosure agreement with Lund.

At the end of the audit, Cooper recommended that Plastics: 1. Cease producing and selling SaniSeat until all deficiencies in the audit had been cured; and 2. Inform all customers who have purchased SaniSeat that the product was developed without complying with the Lund New-Product Development Process. In Derek's mind, this confirmed Cooper's mental infirmity.

After completing the responses, Derek e-mailed them to Cooper, who appreciated the quick turnaround and complimented Plastics for agreeing with all the findings and admitting responsibility. Cooper's quartet was clearly missing a cello.

30

BRIGHT LIGHT, BIG CITIES

A few weeks after Derek's audit response, Dave Lund called him.

"Derek, this is Dave."

"Hi, Dave, how are things in the big office?"

"Not bad these days. It helps a lot that Plastics is doing well."

"I'm glad we can help, for a change. It's been exciting around here with the explosion of SaniSeat."

"That's really great, Derek. Congratulations to the team. How much are you selling now?"

"We sold two hundred thousand gallons last month, a new record, and our cumulative total is about to hit one million. And—get this—it is so popular that we raised the price by 10 percent."

"No wonder your profits are increasing so rapidly. That's excellent."

"It's much more fun this way."

"Speaking of SaniSeat, Derek, there is something I need to talk to you about."

"What is it?"

"The board and I received a curious audit report from Cooper Forton."

"The one concerning SaniSeat?"

"Have you seen it?"

"Of course. I wrote our management response to a draft."

"Well, it's the longest audit report with the most findings any of us have seen. And Cooper's recommendations are way over the top. They would kill your business."

"Agreed."

"But did you really hire Cher?" Dave asked.

"Yes, she's a great team-builder and surprisingly affordable."

There was silence and then a chuckle. "I hate to ask."

Derek explained the Miami Beach outing and could hear Dave trying not to laugh on the other end.

"That's amazing, Derek. Why in the world did Cooper think it was serious?"

"I don't know—it is a little unconventional."

"No doubt. Still, I had no idea Cooper was doing this kind of thing. It's a little embarrassing for the board to be reading this. They'll think he's an idiot."

"It wouldn't be a stretch."

"Unfortunately, all audits go to Miles and the Board Compliance Committee, so I can't squash investigations, like I would do with this one. They are not finding humor in any of this."

"What do you mean?"

"The compliance committee would like to see you."

"Uh, oh, not again."

"Just like with the Nashville office thing, which was a Mongolian cluster fuck."

"I'm sorry they didn't think the whole prairie-dog thing was amusing."

"For them, nothing is funny. Derek, you are a compliance committee recidivist. Hopefully, you won't need to discuss urinals and foo dogs this time."

"Will Miles be there?"

"He's the executive liaison with the compliance committee, so he'll be there, probably leading the inquiry."

"Shit."

"Shit is an understatement."

"Dave, I don't think Miles likes me too much."

"That makes two of us."

"You don't like me?"

"No, I mean Miles doesn't like me, either. Unfortunately, he has too much board support for me to do anything about him. He loves every opportunity to make me look bad. And when he makes you look bad, it also makes me look bad—a twofer."

"It should be an interesting meeting."

"You might want to bring Chen, Tr—, I mean, B'linda, and a good-luck charm."

A week later, Miles sent Derek an e-mail:

Vogel,

The Board Compliance Committee and I received a very disturbing report from Cooper Forton regarding Plastics' flagrant disregard of the well-established corporate new-product development process. This is a very serious matter that requires your presence at the next Board Compliance Committee meeting, which will be held in New York City. You should also bring that Chinese so-called scientist of yours.

Vogel, your flip, cocky attitude about serious corporate issues, like Lund office protocol, has been noted and is a sore spot with many of us.

Miles Templeton
Chief Financial Officer

Darth Vader had invited Derek to his own ritual slaughter.

A ritual slaughter had its upsides, though, like requiring a road trip to New York. In addition to Chen, Derek invited Trophy because she would relate well to the compliance committee. *They are all lecherous old men*, he thought.

When Derek called Chen, he was delighted.

"Derek, I've never been to Manhattans."

"Let's go a day early with Trophy and enjoy it."

"Okay. Bright light, big cities."

"What? Oh, yeah. By the way, Chen, the compliance meeting may not be enjoyable."

"Will Toes be there?"

"Unfortunately, yes. He's looking forward to it."

"I better bring some foo dog to keep away the evil spirit."

"They haven't worked yet."

Chen, Trophy, and Derek arrived at the Waldorf Astoria on Park Avenue in the late afternoon. Since Derek had worked in Manhattan before business school, he gave Chen and Trophy a walking tour, and they dined near Central Park. On the way back, they walked past 30 Rockefeller Plaza. When Chen saw signs for NBC Studios, he asked, "Derek, is this the place for some NBC TV show?"

"Yes. What's your favorite?"

"*The Todays Show* with Al Roker, the weathersman."

Pointing to Studio 3B, Derek said, "Well, that's where Al Roker does his street reports."

"Where the people have some sign?"

"Yep, that's it."

"I've never been on televisions before."

"Just show up with a sentimental message, and you will," Derek joked.

On the way back to the Waldorf, Chen bought a Yankees baseball cap. He wore it in the hotel bar, where they had a nightcap. All the men in the bar stared at Trophy, which Derek hoped augured well for the compliance committee meeting. The three agreed to meet at 9:30 a.m. to visit museums and the Empire State Building.

The next morning, Derek turned on *The Today Show* to catch the news. The weather report with Al Roker followed the news. He was outside Studio 3B, and as usual, tourists lined up with signs and wore shirts from Midwestern high school sports teams. They screamed and waved to the cameras.

Derek wondered if Chen was watching and chuckled.

Trophy and Derek met for coffee in the lobby at nine. As they sipped their coffee, they noticed Chen enter the hotel around nine fifteen. He wore his aviator glasses and new Yankees baseball cap along with white athletic socks and running shoes.

Trophy said, "That's some get-up of Chen's."

Derek noticed Chen was carrying a sign and said, "Tell me he didn't go the *The Today Show.*"

Chen's sign said, "I love the United State."

Trophy said, "Chen, did you try to get on *The Today Show?*"

"There were already too many peoples there, but Al Roker gave me some autograph."

"Just as well, Chen—being on TV can be dangerous."

After a great morning touring New York and a street-vendor lunch, the threesome dressed for the compliance committee meeting in the afternoon. Trophy wore a nice dress and her trademark stiletto heels. Dave Lund met the team outside the room to wish them luck—he was not invited to attend the meeting.

In the conference room, Miles Templeton sat at a table in an expensive suit with suspenders, greased hair, and a sadistic smile. He was relishing this moment, like a lion about to maul Christians in the Roman Coliseum. The committee chair, Langley Kingston, motioned for the group to sit on the opposite side of the table. Langley was in his mid-sixties with gray, immaculately groomed hair and a dark-gray suit. He was the retired chief financial officer of American Gas Company, a Fortune 100 energy behemoth. According to rumor, Langley was the power of Lund's board and a colossal asshole.

Three other members of the compliance committee sat near Langley. They were all quite old. One was Dave Lund's great-uncle, Stefan Lund, who had massive gray eyebrows that almost grew up to his hairline. He was about ninety and looked like he might expire at any moment. Derek hoped he wasn't too old to be swayed by the sexiest vice president of finance in all of Lund. The other two gentlemen weren't much younger.

Langley dryly said, "Welcome back, Derek."

"Thank you, Langley and committee. I believe you all know B'linda Mae Jones, our vice president of finance. But you probably haven't met Dr. Chen, our director of R & D. Dr. Chen led the SaniSeat project."

"Hello, Mr. Langley," Chen said. He quietly pulled a Chinese foo dog out of his briefcase, but kept it out of view of the committee. Derek hoped the foo-dog mutts would finally keep away evil spirits.

"Hello, Dr. Chang. Let's get to it, shall we?" Langley said. Miles sat up and grinned. "Derek, in the history of this committee, we have never seen such an audit. Do you have any opening remarks?"

"Dr. Chen, B'linda and I are really proud of Plastics and SaniSeat. We—"

"Hold on, Vogel," Langley interrupted. "You're proud of *this*?" Langley held up Cooper's audit report.

"Not so much the report, Langley, but SaniSeat."

"You and your so called 'Moons' violated every aspect of Lund's new-product development process, and your responses made a mockery of Dr. Forton's report."

Chen spoke up. "It's the Moon Landings, Mr. Langley."

"That's irrelevant, Dr. Chang."

Chen clearly had undue confidence in his foo dogs. "Mr. Langley, Lund has sold more than eight hundred thousand gallons of SaniSeat, and we are now selling more than one hundred fifty thousand gallons each months. It's our best new-product developments."

"Eight hundred thousand gallons? Do you know what that means to Lund?" Langley shouted. Miles grinned.

Derek interrupted to save Chen. "Yes, SaniSeat has made Plastics profitable, despite the Great Recession."

"What about the liability for not following our process?"

"Liability?"

"Of course. Don't you think plaintiff lawyers will sue because we didn't follow our process?"

"Sue for what?" Derek asked.

"False advertising."

"What advertising?"

"Claiming our product was certified by the Lund process."

Trophy butted in. "But we didn't claim this. We didn't even know about the process."

"Miss, do you think your ignorance will hold up in our litigious society?"

Trophy changed tacks. "But everyone loves the product; it works beautifully."

"Especially for the lady at the baseball game," added Chen.

"What?"

"The lady at the game do not need to wait in the lines because the plastic seat cover gets tangled," Chen explained.

"Let's get into the report. Did you all really hire Cher?" asked Langley.

Derek explained, "Yes, Chen hired her for the team kickoff meeting in Miami Beach."

"Plastics was bleeding money, and you hired Cher in Miami Beach?"

"That is some truths, Mr. Langley, but we saved moneys at the Marriott Hotel with my presidential discounts," Chen added.

"Presidential discount? What the hell are you talking about, Chang?" Langley asked. He was getting really irritated. The foo dogs must have been chasing squirrels.

Derek broke in. "Langley, it was all for a team-building event—and it wasn't really Cher."

Chen said, "It was only some mans dressing like Cher, but he did not shave his leg and had some five-p.m. shadow."

"Are you saying Cher was a man?"

"Yes, Mr. Langley, but with good mascaras."

Langley stopped and stared at Chen, Trophy, and Derek. Then he looked around the room for support. Stefan Lund only stared blankly. He may have passed. Miles nodded, encouraging Langley to go for the jugular.

Derek explained The Celebrity Roller Blading Scavenger Hunt but left out the condom story for obvious reasons—and he didn't know if Langley liked former President Clinton.

"Vogel, Lund is a serious company, and your division was in deep trouble, yet you allowed this?"

"Yes, Chen and his team had already been very successful with antimicrobial siding, and toilet seats were a bigger opportunity."

"But you let them travel to Miami Beach and roller blade with a cross-dressing half-breed?"

Half-breed? Derek wondered, before remembering the Sonny and Cher song.

"Well, yes, in part as a reward."

"Vogel, this is the most irresponsible, unprofessional crap I've ever seen."

"Sorry, sir, but it worked."

"We have eight hundred thousand gallons out there, on God knows how many toilet seats, just waiting for a lawsuit," Langley responded, and then he shifted gears. "Cher was bad enough, but what's this about Jeff Gordon and NASCAR?"

Chen spoke up. "Jeff Gordon was part of some field test."

"How was Jeff Gordon involved with SaniSeat?"

"He drove one of the prototypes—and ended up winning," Derek explained.

"What?" Langley asked.

"They made each prototype floor into a make-believe NASCAR and turned it into a race to see which car would have the least amount of bacteria. The whole plant got involved with scoreboards and sponsorships and everything. Jeff Gordon drove one of the cars."

"You had Jeff Gordon under contract?" Langley asked, losing patience rapidly.

"No, Mr. Langley," Chen said. "Jeff Gordon was already some employee."

"*What*? What are you trying to pull, Chang?"

Derek explained. "It wasn't really Jeff Gordon, but a maintenance worker who dressed as Jeff Gordon. Does that clear things up?"

"Not one bit, Vogel."

Langley paused and then spoke. "Vogel, Belinda, Chang, we don't have time for this nonsense, but before we deliberate on what to do, I have one more question."

"Okay."

"Near the end, there's a Level-1 finding about the name 'SaniSeat.' It says that a marketing firm you hired recommended the name 'WifeSaver,' but you fired them after margaritas without any market research."

Derek answered. "As I wrote in my response, that's true. The name was crazy, and we didn't need market research to know it."

"Why the hell did you need margaritas first?"

"We didn't—Cooper Forton got a little confused." Derek explained the story without elaborating on Bob Davis's date with Jane.

"But no one actually fired the firm while drinking margaritas?"

"That's right."

"I've had enough of your crap, Vogel," Langley continued. "You and your team have made a circus of the Lund process. We'll let you know what we decide."

Trophy had heard enough and jeopardized her career by stating, "Langley, Lund Plastics was in big trouble. The market was in the dumps, and we had no competitive advantage. We went for it with new products. It worked. Our new products are rapidly gaining volume and are turning us around."

"You're way outta line, Ms. Jones."

So ended the meeting. On the way back, they ran into Dave Lund in the lobby and related the story.

He responded, "Not good. I guess you forgot the good-luck charms."

"We brought foo dogs, but they screwed up again," Derek said glancing at Chen.

"What?"

"Never mind."

"I'm really sorry," Dave said earnestly. "Y'all've done a great job with SaniSeat. I hate that this investigation got out of hand."

"It's not your fault, Dave."

"Still, you all shouldn't get punished. Is there anything else I could do to help you and the Moonies?"

"Do you by any chance know Dolly Parton?" Derek asked.

31

FAN CAM

SaniSeat sales passed one million gallons in a blur. Chen started agitating about contacting Dolly Parton, and Derek had to live up to another stupid bargain. While Derek contemplated the "Dolly Dilemma," Trophy came to his office. She wore a low-cut, short, tight dress that showed her impressive figure and her spiked heels. Her hair was thick, wild, and curly as ever. Trophy was a real stunner, in a sultry, *Hee Haw* way.

"Derek, want to hear something interesting?" she asked.

"I could use it."

"SaniSeat sales are now 25 percent of our volume."

"Are you serious?"

"We just crossed the line. Coupled with antimicrobial siding, our business is 50 percent new products now."

"We're already hitting our stretch goal for Plastics?"

"Can you believe it? No offense, Derek, but when you talked about 50 percent new products, we thought you were off your meds."

The phone rang and Trophy excused herself. From the caller ID, Derek knew it was Chen.

"Hello, Mr. President."

"Derek, how is the businesses?"

"Things are going great, Chen. Trophy just told me we passed our 50 percent new-product target, all because of SaniSeat and Bug Off."

"Great new."

"I couldn't have said it better. Cher would be proud."

"I will tell her, but only after she signs some nondisclosure agreements."

"You can't be too careful with new-product secrets. So, what's up, Mr. President?"

"Derek, I'm calling about some personal matter."

"What is it?"

"Hong Hanh is going to be my brides."

"You're engaged?"

"Yes."

"That's the best news I've heard in a long time. Congratulations! I am so happy for you."

"All because of the Dollywoods roads trip and not going to eat at Applebee."

"Fuji gave us Hong Hanh and *uni*. So, when is the wedding?"

"In a few month. Derek, can I ask you some question?"

"Sure."

"Would you be my best mans?"

"It would be a tremendous honor, but what about your brother, Cleveland?"

"He may be a best mans too, but I really want you—so does Hong Hanh."

"I would be honored. Thank you, Chen, and please thank your fiancée for me."

"Okay. Derek, can I ask some other favor?"

"Sure."

"We would like to have the wedding and receptions at Dalton Hills Country Club. Hong Hanh and I would like to invite the whole plants."

"Everyone?" Derek asked.

"Yes, plus some from the Nashville offices."

"It's a great idea, Chen, except maybe for one thing."

"It means a shutting down the plants that day," Chen surmised.

"Chen, come to think of it, the event would be a big morale-building event, bigger even than the NASCAR party. We can do that."

"Thanks, Derek. I would also like to send Dave Lund an invitations. Does he have some wifes?"

"Just one."

The weeks passed, SaniSeat sales boomed, and myriad wedding plans jelled. While Chen and Derek were at a product-development meeting in Dalton, Derek asked him, "So, Chen, are you and Hong Hanh going someplace special for your honeymoon?"

"Niagara Fall."

"Of course."

Later that morning, Chen called The Silver Mist, Niagara Falls' most elegant hotel. After being transferred to reservations, Chen was greeted by a young woman with a nasally, western New York accent.

"Silver Mist reservations, this is Brenda. How may I help you?"

"Hello, I would like to make some honeymoon reservation," Chen said.

"You called the right place. The Silver Mist has beautiful honeymoon suites," Brenda explained enthusiastically.

"My brides and I will be happy; we have never seen the Niagara Fall."

After a brief discussion, Brenda continued. "Okay, we have the deluxe honeymoon suite with champagne greeting package for those dates. Would you like me to reserve it for you?"

"Yes, please."

"May I have your name?"

"Dr. and Mrs. Chen."

"How nice, Dr. Chen. How do you spell your name?"

"The first letter is some *C.*"

"Pardon me?"

"*C,* as in *Commie.*"

"Commie?"

"Yes, Commie."

"How do you spell that?"

"*C-O-M-M-I-E.* Commie."

"Commie, got it—like a Communist?"

"Yes, the same."

"Okay," Brenda giggled. "The first letter is *C.* What's next?"

"*H,* as in *hors d'oeuvres.*"

"Oar dewars?"

"Hors d'oeuvres, like some spring roll or cheese and cracker."

"Okay. Doesn't that start with an *O?*"

"No, it's some *H.* The French do not say the *H.*"

"You sound foreign. Are you French, Dr. Chen?"

"No, I am from China."

"China?"

"Yes, Beijing, the capitols."

"Do you like Bruce Lee movies?"

"Yes, he is some very good actor."

"I agree. Okay, so we have a *C* and an *H.* What's next?"

"*E,* as in *excellent.*"

"That sounds more like an *X.*"

"*X* is the number-two letter. The first is *E.*"

"You're pretty smart, Dr. Chen. I bet you went to college."

"Yes, Beijing University."

"Wow, you're a doctor and you went to college!"

"Yes, but I don't have some nurse."

"Maybe I can apply? I always thought I'd be good in medicine."

"I am some plastics doctor."

"Well, plastics need doctors too. Okay, we have a *C,* an *H,* and an *E.* What's next?"

Chen had caught on. *"N ...* as in *engagement."*

"N, got it. *C-H-E-N,* Chen. Is that it?"

"Yes."

Chen was happy to be going to Niagara Falls, the archetypical American honeymoon, but had serious questions about the American educational system, as well as Silver Mist hiring practices.

The next major wedding event was the bachelor party. As the co-best man, Derek volunteered to organize it. He wanted to provide a new American cultural experience for Chen, as well as for Cleveland, Dr. Miao, and Hong Hanh's brother from Vietnam, Thuc. And of course, he wanted to make sure it didn't create an HR incident.

After considerable debate, Derek chose Atlanta. Spring was the perfect time for a bachelor party in Atlanta with the Braves, excellent bars and restaurants, and world-class gentlemen's clubs.

The Saturday before the wedding, the team gathered at Turner Field, where the Braves hosted the Dodgers. It was the perfect venue for a crew of Chinese men (Chen, Cleveland, and Dr. Miao), a Vietnamese man (Thuc), a Yankee (Derek), and several Southerners (Bobby, Travis, and Bob). To round out the squad, Cher flew in from Miami. Conditions were ideal for Cher to sign the nondisclosure agreement, which Derek planned to frame and present to Cooper Forton and Toes with an autographed picture.

Hong Hanh's brother, Thuc, was about thirty years old, thin, only slightly taller than Trophy, had dark skin and straight, black hair, and wore a long, loose, white Vietnamese shirt. His English was worse than Chen's. Thuc was excited to be in the United States for the first time and was keen to learn American culture. Travis brought extra Red Man Chewing Tobacco and convinced Thuc to try some in the parking lot. Thuc's first wad caused severe whirlies, and he nearly toppled over. Travis caught him and encouraged further testing, explaining that Dr. Miao had experienced similar start-up issues. After a few wads, Thuc got the hang of it.

Chen's brother, Cleveland, flew in from Hong Kong, where he worked as a trader for Pan Pacific International Bank. He had a sophisticated air and wore bespoke clothing from Hong Kong tailors. Cleveland had left behind his boots and orange hunting hat from "L. Beans," but despite working in an international city, Cleveland had experienced little of the West. His English was no better than Chen's.

Dave Lund had generously given Chen tickets to the game in the prestigious club seats behind home plate as an engagement present. Club seats had outstanding views and included free beer and food.

They were seated less than a minute when Bob ordered beers for the group and a Coke for Bobby. A few minutes after the beers arrived, Bob toasted Chen and the visitors from the Far East, now known as the "Asian Contagion." Dr. Miao proceeded to "clink and chug" Chinese style. Cleveland was used to this practice and followed Dr. Miao enthusiastically. Thuc had a huge wad of Red Man in his left cheek, but he still followed with gusto.

After the first beer, Thuc struck up conversation with Cher, who wore a casual dress and attractive silver bracelets to accent her darker coloring and mascara. Thuc was not used to tall women in Vietnam, nor curly hair. His fascination turned to flirtation until Chen set him straight.

"Thuc, I hate to burst your bubbly, but Cher is some man in lady clothes."

Thuc did a double take, looked into his beer cup, and then examined Cher's hairy legs and impressive biceps before believing Chen.

Free beer was a great perk, but a superior one appeared: four beautiful young women sitting right in front of the group. They each had long, blonde hair, a beautiful face, and an outstanding figure underneath Braves jerseys. At first, Derek suspected that Dave Lund had arranged the happy coincidence. Bobby and Travis wanted the Asians to fit in and bought them Braves jerseys and foam-rubber tomahawks. They also bought a catcher's mask and helmet for Dr. Miao.

Bob ordered more beers, including four for the blondes. When the beers arrived, the blondes thanked Bob profusely, blowing kisses to him. Bob was visibly excited.

Derek turned to Bob and said, "Bob, they don't know the beer is free."

"You know what that means?" he asked.

"They're genuine blondes?"

"One hunner percent, Derek. Time to party!"

The National Anthem interrupted the festivities. As the anthem played, the Asian Contagion, resplendent in new Braves jerseys, held their right hands over their hearts. Chen belted out the first stanza:

"Okay can you see, by some dawn's early lights?
What so probably we hails by the twilights last gleamings.
Whose broad stripe and bright star thru some perilous fight,
Over the dram parts we watched were so gallantly steamings?"

He rose to a crescendo at the end:

"O'er the land of the freeeeees …, and the home of some brave!"

As the anthem was ending with an accent on the word *brave*, the Asian Contagion performed tomahawk chops in unison, the trademark move of Atlanta Braves fans.

"I always knew Francis Scott Key was a Braves fan," Bobby said to Derek.

Afterwards, the blondes complimented the Contagion on their rendition.

"Y'all did great, didn't they, Jasmine?" the first, Bianca, said to the other.

"I'm surely impressed," Jasmine said to Chen. "Honey, where are y'all from?"

"I am from China; he is from Vietnam," Chen said, pointing at Thuc, who sat wide-eyed, staring at the huge breasts turned toward him.

"Oh, my God, Bethany, these guys are from Vietnam!" Jasmine exclaimed to the third blonde.

Bethany beamed and said to Thuc, "Honey, don't y'all just love those *Rambo* movies?"

Thuc stayed in his trance with a slight dribble of tobacco juice running out the left corner of his mouth.

Bob kept the Asian Contagion and blondes on an impressive beer pace. After the fifth inning, with the Braves leading 4 to 2 on a Chipper Jones home run, Thuc talked with Bethany and Jasmine. Jasmine asked Thuc, "So, Thuc, what brings y'all to Atlanta?"

"Some wedding," Thuc answered through tobacco juice.

"How nice! Who's the guy next to you?" Jasmine continued, nodding at Chen.

"He is my grooms."

"Really? *Your* grooms?"

"Yessss, ma'amssss," Thuc answered, struggling with tobacco juice.

Bobby explained that Chen was marrying Thuc's sister, and this was a bachelor party.

"Bachelor party?" Jasmine asked.

"That's right. Chen is getting married next Saturday."

"Hey, girls!" Jasmine yelled to her companions. "It's time to show Chen and these Oriental boys a good time!"

Bob pounced. "Hey, ladies, can I buy y'all another round?"

At the seventh-inning stretch, Thuc sat between Bianca and Bethany, who repeatedly sandwiched Thuc with kisses on both cheeks. The pressure from simultaneous kisses caused spurts of tobacco juice from his mouth, which made the girls laugh. At the same time, Dr. Miao initiated frequent beer-chugging toasts with Cher. His new catcher's mask was only a minor impediment—he just raised the mask for each chug. He had to do the same to spit tobacco juice but sometimes forgot.

Jasmine sat next to Chen and tried to get affectionate. She put her arm around him and let her long, blonde hair fall over his shoulder. Chen squirmed when Jasmine nibbled on his right ear and whispered something, most likely unrelated to baseball.

"Bobby," Derek asked, "do you feel kinda left out?"

"A little, but this is solid entertainment."

"No doubt."

A big message suddenly appeared on the gigantic Center Field scoreboard:

"CONGRATULATIONS, DR. CHEN, ON YOUR UPCOMING WEDDING!"

At that moment, the crowd camera ("Fan Cam"), which displayed pictures on the large centerfield scoreboard, found Chen and the Asian Contagion. Dave Lund had undoubtedly arranged the whole thing. In front of thousands of fans, the scoreboard displayed:

- Chen being reluctantly nuzzled by a beautiful blonde, who was nibbling his ear.
- Thuc getting simultaneously kissed by Bianca and Bethany with spurting tobacco juice. His new Braves jersey had a trail of brown juice down the front.
- A strangely male-looking Cher interlocking elbows and chugging beer with an Asian wearing a catcher's mask and helmet.

- Derek's mouth hanging wide open in sheer terror.
- Bobby pointing at the scoreboard and laughing uncontrollably.

The crowd noticed and cheered wildly. Chen pulled his ear away from Jasmine and gave a big thumbs-up sign to the camera, eliciting more cheers. The crowd was on its feet, laughing and cheering Chen. The Braves and Dodgers stepped out of their dugouts to view the Contagion with their own eyes. They all laughed and returned Chen's thumbs-up sign.

A minute later, Derek's cell phone rang.

"Hello."

"Hey, Honey." It was Carol.

"Hey, Hon. How are things at home?"

"Nothing special. How's the game?"

"The Braves are ahead 4 to 2, and the Asian guys are really getting into baseball."

"Really?"

"Yeah, we bought score books to keep track—they are being quite cerebral about all this—and the American guys are spending a lot of time explaining the rules to Chen, his brother, Dr. Miao, and Thuc."

"Cerebral, huh?"

"Yes. They're very serious about learning American culture."

"I can see that," Carol commented.

"I sure wish you could."

"No. I can. Do you know that all Atlanta Braves games are televised nationally by the Turner Broadcasting System?"

"You don't say."

"Including in Nashville."

"No kidding."

"Well, the kids and I have been watching it."

"You're watching it now?"

"Yes, we've been watching the whole game, including a few minutes ago."

"A few minutes ago? What'd you think about Chipper Jones's home run?" Derek's voice betrayed total fear.

"Great, but not as good as the recent fan-cam shots."

"Fan cam?" Derek asked, his voice now several octaves higher.

"You know, the stadium camera that flashes images on the scoreboard."

"Oh, yeah, isn't that fun?"

"Fun and enlightening."

"Oh?"

"Derek, it showed some buxom blonde nibbling Chen's ear."

"Really ... where?"

"About two feet in front of you. It was on national TV. The announcers loved it."

"Is that so?"

"There was also an Asian guy with tobacco juice all over him getting kissed by two girls, and another chugging beer with a catcher's mask. Was that Dr. Miao?"

"Yes. The other was Thuc, Hong Hanh's brother from Vietnam. They're learning American culture really fast, aren't they?"

"They have some excellent mentors."

"Well, um—"

"Who was drinking beer with Dr. Miao? It looked like Cher with a five-o'clock shadow."

"That's Chen's friend from Miami. We don't even know his real name."

"You run a fascinating organization, Derek."

"You're catching on."

"Another thing, Derek."

"What's that?"

"I hope Hong Hanh doesn't watch the Braves."

After hanging up, Derek turned to Chen and asked, "Chen, do you still dream of being on TV?"

32

CHEETOS

After the game, the blondes joined the party, and they all piled into the van. Space was limited, so they doubled up. Bethany sat sideways on Thuc's lap; her large breasts lined up perfectly with his eyes, which never blinked. Jasmine cuddled Chen, and Bob blanketed Bianca, like a dog on dead fish. Cleveland had gotten friendly with Keri, the quiet fourth blonde. Dr. Miao wore his catcher's mask, which now had tobacco stains along the bottom. Derek sat with Cher. Bobby, who never drank alcohol, drove.

They stopped at an outdoor café in Buckhead, a posh section of Atlanta. The outdoor crowd was awestruck when the van emptied its contents like a circus car.

After piles of appetizers and copious beers, Jasmine asked Chen, "Honey, what's the plan for the rest of your bachelor party?"

"We go to Cheetos."

"Cheetos? What's Cheetos?" Jasmine asked drunkenly.

"It's some stripping club."

"A strip club?"

"Yes, some place where the girls do the dance without their shirt."

"Do you mean Cheetah, the strip club downtown?"

"Yes, Cheetos, the strip clubs," Chen confirmed (sort of).

"Honey, y'all don't need to go to Cheetah—you have us girls."

Bob rocketed straight up in his chair.

Jasmine continued. "Bianca and I even worked there for a while."

"Were you some bartenders?"

"Honey, we were *some* dancers."

"Do you have your own strippers club now?"

"No, darlin', but we share a large condo nearby—it even has a hot tub. Why don't we all go there?"

No further discussion was needed. They paid the bill and hopped in the van. After a short drive, the van arrived at a two-story condominium in a circular complex with a large swimming pool and steaming hot tub. Bob stared at the hot tub in longing wonder. Travis asked the blondes if they had beer, and they directed him to a spare refrigerator in the back hallway. He returned with a twelve-pack of Bud Light. Jasmine blasted party tunes on the CD player. Everyone danced and made quick work of their beers. Travis fetched more.

Jasmine, Bianca, Bethany, and Keri displayed their exotic-dancing skills. It was almost like being at "Cheetos." And like at Cheetos, the girls started removing layers. Under the Braves jerseys, they wore skimpy, black-lace bras and thongs. Cher was a little jealous. Bob beamed with anticipation of possible groping, but the girls directed their complete attention to the Asians.

Jasmine announced, "It's hot-tub time, y'all!"

The girls changed into skimpy bikinis. The men had grossly underappreciated the ladies' stunning figures.

Even Chen responded positively but raised a sticky issue: "But, Jasmines, we do not have some bathing suit."

Bianca jumped to the rescue. "Chen, darlin', y'all can just go in your undies."

The Asians stripped, exposing bony legs and four pairs of tighty-whities. Cleveland, Thuc, and Dr. Miao had skinny, hairless bodies and wore nothing but their underwear, except for Dr. Miao's catcher's mask. Chen was slightly pudgier but equally hairless.

Bob unbuckled his belt and Cher gasped before Jasmine interceded. "Sorry, Bob, the hot tub only has room for eight, and these guys are our special guests."

Bianca retrieved two bottles of champagne and eight glasses, and they did a line dance out to the hot tub. While Bob pouted, Travis returned from the back hallway with sad look.

"Travis, is there a problem?" Derek asked.

"We're outa beer," he said sadly.

This was a bad time for sobering up.

"Are you sure?" Derek asked.

"Yes, there was only a case and half when we got here, and it's all gone."

Bobby jumped to the rescue. "Let's go on a beer run. I'll drive."

They found a 7-Eleven and bought two cases of beer. On the way back, they stopped for pizza, figuring the Asians wouldn't notice their absence. Everyone in the restaurant stared at Cher.

After finishing the pizza, they returned to the condo. Chen was standing in the family room in wet tighty-whities. He looked distressed, as well as in need of some serious abdominal training. Bianca stood next to him clad only in her bikini.

"Hey, Chen; hey, Bianca," Derek said. "What's going on?"

"Derek, we have some problem," Chen replied with a very worried look.

"What's wrong?"

"I lost Cleveland, Thuc, Dr. Miao, and the other girl."

"In the hot tub?"

"No, outsides of it."

"Where?"

"I dunno; we lost them."

"Start from the beginning, Chen. What happened?"

"We ran out of champagne, so Bianca and I came back inthesides looking for more and some towel. When we got back to the hot tubs, they were gone. I looked in the pools and did some yell, but it was no use."

"Maybe they went to the bathroom or something."

"Derek, they have been away forty-five minute."

"Did you see anyone else out there?"

"Many peoples. They came out on their balconies to watch us and say hello. They were very friendlies."

"I can imagine. They were all men, right?"

"That's why you're some boss, Derek. How did you know?"

"Lucky guess. Bianca, do you know people in the complex? Maybe we should ask around."

"They may have gone over to Ted's condo," Bianca said. "He and his cousin live in the condo opposite ours, and they like to party."

"Let's start there."

Bianca put a towel over her shoulders and led the group over to Ted's place. As they passed the hot tub, they noticed empty champagne bottles with a couple bikini tops draped over them.

Bianca knocked on Ted's door, but there was no answer. She opened the door and shouted out to Ted. They smelled cigar smoke; empty beer cans and shot glasses were everywhere. Ted and his cousin were both passed out on the couch with the TV on.

Bianca shook Ted and said, "Ted, have you seen Jasmine, Bethany, and Keri tonight?"

Ted groaned.

As Bianca revived Ted, Bobby looked around the condo.

"It looks like they've been here," Bobby said.

"Why?" Derek asked.

"There are puddles of water around the kitchen island and six empty glasses, not to mention chewing-tobacco residue next to one glass."

"I wonder where they went?" Bianca asked.

Just then, Bob spoke up. "Where is that music coming from?"

They heard muffled music. Bobby found a door to the basement. When Bianca opened it, the music got much louder, and they heard laughs and shouting.

"Eureka!" Bobby exclaimed.

They went downstairs. There was a ping-pong table, and on one side, Jasmine and Bethany stood topless with paddles in hand, two cups of beer placed before them. Cleveland and Dr. Miao, in wet tighty-whities, were their opponents. They held their paddles with the famous Chinese-style pen grip. Keri and Thuc watched and cheered.

Jasmine and Bethany showed outstanding form against highly skilled Chinese ping pong players. Cleveland and Dr. Miao were clearly experienced in ping-pong but had trouble hitting the girls' cups. Jasmine and Bethany played defense, returning smashes with lobs aimed at the Asians' beers. The Asians were oblivious to the dangers of beer pong. Bethany ended a long rally with a soft underspin forehand that landed softly in Dr. Miao's cup. High-fives, hugs, and chest bumping between Jasmine and Bethany followed.

Cleveland and Dr. Miao were confused until Keri explained the rules—they had lost and had to chug their beers. The Chinese complied.

Chen and Travis challenged the victors to another game while Cher fetched more beer. As Jasmine and Bethany's breasts shook with each shot, Bob said, "Y'all, this is far better than High Beams."

33

DRAGONS AND FOO DOGS

A week later, the debilitating hangovers from the bachelor party were long gone. The focus was on the wedding and reception at the Dalton Hills Country Club. For the ceremony, Chen and Hong Hanh had chosen a grassy area next to the club's gigantic pool with rows of white chairs and a beautiful flowered arch. The reception would take place by the pool, with dozens of floating Chinese lanterns in the water.

Chen had invited every employee from the Dalton plant and several from Nashville headquarters. Hong Hanh had invited the staff from Fuji, including the two Philippine sushi chefs. Dave Lund brought his Norwegian wife, Margrethe.

Derek's decision to shut down the Dalton plant for the wedding had unforeseen repercussions. A few days before the ceremony, he received an e-mail from Commie.

Derek,

It has come to our attention that you will close the Dalton plant so every employee can attend Dr. Chen's wedding. By showing such bias in favor of Dr. Chen, you are violating Lund rules and tacitly endorsing the wedding as a Lund event. As such, you and Lund Plastics will be responsible for all behavior at the wedding.

Any reports of excess or abusive behavior will receive
swift and thorough review by Corporate Human Resources.
Connie Schmidt
Corporate Human Resources

An hour later, he received another missive.

Vogel,
I have learned that you will shut down the Dalton plant
for an employee wedding. What the hell do you think you're
doing? You have no authority for such action, which will cost
Lund tens of thousands of dollars and affect our bonuses.

I have alerted Dave Lund, as well as the Board
Compliance Committee.

Miles Templeton
Chief Financial Officer

This warranted a reply.

Miles,
I will be sure to discuss the Dalton plant-closure matter
with Dave Lund and his wife during the wedding reception.
Best regards,
Derek

Chen and Hong Hanh had decided on an Asian-style
wedding with traditional dress and Chinese decorations. Hong
Hanh looked stunning in her silk Chinese robe. The American
groomsmen wore the traditional Chinese garb of decorative shirts
with priest collars. Carol thought they looked funny.

The guests dressed informally. Several men wore shirts and
ties with blue jeans. The ladies wore sundresses with thin straps,

revealing many tattoos. As the guests were being seated, there was a strong buzz in the air. This was the Lund social event of the year.

The minister stood in the center of the arch holding a book. He was an older Chinese man, barely five feet tall, with small, round glasses. Chen stood to his left. To Chen's left were his co-best men, Cleveland and Derek, followed by the other groomsmen: Bobby, Thuc, Travis, and Dr. Miao. Cher sat on the groom's side, sporting her signature five-o'clock shadow.

The processional was distinctly Chinese. First down the aisle was a long, red dragon with giant scales, like in a Chinese New Year's parade. Two people manned the dragon costume. The lead person had trouble seeing and missed the left turn at the end of the aisle. He bumped into the minister and stumbled before turning suddenly. The trailing person had too much momentum to turn and sideswiped the minister, who had just recovered his balance from the initial bump. Both the minister and the dragon's tail tumbled. The falling dragon tail pulled the head backward, but it stayed upright. The dragon recovered and assumed the proper position to the right of the minister. The only signs of mishap were grass stains on the dragon's knees, a green smudge on the minister's backside, and his slightly bent glasses.

Next came a giant foo dog, about seven feet tall. As guests roared in approval, the foo dog skipped down the aisle, waving its front claws. In its zeal, the foo dog missed the turn at the end of the aisle, tripped, and wiped out the minister.

Chen and Derek helped the minister back to his feet, who said: "Fucking *foo dog!*"

The bridesmaids followed. The first was Hong Hanh's friend and fellow waitress from Fuji: Kong, who was originally from China. Kong had classic Chinese looks with long, jet-black hair and a beaming smile. She looked completely normal in a beautifully colored silk Chinese robe with a dragon on the back. Trophy was second, resembling a mix of Ellie Mae of the *Beverly Hillbillies* and a nineteenth-century Chinese empress. Cher stared as Trophy sauntered up the aisle, slowly swinging her hips and taking her place next to Kong. Sophie followed, looking like a young Sophia Loren playing a Chinese princess.

Then came the vows. The minister read them to Chen in short chunks for easy repetition, and Chen responded.

"I, Chen, take you, Hong Hanh, to be some wedded wifes, to have and to holds, from today forwards, for better, for the worst, for richer, for the poorer, in some sickness and in some healths, to loves and to perish, 'til death do us apart."

When Chen and Hong Hanh kissed as husband and wife, the crowd cheered. Cher fought back tears.

During the recessional, the dragon fared better but still sideswiped two guests in the front row. As the guests clamored around Dr. and Mrs. Chen, the throng moved toward the pool like a rugby scrum. At the pool, waitresses dressed like foot-bound Chinese ladies handed out champagne. Cher downed two glasses from the same tray.

There were two bars around the pool. For the Dalton plant people, an open bar was like Christmas in May. A warehouse worker shouted to his colleagues: "Y'all should get two drinks—they're free!"

Off to one side, Travis, Dr. Miao, Cher, and Cleveland did "bottoms-up" toasts along with some other Dalton folks. They yelped after each toast. Bobby watched and laughed.

After an hour, Dr. Miao put on his catcher's mask, an odd complement to his Chinese garb. He and Travis had significant bulges of chew in their cheeks, and Thuc tried to mimic his cultural heroes.

The band, Rebel Yell, played a series of Southern rock songs. They sported long, straight hair, and a couple wore Confederate Army hats. All had string ties with long-sleeved denim shirts.

The combination of open bar and Southern rock made the plant folks go wild. They drank and danced without inhibition. The dragon and foo dog drank in costume and danced with gusto.

As the music blared, the giant red dragon did a jig with the bizarre, haunting-looking foo dog.

Dave and Margrethe Lund enjoyed the champagne and mingled with the Plastics people. Things went well until Dave addressed B'linda as "Trophy" in front of Margrethe. In an instant, he had two women aligned against him.

After an hour of dancing, the band announced dinner, a generous buffet of Southern cuisine. One blending operator shouted to his pals from maintenance. "Hey, y'all, there's mac 'n cheese!"

Once everyone was seated, it was time for toasts. Chen took the microphone first.

"Dear guest, thank you for coming to our weddings. Hong Hanh and I are very happys you all are here. I would also like to thank Dave Lund and his wifes, Maggots, for coming to the weddings. We are all proud to works for Lund Plastics. We are all some family."

Carol turned to Derek and said, "*Maggots?*"

"It's a Chinese term of endearment, Honey. They used to eat them."

After several toasts, Dave Lund and Derek went to the head table and pulled out a package they had hidden earlier. Dave took the microphone.

"Dear fellow Lund colleagues, Margrethe and I are honored to be part of this great ceremony with you. At Lund, we are a family company, and nowhere is this more apparent than here ... because of all of you."

There was huge applause and cheering. Dave continued.

"Dr. Chen, you are a special person and an extraordinarily successful leader at Plastics. Just a few years ago, Plastics was just a small player in our industry. Today, thanks to the efforts of all of you, we are the clear leader in high-value plastics. Thanks to SaniSeat and antimicrobial siding, our sales of new products are approaching 70 percent of the business. It's amazing."

More huge applause, cheers, and high-fives.

"Dr. Chen, you were the president of Bug Off and the Moonies, so we wanted to get you a special wedding present to commemorate the teams' achievements."

Derek handed Chen a large, flat package while Dave continued. "Derek and I are honored to present this to you."

Chen unwrapped the present, which was a framed picture. When Chen saw the picture, he yelled, "Dolly Partons!" and held it above his head. It was a large photograph of Dolly Parton with a personal note that said:

Chen, congratulations to you and your team for selling 1 million gallons of SaniSeat. You are special, and I look forward to seeing you when I visit the Dalton plant.

XOXO, Dolly

Chen asked, "Is Dolly Partons coming to our plants?"

"Next month," Derek said, "as you would say, a bet is some bet."

The band Rebel Yell resumed their play, even louder than before. Travis, Dr. Miao, Cleveland, and Cher led bottoms-up toasts. Dave Lund even joined them for a couple, and so did the Chinese minister, still wearing his bent glasses.

Everyone followed Chen and Hong Hanh onto the dance floor. When the band played "Sweet Home Alabama," the guests screamed the lyrics while dancing. Even the dragon and foo dog sang, though the costumes muffled them. After a few songs, the band played "Gimme Three Steps." Chen and Hong Hanh started a line doing the bunny hop. It was quite a sight: dozens of lit lanterns floating in the pool and two hundred people doing the bunny hop, led by Chen and including Dr. Miao in a catcher's mask, several Chinese people, Thuc, Cher, two Philippine sushi chefs, the minister, Dave Lund and Margrethe, Carol, Kong, Travis in a Red Man hat and Chinese shirt, Trophy, Sophie, Bobby, a giant red dragon, and a foo dog.

Between songs, there were several more "bottoms-up" toasts led by Travis, Dr. Miao, and Thuc. Even Margrethe Lund and Carol enjoyed this Chinese custom. When the band played "Ramblin' Man," the crowd went wild with frenzied dancing.

Halfway through the song, the dragon tail accidentally hip-checked Cher into the pool. Her white blouse turned transparent and clung to her chest, revealing a bra and impressive biceps. Cher's mascara bled down her cheeks. Thinking this was an American wedding tradition, Thuc leapt into the pool next to Cher. Travis tossed Dr. Miao, flailing, into the pool. He hadn't finished his follow-through when Bobby nudged him from behind into the water.

Several plant workers launched Dave Lund into the pool. There was a slight hush as people stared in shock, wondering how Dave would react. He broke the surface with a huge grin, got out of the pool, and threw Margrethe in.

The dragon pushed the foo dog into the pool. As Derek stood laughing, Chen shoved him in.

Moments later, the minister got thrown impossibly far into the pool, landing with an impressive belly smacker. Monique pushed Chen, who landed with a big splash next to Margrethe, followed by the dragon. Trophy pushed Monique, whose 'FroHawk repelled water perfectly. She then got Carol and was, in turn, tossed by Sophie. Hong Hanh crept up behind Sophie and with all her strength, pushed her into the growing mass in the pool. Kong got Hong Hanh from behind and was in turn shoved.

Rebel Yell played on.

After less than two songs, every guest was in the pool, laughing, splashing, and dancing. The dragon and foo dog weaved in and out of the crowd and glowing lanterns, like silent, eerie monsters. Rebel Yell played "Shout!" and the crowd leapt with every instance of *shout*.

Derek danced with Carol and others in four feet of water, laughing and screaming *shout*! Bobby danced with a grinning Sophie. They both beamed and gave enthusiastic thumbs-up signs, as did Travis and Trophy. Chen, Hong Hanh, and the others were having the time of their lives.

Dave Lund and Margrethe danced with everyone else. After a while, Dave splashed over to Derek and said, "Great party, huh?"

"Yea, Chen and Hong Hanh know how to do it."

"It's a good thing Connie isn't here."

"No kidding."

"Your Lund career probably couldn't survive a third trip to the compliance committee, even with my air cover."

"Thanks for the confidence."

"Actually, I wanted to talk about your career, and now is as good a time as any."

"I can't imagine that's true. We're in a pool, dancing in our clothes."

"It's just an expression. I wanted you to know how proud I am of the Plastics team and what they've accomplished. Even with— let's say—very unconventional methods."

"Like Cher."

"A good example. She's a lot more attractive than I expected, at least when she's dry."

"She'll be flattered."

"Anyway, I was thinking now might be a good time for you to move on."

"What? Where?"

"Our international operations. How would you and Carol feel about moving to Paris?"

"Are you serious?"

"Totally. It'll be great for your career—and Lund."

"But who will run Plastics?"

"Dr. Chen, I presume."

AUTHOR'S NOTE

Buzz Kill is a work of fiction. The names, characters, places, and incidents portrayed in the story are the product of the author's imagination or have been used fictitiously. Any resemblance to actual persons, living or dead, businesses, companies, events, or locales is entirely coincidental.

ABOUT THE AUTHOR

William Goodspeed began his writing career as the secretary of Baccus, a prestigious wine club in Charlotte, North Carolina, with up to twelve members. Baccus catapulted William to his first publishing blockbuster: *The Point*, a seasonal newspaper in Northwestern Michigan with 125 subscribers (all unpaid) and no advertising revenue. Despite earnest pleas from his newspaper subscribers to quit writing, William moved to novels and wrote *Buzz Kill*.

Bill was a longtime resident of Charlotte and now lives in Maine and Michigan with his wife, Jen, and three badly behaved dogs.